The 3 U-Turns of My Life

• LOVE-RACE-DESTINY •

Srishti
PUBLISHERS & DISTRIBUTORS

Srishti Publishers & Distributors
Registered Office: N-16, C.R. Park
New Delhi – 110 019
Corporate Office: 212A, Peacock Lane
Shahpur Jat, New Delhi – 110 049
editorial@srishtipublishers.com

First published by
Srishti Publishers & Distributors in 2015

10 9 8 7 6 5 4 3 2

All characters in this book are fictitious, and any resemblance to real persons, living or dead, is coincidental.

Printed and bound in India

About the author[*]

Jitendra Gianchandani (Jeet Gian) was a happening person till he became a chartered accountant (and got married). He has been practising accounting, auditing and business advisory services under JCA Consulting Group in Dubai-UAE since 2001. He is CEO and Chairman of the company with offices in Dubai, Sharjah, Jebel Ali Free Zone, Hamriyah Free Zone and...perhaps planet Mars (by 2019).

He is a great communicator and on good terms with clients, media, and almost everyone around him, except his in-laws. He has been interviewed by Dubai TV, Zee TV-Gulf Pulse, CNN Arabia, Radio 103.8 and on many occasions by his mother-in-law!

Divya, his life and business partner – only in profit – is also a Chartered Accountant. Both are blessed with two kids: a daughter Falguni and a special needs son Krishna. For Divya, children come first; the rest of the world is just Tom, Dick and Jitendra.

He is up by 5 am – even if holidaying on Star Cruise – and is a fitness buff. Plus, he eats every two hours, like babies do. He is well-organized and futuristic; even knows what he will have for breakfast on 12 June 2020 (oatmeal and six eggs without yolk). His parents feel proud of him for...marrying Divya.

---

* *In his wife Divya's words*

To my wife, editor, publisher, personal trainer, my office team and my in-laws who were continuously behind me
to make this book
a mission impossible!

Note for the readers

Here is a small brain training opportunity for everybody. I am saying "opportunity" not "quiz", so have fun and stimulate your brain before you start reading the book.

Warning! Warning! Warning! There are no rules to follow, neither for you, nor for me.

Anyway, here are the questions:

Who let the dog out?

Oops! Sorry, this one is wrong.

Is there any formula to succeed in life? If yes, what is it?

1. ______________________________

2. ______________________________

3. ______________________________

4. ______________________________

5. ______________________________

What should be one's priority in life – Love, Career or iPhone?

____

Is race or competition good to excel in one's career? Yes /No.

____

The best answer will stand a chance to win a romantic trip – accommodation and airfare – for two for three nights and four days in a breathtaking location – Iraq.

Thank you.

Note: Economy class passengers are permitted one piece of hand baggage: a laptop bag or an A.K. 47!

Acknowledgements

I had thought writing a book would be cakewalk, but it's an extremely slow process. Many state governments changed in between. Even government at the center changed. MoM-Mars Orbiter Mission Spacecraft entered planet Mars. Prince William and Kate got married; she delivered a baby boy and became pregnant again!

But all that apart, now that the book is over, it's time to remember all those people.

Let's start with our wonderful Indian politicians (aargh!) who inspired me to write this book; who, in spite of all the uproar can sleep in the parliament, especially when it is in session.

My wife Divya, also a Chartered Accountant, gave me whole hearted support throughout this grueling journey of writing a book, by supporting me in office work, sparing me from the parental odd jobs, and calling up my mother a million times to complain that I am selfish!

Ha ha! I am kidding.

My daughter, Falguni, loves whatever silly thing her father does, even if there are hundreds of grammatical mistakes.

My son, Krishna, whose arrival has made our family complete. We are lucky to have him. He is a child with special needs. Since his birth, my life has been filled with positivity and Magic tape diapers.

My parents, my brothers and the Humongous Gianchandani Circus! Hundreds of my uncles, aunties and cousins (more information available on request).

My in-laws who are still in trauma to see their daughter handling home affairs, office, children – including me – and grocery shopping three times every day!

I am deeply indebted to my diligent office team in Dubai, which we call the JCA family (for more information email haha@ iamkidding.com). Without them, this book would have been in bookshelves last year itself.

My gym personal trainer Mr. Antonio Francisco de Morais Teixeira alias Tony for making this journey of writing further torturous by recommending delicious diet and Quinoa in particular, which makes me throw up even when I think of it.

I thank my publisher and team Srishti to have mercilessly cut out many words I had so painfully typed during day time and staying up various nights. I was petrified for 48 hours. My dream of becoming an author sank like Titanic before completing its maiden voyage. But being a Gemini, I sprang back!

Lastly, thanks to the proficient people of our CA fraternity and MBAs. Without you guys, this book wouldn't have existed. So, if there are any mistakes in the book, they are simply because of you all.

Hey guys! I guarantee this book will help millions of people – and I don't mean politicians here – fight insomnia.

Prologue

Conference room at Falcon Realty Ltd, Powai, Mumbai.
20 January 2010, 6:30 pm.

I was eagerly waiting in the conference room for the meeting to finish. It had dragged longer than the World War II. I think the concept of conference rooms was invented by ex-Nazi administration as means of maintaining office discipline in the corporates.

And when the meeting finally ended, I ran to my cabin to pick up my cell phone and hurried to the lift to leave for CST airport. I had a flight to catch to Dubai, where my best friend was getting married, for better or for worse. Soon the car hit the road. I sat in the back seat wearing blue jeans and a slim fit black V-necked T-shirt. The white Honda Accord was moving slowly in the traffic like a tortoise, so I decided to submerge myself in a magazine, *Business India*. The cover stories were:

FII sceptic about investment in India.
Current account deficit widens: India's love for coal, gold, oil on rise.
Corruption v/s Growth: Corruption chucks growth in India.
Generation 'Y': Interview with youngest CEO, CA Manav Arvind Modi, Falcon Realty Ltd, the man with the Midas touch and a golden tongue.

My eyes were transfixed on my photograph on the cover page. I was clad in a black suit with a red tie, just like a Bollywood actor. I was a shy and simple person, but the media had labelled me a man with the Midas touch and a golden tongue. The power of the media is amazing. They can make you or break you, like a wife can make your home heaven or hell.

In Ahmedabad, my father Arvind Modi had bought one hundred copies of the magazine to distribute to our extended family in India and abroad. My mother Roopa Modi, who I lovingly called Ba, had wanted to distribute even more, but couldn't find any in the bookstores in Ahmedabad; they had all been raided by the Modis.

The driver honked the car horn, breaking my reverie. We were stuck in traffic.

"I have been living in this city since the last thirty years, but the traffic situation is the same! I don't know where these people are coming into this city from!" Usmanbhai, the chauffeur, wearing a white shirt and cap screamed, his face resembling that of an Angry Bird.

"Easy Usmanbhai, we cannot do anything about it," I said quietly glancing outside at the incredible traffic. I looked down at the magazine. The car moved and I read and re-read all the articles again; after all I am a nerdy CA – a born mugger.

I kept an eye on the traffic. The city turns into a wildlife park during the rush hour, but with only one human species. Mumbai has given me everything but it has taken my heart. My love! And a human without a heart is like a machine. Yes, Mumbai makes you work like a machine. Everybody runs after money, and I am no exception to it. And everybody is ready to give away everything for the sake of money. But I was ready to give money and everything for the sake of my love. Alas! Why do we repent for loss of loved ones after we have money and everything else? Why not before that?

It is righty said that one cannot have everything in life. I think this phrase was made for people like me only. I cursed myself again.

But I cannot curse Mumbai traffic; it is the sign of progress and the strength of India (see, how reading the same article repeatedly impacts the mind – I was thinking like an economist). Once upon a time, India's population was a curse, but it has now turned out to be a blessing in disguise for India, as western countries have no buyers to buy their products and their average older population is increasing.

"Sir, your interview in the magazine is very nice. Now you should have a nice car – a BMW or Mercedes," Usmanbhai spoke politely. He always flatters me like my hair stylist when I am alone.

Though Usmanbhai was in his mid-forties, he looked older than sixty. This is the drawback of having two wives and six children. Normally, an aircraft has two engines or at least one engine; but in Usmanbhai's case, there were two aircrafts with only one engine. He was depreciating at an alarmingly fast rate. I am sorry about bringing my accounting fundas into his personal life and the aviation business.

"Did you read the interview, Usmanbhai?" I asked, returning from my weird thoughts.

"No, sir. You know that I don't have time. I am on the road the whole day, and the Mumbai traffic doesn't allow me to read anything," he said with a shy smile, looking at me in the rear-view mirror and also peering into the side mirror to monitor the traffic.

I wondered if he did not have the time to read, then how did he have the time to have six children!

"Sir, Rita Madam told me that your interview is very nice and you look very smart in a black suit," he said, flattering me again.

It's quite incredible that chauffeurs, hair stylists, and women have a natural divine art – they do their job best if they are free to chatter. Anyway, I love all of them.

"Usmanbhai, don't believe this. I am not a big man. I am the same person working like you from 5:00 am till late evening," I said and thought, *not after that.*

◎

I moved to the check-in lane. To my surprise, there were fewer people at the check-in lane of Indian Airlines, as opposed to Emirates Airlines where a lot of passengers were queuing up, as if to see Vidya Balan's *Dirty Picture*. Moreover, unlike European countries, our country doesn't protect the civil aviation industry from foreign airlines. It's sad. Add to it the sorry condition of aircrafts of Indian Airlines – poor quality of service and ageing air hostesses – which is why they are struggling to get passengers in their own country.

"Fella, move on!" an aggressive passenger, chewing gum, wearing his cap backward said from behind me. His accent and look made me feel like an extraterrestrial.

I shook out of my thoughts; all the articles I had read in the magazine were hovering above my head. Why can't we keep our brain at home while travelling and just relax and enjoy? We CAs are real chumps.

Suddenly, my phone rang once and got disconnected. Missed call from Dubai?

I dialled after waiting for a few more seconds.

"Good evening, Manav Sahib, NK Gupta, Chairman of the Dubai Chapter of Chartered Accountants. I wanted to remind you that the annual conference is tomorrow. Your speech is at 2:00 pm, Thursday after lunch."

Missed call for reminder? I think they have invited me to save their travel and hotel cost because I would be in Dubai to attend the wedding anyway. We CAs are real penny-pinchers!

"Don't worry, I will be there on time," I said and disconnected the phone.

I reached Café Coffee Day after a rigorous immigration security check.

Just when I went ahead to place my coffee order, I heard an announcement being made, "Flight IC-787 will be delayed due to a strike by the ground staff. Kindly be patient until the next announcement."

Even before I could react to the announcement, I heard a thud. A young guy in his early twenties standing next to my table had thrown his bag on the ground; he seemed very upset by the announcement. I couldn't control my urge to talk to him. He was unshaven and looked tired. *He might be a CA aspirant*, I made a wild guess.

"Hi, can I help you?" I asked, looking at the boy. I am a boy too, a bachelor.

"Indian Airlines needs help, not me. I think India is growing only on paper; this country is practically backward! It will never change even if they achieve any amount of growth. India is expected to be the engine of growth, but if they cannot run one airline, how will they become a super power? It's bull shit!" the young boy shot out.

I gasped at his outburst but remained quiet.

"If you travel by Indian Airlines, you don't have to visit villages in India," the boy said again in disgust. "It still reminds one of the 1940s. Everything is the same, including their mentality."

This time I felt like laughing; the boy had good powers of observation but he was so negative and cynical.

"You have a point, but nowadays even European airlines have strikes, why hate only our country?" I asked, still standing.

"I know that," he said softly. "I am just upset."

I remained silent. Thank god he did not mean it.

But then I wondered why this boy was so upset. I gazed at the *Business India* magazine on his table, the one with my interview. The boy must have been reading too much and his head must now be filled with negative articles.

"Why get upset, my friend? Let's have some coffee and enjoy the evening," I said and sat down facing him. He nodded.

I gestured to the stewardess and ordered two coffees.

"Hi, I am Manav Modi, CA and CEO of Falcon Realty Ltd," I said and extended my hand.

"What? Really?"

The boy's eyes widened; he looked dumbfounded and stared at me, as if he had just seen Britney Spears in a bikini at the airport.

"Are you the same one... who is on the front page of this magazine?" he asked and stared hard at me and back at the cover of the magazine. Maybe he was not impressed by my face in person, as my photograph had been photoshopped on the cover.

I smiled, but didn't react to his silly response.

"Oh, nice meeting you, Mr Modi! I am Jiten Goswami, and I am sorry for being so harsh about India," he said and took my hand into his quickly.

I remained silent.

"Your article was inspiring to read. I can't believe that a simple and shy person is the leader and CEO of a big company," Jiten said, sounding excited.

"Why not? Doesn't God give equal opportunities to every human being?" I said.

"I don't know. You are talking like Ba, my mother. She believes in God as well," he said.

I suddenly wanted to get to know the boy now.

"What do you do for a living?" I asked after a few seconds of silence.

"I am going to Dubai for my first job," he said and paused, as if he was hesitant to say something.

"What are your qualifications?"

"I am B.Com, Intermediate CA; I couldn't get through the CA final exams. And..." he trailed off, gazing at his shoes.

Here we go, my guess was correct; all accounting professionals have identical melancholic looks.

"Why didn't you clear your CA final?" I probed, my voice sombre.

"I failed twice in the final; now I want to earn quick money," he said, "Any unschooled loser can earn money in Dubai."

Whether he was mocking at himself or the NRIs in Dubai, I'm not sure. But for sure he was in a fool's world if he thought Dubai was the land of milk and honey.

"So, how quickly do you want to make money in Dubai?" I asked like an auditor.

"I will see... six months to one year. If I like it, fine, or else I will go to Lagos in West Africa. I know life is not good there, but it gives you lots of money," he said without hesitating.

My thirst for coffee matched my wish to knock him down with a solid punch, but I controlled myself. I didn't want to be labelled a bad boy, like the one in Bollywood. I hope you understand my drift.

"And if you don't like Lagos?" my voice turned stern as I looked into his eyes.

"I don't... know." he said, looking down.

The stewardess brought the coffee. She was wearing a red top with white shirt inside and had applied stark red lipstick. She reminded me of a traffic cone. She came very close to us as she placed the coffee on the table.

"The flight is delayed; you will have more sales today," I said to the girl, keeping the cash on the tray.

She gazed at the cash and looked offended.

"Sir, even if we work extra hours, we get the same salary," she replied bluntly, blowing me off. I wondered if she would still have been bitter if I had given her a nice tip.

Jiten looked at me and we smiled at the girl's comment.

"See? How will India grow if we have such an attitude?" Jiten said and poured sugar in his coffee.

"But she brought a smile to your face," I said and took a sip of the coffee. I felt better as the aroma of coffee reached my nostrils.

"Sir, I read in the interview that you are a fitness buff and wake up daily at 5:00 am. This is amazing! How do you manage to find time?" Jiten asked, taking a sip of the coffee.

"Well, it's a lifestyle," I replied briskly, taking another sip of the coffee. "Tell me one thing, will you be appearing for the CA final exams in Dubai?"

"I don't want to think about the future. I don't even know when this plane will take off. Or even if it flies, will I land safely in Dubai? How can I say anything about the exams? I have given up; my destiny and future, both are bleak," Jiten said and smirked. He guzzled down his coffee. While I took a sip of my coffee, I could see that he looked dejected.

"Sir, my story is not inspiring, I am loser. Please tell me your story. How did you become the CEO and how did you achieve success at such a young age?"

Before I could say anything, his cellphone rang.

"Hello, Ba, I am at the airport. Flight is late due to a strike at the airport," he said.

He paused. The mention of his *ba* intrigued me further.

"Ba, you know that I am hapless, but it's not my fault this time. I hope my stars change in Dubai." His voice cracked and his eyes filled with tears. He looked up, pretending to complain to God or maybe he expected God to give him a tissue paper.

I inhaled as I listened to his conversation.

"Don't wait at the airport. Go home, and don't expect too much from me. Let me live my life, your Ashapura Ma cannot do anything for me. I will try to do something for Bapuji. I will earn and send some money soon, and for god's sake, don't talk about CA. For me, it's over!" he said and disconnected the phone. Suddenly my Ba's image flashed in my head, and I became sentimental.

Jiten was weeping loudly. I was confused and annoyed too. I looked at the people staring at us. I patted his shoulders in confusion, not sure what to say.

After a few minutes, he stopped crying.

"Sir, I have botched up my career," he paused, clearing his throat.

"Today all my friends are well settled. I joined CA and passed Intermediate CA in the first attempt, even before I qualified for final year exams in college. But I realised that I was stretching myself too thin with my final year B.Com studies, daily eight hours articleship training, and the CA final exams. I was beleaguered."

I wanted to tell him I was a mugger like him. Our institutes don't spare anyone; they suck the blood out of you.

"And before I could correct my mistake, life changed; my father lost a lot of money in the share market due to one wrong decision or maybe his greed. And if that was not enough, my father got a paralysis attack. We had to sell our home and our office. He has still not recovered from the shock and has been at home since the past six months."

I was stunned. My body shook. I felt a sense of déjà vu.

"I felt the pressure to earn money as things were going from bad to worse. The medical expenses of my father increased, and all our relatives and friends were laughing at me. After two failed attempts, I stopped appearing for the exams and finally decided to go to Dubai to earn some quick money. Ba was against my decision, but I couldn't bear to see them like that any longer."

I could see myself in Jiten. We didn't speak for a while.

He broke the silence. "Sorry, I became emotional. I told you that my story is depressing. I am sure you must have been lucky throughout your life, unlike me," he said, sounding low.

"Do you think I have everything in my life?"

"You are the youngest CEO of a big company. What else do you need in life?" he asked.

"No, that's not the case; we all are in the same boat," I said seriously.

"You mean you also faced problems like I have? How did you handle them? How did luck favour you?" Jiten asked with excitement and faith in his eyes.

I went into deep thought; Jiten had touched a nerve once again. I took a deep breath and looked at Jiten.

"Are you ready to listen to the long-drawn-out experience of my life?"

Jiten bobbed his head in excitement.

I took a deep breath and continued, "On 10 January 2001, when I was in the 12th standard, I got a vision to become a Chartered Accountant and on that day, my life's race began. A race between CA and MBA, as our CA fraternity taught us. Or the race between me and Deepak Mehra, an MBA."

Vision CA

10 January 2001.
School, Ahmedabad.

"Good morning, Madam!" the students greeted Mrs Ushaben Vaghela, our Accounts teacher, as she entered the classroom carrying a bunch of papers in her arms. She was wearing a purple sari and looked pretty as always; the boys held their breath and were speechless, and the girls envious. It was the day of the results of the internal test paper for Accounts subject and the last day of school before the final exams for 12th standard due in mid-March.

"Gooooood Morning," she drawled and kept the papers on the table, looking at her fans, I mean the boys.

"Shh…" Ushaben gestured with her index finger touching her lips and all of us fell silent.

Ushaben, I think, was in her mid-thirties. She was beautiful and charming. Very fair and tall, she had waist-length hair and was polite and friendly. She was adored by all the boys, including me. On the other hand, most of the girls were jealous of Ushaben, as she received more attention from the boys when she was in the classroom.

I never thought about her in the way other boys did, but I think I was turning mature like junior Raj Kapoor in *Mera Naam Joker* in the company of Deepak and Urvi. I wondered where they were as I was busy looking at my favourite teacher. She was to announce the results of my favourite subject, Accounts and I had topped the class through the present year as well as the previous year; I was a mugger.

All the students started whispering amongst themselves as she settled in.

"Can you guess who has topped?" she asked smiling, and moved in front of the first row, causing everyone to move their necks.

The class boomed "Manav...Manav... Manav!"

"Shhh..." she shushed, widening her eyes, and raising a finger to her lips again.

"Yeah, it's Manav again. You have scored 100 out of 100!" she said excitedly, looking at me and clapping, acting like one of us. We rookie lads liked it. She was more like a friend, a mentor and a guru to me. Once again, all the students started applauding.

I was on cloud nine. Somebody patted my shoulder hard from behind; it was none other than Deepak. He somehow pretended to be ignorant of his own strength. He was the son of a well-heeled businessman-cum-politician. His house, sorry, palace, at the posh locality of Satyagrah Chavni in Vastrápur was large enough to have a gym. And let me be clear, people who live in Satyagrah Chavni have no connection to Gandhi's satyagrah; they are the purely commercial and successful people of modern Ahmedabad.

"You geek! See how excited she is, as if you have topped the board exams. She always favours you," he sulked from behind. Had he just complimented me? He was like that – bold and blunt.

He was born and brought up in Delhi. After his mother's and sister's deaths in an accident (or suicide as some rumoured), they had shifted to Ahmedabad some five years ago.

Deepak Mehra was born with a silver spoon in his mouth. He was always full of beans. I liked him because he was always positive and thought big. He excelled in public speaking, which was my biggest weakness. He had developed a huge ego, thanks to his father, Ranjit Mehra, who had given him all the comforts which Junior Mehra misused. Perhaps it was Senior Mehra who had spoilt him, though they didn't get along very well.

I looked back, smiled in pain and nodded before he hit me again.

I was sitting in the middle row in the class; students were teeming around me to wish me, but my eyes were looking for Urvi. She was waiting for her turn to meet me. We had grown up together, right from when we were in nappies.

"Hey wonk! We want a party tonight, Manek Chowk!" Urvi said, shaking my hand firmly. I was expecting a hug, but girls are very smart; they don't do it at the wrong place or when the guy wants it. However, I agreed to a party readily.

Urvi, alias Urvashi Raman Doshi, looked like a doll in two pony-tails, a white skirt and red shirt. She was five feet six inches tall, slim and fair. She was inquisitive and loved to talk. She liked Gujju food and chaat like all Ahmedabadis. She also loved reading and travelling.

She had enjoyed all the luxuries of life as her father, Raman Doshi, was the branch manager at ICICI bank (which is better at sales than real banking, as my Bapuji had said many times). Uncle was a foodie and chaat was his biggest weakness. Chaat was banned by Mrs Ramola Doshi in their home as it contributed immensely to Ramanbhai's weight. Getting booze in Ahmedabad was easier (though it's prohibited) than getting chaat in Urvi's house!

Aunty was an ex-NRI, disciplined, good looking and charming. She was interested (like most other women) in interior design and was also very health conscious. Her forefathers, originally from Gujarat, lived in Kenya. She had had a crush on Uncle, as he looked like Anil Kapoor in those days. Now he resembled Boney Kapoor with a balding head and a big belly. Uncle had worked in Kenya after he dropped out of CA, but after winning a jackpot – marrying

Aunty – in Kenya, he returned to India to serve his motherland, and his hundred and fifty-year-old sick mother.

Urvi was a combination of her parents; I can confirm that without a DNA test. They lived in the upper middle class Aradhna Arcade, near Kankariya Lake in Maninagar.

After their interesting profile, you will find my sketch undersized, but I have to tell you and stretch it to make it noticeable. I am Manav Modi, five feet eleven inches tall, fair and slim. I was good at studies and especially brilliant in Accounts. A bit of an introvert, simple, straightforward, down-to-earth, and honest guy (read, not-so-practical in the ways of the world). This was something Deepak accused me of various times. But then, everyone knew we both were different, like apples and oranges!

And most of my grand family members never even dreamt to pursue elite professions such as doctor, engineering, lawyer, IT and journalism. They were into grocery, flour mills, garment and working as clerks in private and government companies.

One of my aunts, Leelaben, though pretty, had an IQ of peas. She never saw school but had nine kids. And one of her sons, my cousin Jignesh, also like his mother, didn't even know how many days there are in a week. And how many hours in a day. But he triumphed by marrying a commerce graduate girl and now they have two sons. Both are following in the footsteps of M.S. Dhoni and Sachin Tendulkar and have dropped out from the school to pursue cricket!

My father, Arvind Harishbhai Modi, was a small-time real estate agent. Modi Investment & Estate Agent, our office, was in Ganesh Plaza, CG Road. He was emotional and had helped many friends in crises, who are all millionaires now. I had a good knowledge of property business, which I had learned while writing the accounts in office and in Bapuji's company. I became very mature and was apparently ten years ahead of boys of my age, as Bapuji would tell Ba. I had no complaints in life; we were a simple and happy family.

We lived in Ridhi Sidhi Apartment, Naranpura, a lower middle class society. It included lower middle class Gujaratis and Sindhis, who had been refugees after the Partition of India. My mother had studied till X standard, but was the best cook ever, as her father, my nana, had been in the restaurant business in Surat. Every meal at our home was like a feast. Bapuji was a potential diabetic patient, thanks to Ba, her passion for food and love for her husband.

Let me stretch my profile further.

Ba had watched the *Ramayana* and *Mahabharata* serials a hundred times. She was a religious lady; in fact, the entire Ahmadabad city was religious. People keep religion ahead of business, unlike people in the metros who keep business ahead of religion.

Anyway, let's get back to Ba.

She was an advisor to our entire extended Modi clan in Ahmedabad; no sorry, all of Gujarat; no, I think all over India, as all my uncles and other kith and kin are settled all over India. And thanks to India's growth in the telecommunication sector, everybody talks every hour.

We have around one hundred Modi family members. The census was taken using Block-Direct-Total Count method during the 80th wedding anniversary of my eldest uncle-aunty; both in their 90s, when all the Modis were present. Every monsoon, like mushrooms, at least half a dozen new are added to the family. There was competition among the ladies' wing of the Modi family; some of my aunties delivered babies along with their daughters. In short, our hobbies and recreations can be summed up in the one word... "sex".

In short, I was nowhere close to Urvi or Deepak. But my rank in Accounts had made me famous in school. I wanted to be successful in life; in fact, the most successful Modi. I wanted to earn more money and give my parents every comfort they desired. Maybe I felt inferior whenever I was with Urvi and Deepak, or maybe inspired. But the big question was how I could be successful. Can I deserve her? Those were the questions that hounded me since I became mature and realised the gap in the financial status between the three of us. But today was the day when I got an answer to my question.

Ushaben had announced the results and the whole class was murmuring. She brought joy to a few and woe to many. Students crowded around her – girls went to her to argue about poor marks and boys went to her to see her more closely.

"Hey, c'mon, take your seats!" Ushaben said, clapping her hands.

"Have you planned your future or do you just want to slog your entire life?" she asked vociferously. The entire class was silent. She looked serious, moving around the front row.

She stopped, looking at me.

"Manav, what are you thinking? What is your passion?"

I was puzzled and everybody looked at me. I didn't know what to say. 'Madam, even I am searching the answer to this question,' I thought.

She stared at me, scanning my face quickly; after all, I was her favourite student.

"Okay, I will tell you," she said finally. I became more nervous.

"You are a number cruncher; you should pursue CA after completion of the exams," she said, looking at me with a smile on her face.

"Crook accountant!" Deepak said loudly and the whole class chuckled with him. Ushaben shushed them.

But to my intense surprise, I saw Deepak flushed and it looked like he really hated CA.

"Sure, madam," I said quietly.

I went into deep thought – "CA", "number cruncher" sounded cool. A million thoughts ran in my head; was this solution to all my worries? I could earn money, look after my parents, and maybe even win Urvi's heart..I think that's when I got the vision to become a Chartered Accountant. I said to myself, *Yes...Yes...I will become a Chartered Accountant.*

But Urvi's impatient voice disturbed my cheerful thoughts.

"Madam, I like travelling and also want to bring change in society, therefore I will either choose the travel industry or journalism," she said.

She had mentioned to me that her mother was pushing her to pursue a modelling career ever since Priyanka Chopra had won Miss World in 2000. But she was more interested in journalism. I think she was more practical than her mother. Well Ba would also not accept her prospective daughter-in-law to show her legs to neighbours, fellow citizens and foreigners.

"Both are good professions, but you have enough time to decide before finishing college. Though you are bold, this is a man's world and you have to be careful," Ushaben warned.

"Madam, I will pursue an MBA in marketing," Deepak said hurriedly.

"Very good. After completing your MBA, you can join your family business as well," Ushaben said.

"No madam, I want to be rich and famous. I want to become the CEO of a big company in Mumbai," Deepak said confidently.

I was impressed with Deepak's confidence, knowledge, and flamboyant style. He was always ahead of the times; because he had travelled a lot. Urvi had told me, travelling is not a cost, it's an investment. I think for men, anything that pleases women is an investment, including shopping! However, Deepak's look, style, and confidence had transformed into selfishness and a superiority complex since the previous year.

"Sounds good, but always be honest and a good person. Make sure that people around you like you as well just like Manav," she said, pointing at me.

"Madam, I don't want to slog and I don't like miserable people, especially accountants," he said, pronouncing the last word loudly, I think, on purpose.

All the students hooted, but I ignored his mockery.

After the class ended, I walked with the madam towards the teacher's room.

"Thank you, Madam. Until today I was not sure what I wanted to do, but you have shown me a way. I will consider CA for sure," I said to her.

"Yes, you can. You need to be more disciplined, but for now, focus on your board exams. And don't take Deepak's remarks personally. He is good at marketing, let him focus on an MBA. But your strength is accounts, so focus on CA. Also, CAs cannot advertise due to code of ethics of the Institute."

Ushaben also suggested that I should not wait until completing graduation, as the Institute of Chartered Accountants of India (ICAI) had started a CA foundation entrance for bright and intelligent students after the 12th standard itself. I could save three years and pursue B.Com alongside CA.

"Maanaaav..." Urvi bawled from behind. I stopped, looking back.

Urvi waddled like a duck, slicing the crowd in the lobby, with slight annoyance on her face. Even that made her look more beautiful.

"Why do you boys have memory the size of cereal! We came together today, no," she gasped, catching her breath.

"Darling, if I forget you, I will never forgive myself," I felt like telling her. But no, I didn't deserve her yet.

"Sorry, I wanted to thank ma'am and ask more details about CA,"I said, and we walked together outside the school.

We reached my scooty, parked next to Deepak's bike; he was sitting on the bike, waiting for us.

"Sorry Manav, don't take it personally," Deepak said, stuck out his hand. "I really don't like accounting. But my purpose was not to hurt you."

"It's fine boss, but I like your ambition of becoming a CEO," I said to him, taking his hand into mine.

"Thanks buddy! But will you practice after CA..."Deepak began asking, but Urvi cut him off mid-sentence.

"Hold on, can't you see I am here too? Let's meet tonight at Manek Chowk and plan our future," she looked at me and snapped her fingers, and then turned towards Deepak.

"I have scored 100 out of 100, so I should get a party from both of you," I said, laughing.

"Hey! You will be the host, don't try to act smart," Deepak said loudly and accelerated his bike – vroom, vroom, VROOM!

"We will eat twofold tonight. Bring lots of money; you will get a big bill today!"Urvi said laughing.

We all laughed. Deepak signalled Urvi to come with him.

"Sorry, I will go with the future CA; they talk less and are good listeners," Urvi said and chuckled.

"But good listeners are not as successful as good talkers," Deepak said and gave me a smug smile. Rascal!

I just stood there and listened to their banter like a dumbass.

"Really? Then let's have a race. The last race of our school days," Urvi said, challenging Deepak.

Deepak looked ready for the challenge.

"Excuse me, Urvi, you know a scooty can't race with a bike," I said finally.

Realising that I had made a point, she nodded in agreement. After agreeing to meet at 10:00 pm at Manek Chowk, Deepak vanished – whoosh – leaving us in a cloud of dust and smoke.

Deal of a Lifetime

"Roopa, today is a very big day. Mehra Sahib has agreed to buy the showroom. We will get a good commission, but we have to invest some money," Bapuji announced in excitement as he came home early in the evening.

We lived on the ground floor in a two-bedroom apartment. The living room and dining room were one, making it easy for Ba to rant at Bapuji from the kitchen and watch television. The walls were dark pink. Family photographs, many pictures of gods and the Gujarati *panchang* (calendar) were fixed on the wall around a small wooden temple in the living room. It gave our home the feel of a mini Akshardham temple.

I had a small study-cum-storeroom where rice, onions, and potatoes were stored under my bed; and one of the corners of the room was crowded by ceramic pickle jars which had been there since Emergency was declared by Indira Gandhi on 25 June 1975! But one thing always gave me strength and peace, and that was Lord Krishna's smiling effigy – a gift from Ushaben – fixed in the corner of the wall near my study table. I used to have one-on-one chats with him, whenever I felt low.

I was flipping through the channels on television in the living room, taking a break from the mugging. I was starving and wanted to hog at night. I kept staring at the clock; it was moving like a tortoise.

Bapuji went straight to the kitchen. Ba was making *dalkhichdi* and *bhinda*, Bapuji's favourite dish. All traditional and contemporary Indian women love making their men's favourite food, especially when their kids are eating outside.

I switched off the television and joined them in the kitchen. Ba was stirring the *bhinda* with one hand and eating some salad with the other. She does that while cooking. She tastes half the sabji, checking the salt and spices, before serving us. Bapuji also joined us and started eating a cucumber. I stood at the entrance of the kitchen.

"Manuda, your Bapuji is dreaming like Sheikh Chilli again," Ba smirked.

"No, I swear on Ashapura Ma, I have really cut a deal," Bapuji said primly.

Ba stopped her work and turned around. "Really? Thank goodness! I will donate a thousand rupees to the Ashapura Ma temple and also celebrate at home once we get the commission," Ba said, closing her eyes, looking up and folding her hands.

But, I know she just needs a reason to invite the Modi clan. Maybe she wanted to announce that I was going to be a CA, to increase our standing in the Modi family. Since the afternoon she had already told more than a dozen relatives over the phone.

"I want to celebrate with my friends tonight at Manek Chowk. I scored 100 marks in Accounts. I need some money," I said, pitching my story at the right time.

Bapuji took out a five hundred rupee note from his wallet and offered it to me and I quickly took it from him.

"This is for my 100 marks and what about your deal? Give me five hundred more," I said, smiling.

"No, give him only 200 more. We will celebrate at home. Invite your friends as well," Ba said looking at me and then turning towards Bapuji. As she added spices to the *bhinda*, the pungent smell tickled our nostrils and we started coughing. Bapuji and I came out of the kitchen.

Bapuji gave me two hundred rupees more, obeying the court order and I took it without complaint.

Bapuji went to the washroom to change and returned quickly. I was waiting for him on the sofa to cross-examine him about the deal, now that I had enough money for tonight's party.

Bapuji sat on the sofa next to me and started flipping through the channels randomly.

"What is the deal? And how much do we need to invest?" I quizzed him.

"One crore," Bapuji said, his eyes on the television.

I read his mind; he didn't answer my second question. He was hiding something.

"But… how much?"

"15 lakhs," he said loudly.

"What? 15 lakhs!!" I screamed, jumping up from the sofa.

Ba came running from the kitchen, stunned.

Bapuji had invested small amounts in similar deals quite often, but this was humongous! It sounded suicidal! If it failed, we would be out on the streets. All of a sudden, the atmosphere in the house changed, like in a scene from a horror movie.

"But *Kamorta* will start soon, it's too risky," Ba interrupted in a meek voice, pulling out a chair from the dining table and sitting on it.

Ahmedabad city is full of superstitious people; they don't buy or sell any properties during *Kamorta*, i.e. 15 December to 14 January, as it is considered to be an inauspicious period. Now you understood why Ahmedabad lags behind other metros where business is done 365 days and where people even chat about business during condolence meetings.

"No risk, no gain, Roopa," Bapuji said, pretending to be Dhirubhai Ambani.

"It's a matter of only four to five days. Ranjit Mehra is a reputed and well-known businessman. He doesn't believe in Kamorta and we know him very well. He is Manav's friend Deepak's father." Bapuji said again.

"But he is a shrewd businessman and has big political connections as well. If anything goes wrong, we cannot do anything to him," I said, worried.

"All business people are shrewd," Bapuji said casually.

"But how you will arrange for 15 lakhs?" Ba asked, raising her voice and looking at her thin gold bangles. She was trying to suppress her annoyance.

"Parthivbhai has spoken to the financier and he has already agreed," he said with confidence.

Parthivbhai Patel, was a chartered accountant and our tax advisor. Their firm (PIA) Parthiv, Indrajit, Ashish & Co. was one of the most reputed auditing and consulting firms in Ahmedabad.

"But why do we have to invest when Mehra Sahib is a big party?" I asked. Maybe Mehra Sahib thinks why buy a cow when you can get milk for free?

"Mehra Sahib is expecting money next week from the sale of one of his farm houses in Mehsana, but he will give us a token, an advance of one lakh rupees tomorrow," he replied. "We need to prepare a Memorandum of Understanding (MOU) for the deal. Manav, tomorrow you have to help me in office."

Bapuji had finalised everything, without taking any advice from Ba, which was his normal practice. I don't know whether he was dreaming like Sheikh Chilli or Dhirubhai Ambani. But lower middle class people mostly have no choice except living on hope.

I don't know why I felt the urge to share this with Urvi, as girls are more mature than boys (of course, in financial matters only). I once again stared at the clock; it had died.

"Can I serve food now?" Ba finally spoke, more like ordered; she was worried and upset. She dashed into the kitchen without waiting for our reply.

Ba tossed the food on the table, like she did when tossing leftover food to street dogs.

Bapuji gobbled his dinner quickly, while I was flipping through the newspaper pages and at the same time watching news.

Bapuji looked confident, or perhaps even overconfident, God could only tell. But for sure, he was doing it for us, his family. I went to my room and offered prayers to Krishna. I gazed into his eyes and murmured, "Krishna, please help us and look after our family. We are honest people. Please make me strong to help my parents and accomplish my dreams,"

At 9:30 pm, the telephone rang and I silently thanked Alexander Graham Bell for his invention. I picked up the phone; as expected, it was Urvi. She ordered me to come out in two minutes. As soon as Urvi's scooty's horn fell on my ears, I hopped towards the door.

I picked up my black leather jacket, unbolted the door and jumped out like a hare.

The Race Begins – CA vs MBA

"Stupid, let's go quickly! It's very cold today and I am very hungry," she said keeping both her hands on my shoulders, and jumping to the back seat to ride pillion.

I sat on the scooty; she removed her helmet and placed it on my head. She was wearing a red sweater and blue jeans. Her perfume smelled fantastic and I forgot my anxieties; her intimacy brought positive vibrations.

The weather outside was extremely cold compared to the warmth inside our home. Some elderly couples were walking on the street after dinner (at 5 pm).

"Harrummph!" an old man walking nearby cleared his throat, and then coughed, bringing up mucus, almost vomiting. He glanced at us from the corner of his eye.

"Come back early!" Ba screamed, sticking her head out of the window.

"Jai Shree Krishna, ba," Urvi said, waving her hand at Ba.

"Jai Shree Krishna," Ba replied, screaming, "Girls are more forward than the boys."

"Okay," I said and we vanished like a space rocket.

"Sorry, Dad took me to the site of a new mall. We are buying a showroom," Deepak said, removing his helmet and parking his bike next to my scooty.

He always showed off his wealth.

Stupid! We Ahmedabadis are so low profile, even if we own a mall, we will call it a shopping complex.

Had I said anything about Bapuji's deal and the two lakhs commission? Nope. Because I was in tension.

Anyway, we were in Manek Chowk now. It was glittering with lights and bursting with chaat counters. It was jam-packed with people as it was the weekend. During day time, Manek Chowk turns into a bazaar teeming with people, cows, scooters, bicycles and surrounded mostly by jewellery shops. In the evening, it turns into Juhu Chowpatty. People enjoy their chaat, either sitting on their scooters or motorbikes or standing at the chaat counters, mostly run by North Indians. Or maybe jewellery shop owners sell chaat in the evening after business hours; we Ahmedabadis are purely commercial people.

As usual, Deepak had come late. He came in clean and debonair as ever and greeted us both. He didn't mention that Bapuji had arranged the deal; maybe he did not know.

"Wow, you will open a sari showroom after college. I will ask my mom to buy saris from your showroom," Urvi said and giggled. I suppressed my smirk.

"Hellooooo!" he drawled, irked by her remarks. "It's just an investment. Ahmedabad is changing. People will visit malls in the future instead of local shops, and we will rent out to *big companies*," he said, stressing the last words. "And it's my dad's decision. He is doing it for me, but I am not interested in small shops or in a small town like Ahmedabad, or even Gujarat for that matter. The future is in Mumbai."

He never spares anyone. Gujarat was small? The birth place of Mahatma Gandhi, Dhirubhai Ambani and Sardar Vallabhbhai Patel. And what about us one hundred Modis?

"Idiot, you know everything about Ahmedabad and Mumbai, but what about us? We are hungry and have been waiting for you since the past fifteen minutes," she said looking Deepak directly in thc cycs.

"Point, sorry madam! I can't argue with women! Now can you please order? I am also hungry," he said, holding his ears.

She smiled, melting like a kulfi. "Okay, stupid! Some panipuri first?"

We sprang to the panipuri counter, *Rajasthan Chaat Bandar*. It was more brightly decorated than the other chaat counters. The bhaiyaji was serving some customers, and gestured at us to wait with a smile.

"So, what is your programme tomorrow, mugging 24x7?" Urvi smirked, looking at me.

"Of course, I have to prepare for the exams," I said. *Otherwise how I can propose to you sweetheart?* I thought.

"Why don't you enjoy yourself before you go into the asceticism mode again?" Urvi said, exasperated.

"Yes boss, she is right. By the way, I will be going to London next week," Deepak butted in, fuelling our guileless banter.

"Wow, you are so lucky! I am sure you will be a successful CEO one day," Urvi beamed and looking at me said, "See Manav, how Deepak is enjoying life. You should relax as you have enough time to study."

She was once again comparing me with Deepak. I was already mad at Deepak as he was purposely trying to swank about himself.

"No, I can't relax!" I screamed, controlling my urge to shout louder.

I realised that the couple ahead of us stopped gobbling their panipuris and were now glaring at me with a mixture of angry and perplexed expressions.

"Take it easy Manav.What is the wrong with you?"Urvi said, looking at me with wide eyes. I softened a little bit.

"I have to focus on my career, CA, and I have to earn money. I can't enjoy life until I become something," I said, more to myself than to them.

Since morning a monologue had been running a hundred times in my head, "My father is not a multimillionaire like Deepak's father. My strength is studies, numbers, and I can propose to Urvi only if I do something in life."

"So, you will become a broker and agent of an income tax officer?" Deepak jeered. He never missed a chance to pull my leg.

"Don't generalise. I will be an honest CA and don't forget, in every profession, there are good people and bad people," I defended.

"Fine, then tell me, how many bad MBAs do you know?" Deepak argued.

"That I don't know, but there are millions of universities providing an MBA degree scattered all over India, unlike one single body, ICAI for CA studies. Moreover, very few of these are recognised MBA universities and all of them have diverse syllabi. Plus, unlike the CA profession, there is no practical training and code of ethics for MBAs," I said, pretending to be the president of ICAI, thanks to Ushaben, who had briefed me about it.

"Accountants are cheap pricks," Deepak said to Urvashi and glanced at me. "Sorry dude, don't take it personally. I mean CAs are very conservative and live meagre lives like cockroaches, unlike flamboyant MBAs."

"Stop these arguments! You both have bees in your bonnet," Urvi said, interrupting us.

"Sorry," I said and looked at bhaiyaji who was blissfully serving his customers. If Urvi would accept me, I would sell panipuri also. To hell with CA or MBA!

"Bhaiyaji, hurry up or else both of them will start fighting," Urvi said and giggled.

Bhaiyaji smiled and said, "Why to fight madam? Whether Chart...err...eed Accountant or MBA or Doctor or chaatwala, we all have to work only for our family," he said, stretching out his hand to give us the plates. "But we should always be honest and hardworking."

"Bhaiyaji, how many children do you have?" Urvi asked, like a journalist interviewing.

"Total five, two sons and three daughters," Bhaiyaji said, smiling.

"What do they do? Do they study?" she asked again.

"My eldest son had finished his MBA and is working in ICICI bank in Jaipur and my second son finished his CA last year in Jodhpur and is now pursuing CS. He wants to study in ICWA before he starts working. And my three young girls are in school in Jodhpur. They will become IAS officers or doctors," he said and laid a panipuri in Urvi's plate.

Urvi looked astonished. We burst into a laugh.

In the next one hour we chomped on panipuris, pav bhaji, and bhel puri.

We then rushed to the ice cream counter. Though it was cold, after eating a lot of spicy chaat, I felt I could eat an entire iceberg! I think bhaiyaji might have asked his MBA son: "Hey! How to make people eat ice cream in winter?"

Marketing people love such tough challenges, and after brainstorming, they would have come up with the idea "double the spices in the fast food!"

"Three faluda kulfis," Urvi ordered, without even asking us what we wanted. All women know by birth how to rule men, and that too without using any external weapon and breaking laws; a very smart species, it comes naturally to them.

"Ask him to serve it quickly," Deepak said, covering his burning mouth with a handkerchief.

"Don't babble, especially when you are with a lady," she said and giggled. "Both CAs and MBAs are equally important for our society, just as journalists are important for the society," Urvi said with confidence.

A small boy brought the faluda kulfis for all of us.

"You know, I am a future journalist, who knows a little about every subject," she said smiling.

Urvi had also spoken to her father about what had happened on the last day at school, just as I had discussed it with Ba, but it had taken the entire day to make Ba understand about CA and auditors. First, she asked me how much I would earn. And then whether I would get a job in the private or government sector. Lastly, she asked me why I was not doing B.Com instead of CA. At that point, I stopped explaining to her.

However, Ba could not resist, and had called Bapuji in office and then he had explained to her that I would become like Parthivbhai, chartered accountant and our tax advisor. After that she had issued the mini evening bulletin, *The Modi Express*, to disburse the news around the world.

"What more did uncle say about CA? He likes CA or MBA?"I asked, gulping down the kulfi. Actually I wanted to ask her, "What about you darling, do you like CA or MBA?"

And if she had ordered me to pursue an MBA, I could have even done that. People commit suicide in love, and doing an MBA for me was not less than committing suicide, as I had already imagined myself as a CA and had bowed myself before the CA profession.

"He doesn't like CAs, because they grill him during the audit every year," she said, and slurped her kulfi.

She continued, "But, he still appreciates them, as many times during the auditing they help him in finding serious mistakes and provide suggestions to improve the internal control systems."

"What does he say about MBAs?" Deepak asked inquisitively.

"That they are smart, but can be tricky," she said and winked at me.

We all chuckled.

We finished the ice cream kulfi and reached our parked bikes.

"So you think CAs are perfect and more trustworthy than MBAs?" Deepak questioned her and sat on his bike.

"Both are needed in business, but ethics and integrity are important. Apart from that, whether you are an MBA or a CA, it doesn't make any difference," she said.

"You prefer a CA or an MBA?" Deepak asked. Idiot! That was my question.

She smiled, gazing at Deepak and then at me. She signalled me to move to the back seat. I obeyed her instantly.

"Business needs both MBAs and CAs. So I would want a husband who is smart and earns like an MBA and is honest and spends wisely like a CA," she said and put the helmet over her head.

She meant MBAs earn more than CAs?

She laughed with confidence; we both laughed in confusion.

"I don't want to have more *pohe*," I said to Ba, holding my stomach. I had already consumed four puris.

We had special breakfast on Sundays, but today was even better, meaning that either the big deal had been cancelled or Ba had given her nod to the deal.

"Manav, I need your help to finalise the MoU for the deal. Can we go to office? We will come back before lunch," Bapuji alias Sheikh Chilli said and gulped down the last piece of jalebi.

Ba offered him more, but he refused. I think globally most of the husbands and kids are diabetic or obese due to the extra mollycoddling by the women, but the womenfolk won't agree and we won't dare argue with them. Anyway, the big deal was still on. I left it to God and decided to trust Bapuji.

"But I have to study now. Can I come around noon and then finish in one hour?" I asked.

"Fine, but don't be late. Today is a very important day. I don't want to take any chances," he said and got up to leave for office.

"Listen, finish the chai before you go, I put adrak in it," Ba ranted from the kitchen, and came running out with a steel flask filled with ginger tea.

"Total area is 2500 square feet and the price per square feet is Rs 4,000. But due to *jantri* rate, the developer cannot accept more than Rs 2,400 per square yard in white, the rest, Rs 1,600 per square feet will be in *kaccha paisa*," Bapuji said, noticing that I was carefully reading about the 40% *kaccha* and 60% *pakka* clauses in the agreement. We were in his office, Modi Investment & Estate Agent, Ganesh Plaza, CG Road.

In Gujarat, while registering property, people avoid paying tax on the property registration due to government rules called *jantri* (official base rate card of land/plot). That also implies that the government's bureaucratic rules also encouraged black money in Gujarat.

Also, if the government tries to correct it by increasing the *jantri* rates, the developers, including the common men like us, will disagree with it. It's a catch-22 situation for the government, resulting in Gujarat becoming a fertile land for black money. Then, we the people are equally responsible for corruption. We should not blame the politicians or the government, I thought, like a social activist.

I scanned the agreement ten times. The deal was for one crore rupees: Rs 60 lakhs *pakka* (white money), was to be paid in three instalments spread over three months, and of the Rs 40 lakhs *kaccha* (black money), Rs 20 lakhs was to be paid in advance (we had to borrow this to finance the advance, which was like suicide in accounting terms) and the balance of Rs 20 lakhs would be paid in one month by Ranjit Mehra before the registration.

Bapuji also explained to me that the actual plot where the mall was to be constructed was actually agricultural land, but it had been converted to commercial through political connections and the payment of a hefty price to the farmers. In India, money can buy anything or everything.

"We have to arrange the twenty lakh rupees *kaccha* Gandhi notes," Bapuji said, pouring some tea into the flask cup.

"Are we paying twenty lakhs or fifteen lakhs on behalf of Mehra Sahib?" I interrogated with some apprehension.

"You know, Maaanav," Bapuji drawled, taking a sip of the chai.

I knew he would try to dupe me with the example of his favourite hero, Dhirubhai Ambani, a virtual relative of every family in Gujarat, obviously because of his huge wealth.

"If I would have told her the actual figure, your Ba would have been more worried," he said, continuing to hypnotise me.

Forget about Ba being worried, she might have tossed you into the hot oil, like she tosses the puris! I thought.

"But, it's a big risk to borrow and invest," I said worriedly, "We don't have our own money."

"It's business. We are using our name and goodwill to accommodate Mehra Sahib to make this deal happen. We are not investing a single penny; the financer will invest. He will also get interest. And Mehra Sahib has also promised to return the money within four to five days. It's a calculated risk; everybody will benefit," he said the last words more stridently, but thankfully without any example of leaders.

I thought he was assuring himself more than assuring me, but I was not mature enough to challenge him. I knew that if this deal failed, we would be nowhere; we didn't have even one lakh rupees at home; we would have to sell our office or home or both, to pay back the financer.

I offered prayers in my head to Lord Krishna again.

The telephone rang and Bapuji jumped to pick it up.

"Hello, what, who?"

Bapuji looked confused. Maybe the deal was cancelled. I thanked Lord Krishna that my prayer had worked so quickly.

"Laxmanbhai, how are you? You have remembered us after a long time. How is Bhabiji?" Bapuji's joy was noticeable.

His best friend had called from Dubai. Bapuji had spoken to me a hundred times about their Dharam-Veer type of friendship. Bapuji had supported him at a young age. Laxmanbhai Gandhi had had a love affair with a girl, now Kalpana Aunty. She hailed from a rich family. Her parents were against their love, as Laxmanbhai was from a poor big joint family and he was not settled. History repeats itself: Urvi and my story will be the same if Mehra Sahib defaulted on his promise.

Bapuji had given him shelter when Laxmanbhai had eloped with Kalpana Aunty. Bapuji had given him a small office for his business, but it had failed and he had lost his money. He then decided to go to Dubai. Bapuji had paid his debt and arranged a ticket for him. I told you, we Ahmedabadis are emotional fools.

"Don't worry, Krishna is like my son. He can study together with Manav. He will pursue CA," Bapuji said with pride in his voice and hung up the phone.

His son Krishna was my classmate till 5th grade, but he had gone to Dubai seven years ago. He was a very good friend of mine. Bapuji had told me that Laxman Uncle had a big business in

Dubai, and had a lot of property in Ahmedabad and in other parts of India.

"Manav, do you remember Laxmanbhai from Dubai? His son Krishna, your ex-classmate is coming back next week to enquire about colleges, as he wants to pursue further studies in India. We need to guide him," Bapuji said quietly.

I nodded. But at the moment, I needed to guide my father first, as I was more worried about that and myself, and not interested in a mortal Krishna.

"Krishna is lucky for his father. Since his birth, Laxmanbhai has minted money like anything and he also won a one-crore-rupees prize from the bank. Nice people, they still remember us," Bapuji said, looking at Lord Krishna's photo mounted on the wall. I felt envious of Krishna for the first time.

"But Bapuji, we are brokers, we should work as a middle man to earn commission, not to invest like an investor, especially since it is such a huge investment," I tried to argue.

He made a don't-worry-about-it gesture.

"But Bapuji, it's not business; it's a gamble," I boomed.

He suppressed his frustration and tried to convince me.

"Beta, if we take some risk, we will make money. We will also spend money in property and other consumables. We will buy an office for you after you complete CA; you can practice there. That is the way it works; money rotates from one hand to another. That is the economy," he said, keeping his hand on my shoulder.

I thought, *was it our responsibility to run the economy of the whole country? It was a bizarre decision.*

The office telephone rang. Bapuji pounced on the phone like a kabaddi player.

"Chetanbhai, Jai Sri Krishna," Bapuji said in style.

"Okay, we will come now to collect the advance token. Thank you very much," he said and hung up. "Manav, let's go."

"But the MoU..." I said.

"Leave it, Manav. We will finish the MoU at home later in the evening." He switched off the lights and we both left in a hurry.

◎

When we entered Gate 24, the security staff stopped us, as if we had entered Prime Minister's residence at 7, Race Course Road in New Delhi. But, that is the way rich people lived in Satyagrah Chavni in Vastrapur. After verification, they let us inside. We parked our scooty next to a Mercedes S-500, which to me was more expensive than the combined value of our house and office, including the gold and cash at home. We quickly made our way into the Mehra House.

We walked through the garden before reaching the entrance of the hall. A puppy was basking under the sun on the rug. A parrot was squawking inside the cage, maybe warning us to run away. They have better sense than humans. A cat was playing (or seducing) wild sparrows. Even the birds knew that the cat will kill them; Mehra was seducing us, but we human beings had less inkling of danger than the birds. These species were living a more luxurious life than the common man of India, I can tell you. I pressed the doorbell.

"Jai Shri Krishna, Modibhai," Chetanbhai chimed, opening the door with a stretched smile, giving us a good view of his red, pan-stained teeth.

Chetanbhai asked us to sit and left. We parked our butts on the sofa and my eyes roved around. I felt as if we had entered the Taj Mahal, built by Mehra Sahib in remembrance of his late wife.

The walls of the main hall were covered with portraits and a beautiful chandelier hung from the ceiling. Mehra Sahib must have spent lakhs of rupees on the decoration of the hall. I wonder why he wanted us to provide the finance to buy the showroom? Was the house and the Mercedes also financed?

"Namaste Modibhai." Mehra Sahib entered in a white kurta-pyjama. He was tall and fair-complexioned. His eyes were red and he had a beer belly. He was around sixty years old.

"How are you, son?" Mehra Sahib asked and smiled at me.

"Fine, Uncle," I said and asked an irrelevant question in confusion, "Deepak is not at home?"

"Beta, in London it's early morning now so he must be sleeping," he said sarcastically. He sounded upset, just as I was upset with him and Deepak.

"What would you like to have, chai or coffee?" Mehra Sahib asked Bapuji (not me, and I didn't like that).

"Chai will be fine for both of us," Bapuji said, without asking or looking at me. Grown ups do that purposefully. We will always be kids to them, even if we become prime minister and have Special Protection Group security!

"No sugar for Papa," I said.

Mehra looked at me and then turned towards Bapuji; he looked nervous and smiled at Chetanbhai.

Soon, some men in grey shirts and black pants who looked Nepalese entered the hall and placed samosas, jalebis, fafda, dry fruits and ten types of biscuits on the centre table.

I think if someone eats all of that; he will feel obliged to say yes. I felt trapped and became suspicious again.

"Hi Manav," Deepak entered, wearing black shorts and a white T-shirt. He looked half-asleep with tousled head. I greeted him and he sat on the sofa next to me.

"Oh good morning, Prince! Why did you bother to wake up early today? There is one hour before lunch is served," Mehra said mockingly, looking at his wrist watch and threw an artful grin at Deepak. He gave him a dirty look. Chetanbhai suppressed a smirk.

"Mehtajiii," Mehra said showing him the scary red eyes.

Chetanbhai gave us an envelope with one lakh rupees. Bapuji passed it on to me, and I started counting the notes. Bapuji picked up a jalebi to celebrate, and I gave him Ba's angry look. He put it back, picked up a samosa and wolfed it down.

"Thank you for understanding, Modibhai, and there are no further secret negotiations. Our dealings have always been above board," Mehra said tossing a few almonds in his mouth. He gave a haughty smile to Chetanbhai, who was standing by like a soldier in attention. I imagined them high-fiving behind our backs.

"Uncle, is it possible for you to give us the guarantee cheque for the nineteen lakhs rupees?" I asked, after I counted the notes and nibbled at a bourbon biscuit without waiting for the tea.

Everyone was startled, including Bapuji, who looked at me in disgust.

"Modibhai, your son is very smart; ask him to teach Deepak as well," Mehra Sahib said and looked at Deepak. "See, this boy is helping his father. You should also help me in my business and in social work."

"Charity begins at home. And I told you Dad, I will not invest in shops and showrooms! I will create big cities and towns!" Deepak yelled, surprising everybody.

"Why not, Prince William?" Mehra Sahib said, frowning.

"Dad, don't make me embarrass you in public," Deepak yelled even louder this time.

Mehra Sahib frowned, "Stubborn, like his moth..." Mehra Sahib started and stopped midway. Deepak glared at him and darted inside before his father could even finish his sentence.

"Today's young generation thinks money comes from the trees or sky," Mehra Sahib murmured to himself. "Is there any business left in India that can be done honestly? Only stupid people can dream of that."

I looked into his eyes and grew more concerned.

"Mehra Sahib can give you in writing on simple paper, as the leaves in the cheque book are over. I will request for a new cheque book tomorrow," Chetanbhai spoke up quickly, smiling.

"It's fine, Mehra Sahib. Your word is more than enough, but if you are giving us in writing, that shows your greatness," Bapuji said hurriedly and turned towards me to say have-samosa-and-keep-quiet.

Two minions entered with chai and served it to us as if we were in a five star hotel. (These two chai might cost us nineteen lakh rupees!) Mehra bragged about the chai saying it had extra masala and milk. I was sceptical about the deal, hence still thinking negatively.

I raised my cup to sip the world's most expensive chai.

We took the envelope and got up to leave. Mehra agreed to collect the guarantee cheque the next day and we agreed to pay twenty lakh rupees to Purshotambhai, Swastik Developers Ltd.

We all came out and started walking towards the gate.

"Nice plants," Bapuji said, signaling at the plants in the compound.

"You can take it if you want," Mehra said sarcastically.

I made a tactful diversion to avoid further embarrassment.

"What about the MoU?" I reminded Bapuji.

Everyone frowned.

"Yes, tomorrow morning, Chetanbhai can collect a copy from our office and before we pay the advance to Purshotambhai, we can sign the MoU. Is that fine?" Bapuji said looking at me, and then turned towards Mehra Sahib. Both nodded.

We waved our goodbyes and I was lost in deep thought all the way home.

Never Lie-Never, have Adadiya

"What did you do in the morning apart from hitting your books on your head?" Urvi smirked and probed as usual.

But I was waiting for this question as I wanted to share my dilemma with her. We were sitting in Shambu Café, a favourite hangout for lovebirds. It was full of coffee addicted youth like us. After some hesitation, I confided in her about the deal.

"Who is the buyer? Give me the name. I will ask Papa to check him out," Urvi asked like a seasoned journalist.

"I don't know who the buyer is." I lied for the first time in my life and regretted it instantly. Married men are good at lying to their wives; I have seen Bapuji lying to Ba occasionally and paying the price for it.

I thought that if she shared this information with Deepak, and he got offended, he might convey it to his monster father who might cancel the deal. That would make Bapuji terribly upset.

"Why don't you talk to Parthivbhai? He is arranging the money and is also your tax advisor," Urvi said, after thinking for a few minutes.

Her suggestion was brilliant! How had I not thought of that?

I wondered why people say that it's a man's world, when it is the women who are so practical and come up with quick solutions. I thought of bowing down and saluting her, like Bapuji does to Ba.

"It's a good idea. Thank you. I will call Parthivbhai first thing in the morning," I said with excitement. I was relieved... at least temporarily.

"You are welcome, my child," she said and giggled.

The waiter brought our coffee too quickly. When a guy is with a girl, he wishes everything to stand still.

But before I could take a sip of the coffee, Deepak entered the cafe. I wanted to have more time alone with Urvi, but there he was.

"Hi dude! I knew you guys would be here," he said as he sat down next to me, and patted my shoulder.

Next time we will go to some other place, I thought.

"Looking super cool!" Deepak complimented Urvi. All women on the planet love such words and Urvi was no exception.

"Thanks! You look cool too," she replied. My heart ached.

I felt like throwing my coffee at Deepak's face. I felt like running away. I just ordered some coffee for Deepak instead.

"When are you going to London? When will you be back?" Urvi asked him.

"Tomorrow morning. I bought the ticket just now. I am not interested in the showroom. Dad will finish the formalities of the deal himself," he said.

Deepak continued, "Dude, I am sorry for today morning. I got upset with Dad. But your dad should make a good commission from the showroom deal with Dad."

He patted my shoulder. I fumbled and the coffee spilled on the table. I was aghast and so was Urvi.

I stumbled to my feet. People around us gazed at me in disgust while I gazed at Urvi. Her eyes were wet already.

"Oh, I am sorry...." Deepak said, "But I wanted to tell you something...."

"I don't want to talk to you about anything!" I exclaimed.

"But, this deal..." Deepak began, but I interrupted him.

"Just screw the deal. I don't want to know anything," I said, even more upset, looking at Urvi.

She turned her gaze away, fighting to stop the tears.

The waiter brought the coffee for Deepak and cleaned the table. Deepak asked me to order another coffee, but I shook my head.

"Cool down, man; have some coffee," Deepak said, offering his coffee. He poured half the coffee from his cup into my cup forcibly. *Stubborn like his mother*, I thought.

I finished the residual coffee quickly. It tasted awful. Urvi didn't sip her coffee thereafter. She said that it was too sweet.

For the rest of the time that we were in the café, neither did she speak to me nor looked at me.

But she and Deepak chatted like they were kith and kin. Deepak finished his coffee and went to the restroom.

"Sorry Urvi, whatever the reason was, I shouldn't have lied to you," I said after composing myself.

"It's fine. I am stupid, Manav, that I expected more from you. All men are the same." She sounded like she had recited a dialogue from some 1950s movie.

"Sorry, I thought you might tell Deepak and then he may tell his father... and Bapuji may get angry," I fumbled again.

She directed her angry eyes at me with an expression similar to Ba's. I lowered my gaze.

"So Urvi, you enjoy your time with this boring accountant till I am back," Deepak said, as he joined us again.

"To hell with accountants! I have a lot of things to do in my life," Urvi said mockingly.

Deepak laughed hard. *Rogue!*

The waiter brought the bill. I looked at him in anger. He had a face that only a mother could love.

Urvi stood up and walked off. I ran after her. Deepak shouted out to me to pay the bill, but I was already on the road.

"I am sorry, baba. I didn't lie, but for the first time I did hide some information from you," I said, getting off the scooty. She had driven the scooty like a maniac.

"Who told you that hiding information is not lying?" she cried out. I was aghast.

She disappeared without waiting for me to respond.

I walked home.

After dinner I went to my study room. I tried flipping through the pages of the accounts book, but it wasn't easy to focus. I opened the Economics book. Very soon I felt sleepy.

"Papa, I think we should ask Parthivbhai's advice on the deal. He has good horse sense," I said, chewing the last piece of chapatti. Bapuji and I were having breakfast (chapatti and alu-bhindi) at home. I had woken up early for my mugging session, but was not able to focus. Urvi's face with tears in her eyes made me flip through the pages unseeingly, and her last words were ringing in my head. But I had to follow her advice, I was firm on that.

"Manav, don't try to bang your head against the wall. Let him do whatever he wants," Ba said mockingly from the kitchen.

"Do you think I don't know anything about business? And now we have already taken the advance from Mehra Sahib and the MoU had also been sent for confirmation, so why do you have to talk about the same thing again and again?" Bapuji said, irritated.

Ba came out from the kitchen and banged down the plate of *adadiya*, a popular sweet from Bhuj Kutch, sent by my Kokila Fui, Bapuji's elder sister. It's dark brown in colour and is made of *garam masala*, saffron, ghee, *khas-khas* and *adadh daal*. It's a winter sweet that we eat in the mornings and is extremely rich and laden with calories. One time, Bapuji had been unable to control the temptation and had had five *adadiya* in the morning. He had not eaten anything for the rest of the day and had been constipated for the next two days! Finally Ba had to use enema to provide mechanical stimulation. However, Kokila Fui says it is a must have for pregnant women. I finally understood why Modi women become chubby after delivering a baby.

Bapuji looked at the plate of *adadiya,* shifted on his seat and pushed it back in disgust.

"It's not like we don't trust your business knowledge, but we should not forget Murphy's Law – anything could go wrong, maybe due to bad luck," Ba said, repeating Manu Mama's words. He was a Development Officer at LIC in Mumbai. Bapuji hated him more than he hated bitter gourd juice.

"Fine, you can talk to him. Parthivbhai has asked us to collect the payment from the financer at around noon," Bapuji said, looking at me in annoyance. He finished his breakfast and left for office early, without touching the *adadiya.* I took one and wolfed it down instantly.

◎

"Hello, Parthivbhai? Manav… from Modi Investments," I spoke nervously and gave him my janamkundali details. He was in Mount Abu; I had called him on his mobile during my break from mugging. Ba was out for her daily bargaining session at the vegetable stalls and to distribute the remaining *adadiya* to her fellow citizens.

Mount Abu for people living in Ahmedabad is like Khandala for people in Mumbai. Only three hours away, most Ahmedabadis go there on short holidays to swim in booze. They are so avid that they even wash hands with beer or gargle with it!

"How can I help you, Manav?" Parthivbhai replied. I could hear a lot of noise made by ladies and kids in the background.

I recited my problem to him.

"Hmm…I know it's risky, but the developer has agreed to sell only to your father, not to Mehra Sahib. So if the deal has to go through, your father has to take the risk and invest the money or else he will have to cancel the deal," he replied.

"But, sir, you know we don't have money to invest. And investment with borrowed money is not the right thing to do," I said. "Also, if Mehra doesn't pay us, the advance will be forfeited by the developer. What about your reputation? The financier might hold you responsible if we fail to pay him back."

"I know that this might be a Himalayan blunder, but I am not in the deal. I told your father about the risk, but he was resolute about going forward with it. Also, the financier is taking the risk. He has agreed because your father has a good name in the market. Both have tunnel vision so let's hope for the best. But it's your call, take it or leave it," he replied, making me even more nervous.

After a couple of arguments, I hung up the phone.

I looked at the clock. It was already 11:00 am and I had only one hour to do something. I thought of calling Bapuji and giving it one last try.

"Hello," Bapuji said over the phone.

"Papa, Parthivbhai says it's a big risk and that you only want to go for it. So why don't you just stay away from the deal and not invest? Why don't you convince the developer to sell directly to Mehra Sahib?" I said as persuasively as I could.

"Son, you don't get such deals so easily. It's a big opportunity, and if we do it successfully for Mehra, we can make in-roads into the group of big investors. He has connections with big business people. I need to give you and your Ba a good life, so let me take some risk. It's a matter of a few days only," he said with confidence.

"Papa, big investors, big people, big connections and a big deal could create big problems and big headaches as well," I said, irritated with Bapuji's philosophy of 'big'.

"Manav, you are still a child; focus on your studies and let me do my job. My intentions are not wrong. I am an honest person and

Ashapura Ma is with us, she has always been kind to us," Bapuji said and hung up the phone.

The doorbell rang.

"Vegetable prices have become irrational!" Ba exclaimed her famous line. "And potato prices are sky rocketing!"

For a housewife, nothing is as important as potatoes. I had been hearing this since I was in grade three, but I never saw any undercutting on the food menu. Ba entered the house, carrying vegetables in a countless number of bags in both her hands.

I came back to my room and touched Lord Krishna's effigy; he was smiling as usual. I felt better. I sat on the chair and suddenly Urvi's face flashed in my head. I didn't know how I would face her; I had never lied to her or kept any secret from her. I thought that the only thing I could do was to seek her forgiveness. That's what we men can do to please women – bow, and bow, and bow at their feet until they are pleased.

I planned to visit her home in the evening, and thought of a number of ways to say sorry to her.

I gazed at the stack of books and randomly and half-heartedly, picked up a book. Oops! Economics! Lord Krishna wanted me to rest. He knew that I was sleep deprived and the deal would go on regardless of whether if I was awake or asleep. Very soon I was in dreamland.

Men are Puppies

"How are you, Manav? Not seen you for a long time," Urvi's mother smiled and signalled me to come in. A nice fragrance reached my nostrils as she opened the door, unlike our home, where the strong smell of fried *bhinda* or *puri* will welcome you as you enter the compound of the building.

Aunty was wearing a pink salwar kurta. All women, irrespective of age and educational background, look pretty in pink, I can tell you. Even Ba looks nice, Bapuji had told her when I was in the 7th grade. Whenever I saw Urvi in a pink dress, I felt a strong urge to hug her. But I had to control myself.

I had reached Urvi's house; it was named 'Bhuvi', meaning heaven. For the first time in my life, I had bought a 'Sorry Friendship' greeting card. On the cover was a photograph of a small puppy, representing me (or all men folk) holding a small red flower in his mouth, with a big 'Sorry' written on it. I wrote inside:

Dear Urvi,

Sorrrrry

My balance sheet of friendship will not tally without my sorry and your forgiveness.

I maybe a good accountant, but this double entry I can't pass without your help,

Yours Manav

"Aunty, I have been busy with studies and helping Papa," I said and sat facing her on the sofa. At the mention of Papa, I became grim and my mind was diverted from the pink dress to the deal and the risk involved.

Bhuvi was a row house bungalow with a mezzanine floor. It was fairly big for three people. The space had been utilised smartly by the lady sitting opposite me. I think women can use the same TV-and watch Doordarshan channel for ninety-nine years, but they would like to replace the furniture every month on a salary day!

Ten artificial plants and five thought provoking pictures were fixed on the wall, so unlike our home, where Ba had hung a calendar with Shiv-Parvati pictures and Bapuji had put a photograph of our grand Modi clan. Urvi called it the Modi Circus, and my cousins call it the Modi Zoo.

"Aunty, I can see that you have again changed the interiors of the hall. It's nice," I complimented her. I know women like praise.

"I would have done better, but Raman is busy in office and I can't go shopping alone," she said disappointed, "He never appreciates this."

"Aunty, where is Urvi?" I asked, looking around. *Come to the point, man!*

"Oh, sorry! They have gone to the library to buy some new magazines. They are late in fact," she replied staring at the clock in anger.

After a pause, she said, "Wait, I will bring some biscuits." She left without waiting for my reply; as the mother, so the daughter.

She brought water and biscuits in a plate, sugar free and low calories. Ba doesn't understand what calories are. She knows that healthy food is food made with ghee. Otherwise, how will women deliver babies or men perform well?

The doorbell rang. Aunty opened the door and Urvi hurried in, Uncle trudging after her.

Urvi was wearing black jeans, a black T-shirt and a red sweater. Her nose was red like a strawberry.

Urvi completely ignored me, like I was some Tom, Dick or Manav. I had expected this. She ran into the kitchen. I think this was the beginning of a more mature relationship, I thought positively, and was ready with my...apology.

"Why so late? Did you eat junk food again? You will never change!" Aunty scolded Uncle, looking at him in disgust. He was wearing a blue tracksuit and a brown monkey cap. He remained silent, his body language and face expression said he was guilty.

Uncle casually sat on the sofa and took off his cap. He winked at me and gestured with both hands to say wait-until-tsunami-is-over. I smiled and sat to face the trial in the court of Urvi and Mrs Ramola Doshi.

"Urvi, you should tell your dad to not have all that *junk food*. I already made sandwiches for you," Aunty exclaimed, "Did you buy the magazines or not?"

Aunty seemed more concerned about the magazines, realising quickly that she couldn't do anything to change Uncle. He gave her a bag full of magazines.

"Why should I give anyone any advice? I don't care! You all go to hell!" Urvi yelled coming out of the kitchen. She ran upstairs to her room.

I realised that I was the reason for her frustration. I revised my apology strategy. A simple apology was not going to be enough, for sure.

Uncle shrugged. Aunty was shocked and glared in anger at Uncle. Uncle shrugged again.

"You have spoiled her," Aunty said.

For all the wrong things, only men are responsible. Let's not argue about it. I have accepted it because arguing with women is like a bowling game – the men are the pins and women are the bowling ball. The ball will knock down the pins anyway.

"But Ramo, what is my fault? Urvi was upset since morning. And you asked me to take her out for a change, so on the way back from the book shop, I thought let's have some chaat, she loves panipuri. I ordered one plate of panipuri for her, but she didn't eat it, hence, I had to finish the panipuri. And I had ordered dahi-puri for myself. Obviously, I had to finish that as well. I don't like to waste food," Uncle said and winked at me. Aunty had already sunk her face in the new magazines, ceasing to worry about Urvi's comments and Uncle's explanations. The court had been adjourned. Uncle survived. Now it was my turn.

"Aunty, she wanted my help in Accounts, but I said no to her as I was busy with Papa. She might be upset with me," I said, and lied once again. It comes naturally to us; menfolk lie to womenfolk to maintain peace and harmony.

Both looked at me and smiled.

"You want to pursue CA after 12th exams?" Uncle asked.

I wanted to pursue your daughter, Uncle, I thought.

"Yes, Uncle. Bapuji suggested that I should practice like Parthivbhai."

"But, only good marks in Accounts will not help you become a successful CA. It's very competitive; you need contacts, good negotiation skills with the clients and income tax officers. It's very challenging. Nowadays, you can hardly do a thing with honesty," he turned serious.

"I will try to be honest, follow the ethics, and maintain the integrity of the profession," I said confidently, as if I was already a CA.

"But you have to be practical in today's time. However honest you are, circumstances, your clients, income tax officers, your own needs, greed, society, and your family demands will force you to disregard ethics and ideologies," he said, gesturing towards Aunty. She raised her eyebrows.

"What family demands?" Aunty censured.

I can tell you, women are gifted with the art of multitasking; she was reading the magazine and listening to our conversation at the same time.

"Every man has to provide basic life necessities to their family, whether you work like Daku Ratnakara or Rishi Valmiki," she scoffed and once again dove into the magazine. I think it is rightly said: all that glitters is not gold. Including women!

Uncle was clueless and gestured at me to go upstairs.

I climbed the stairs towards Urvi's room to apologise.

I knocked at her door. No response as expected.

I pushed the door, realising it was open (for me, I guess).I was greeted by an eerie silence, as though I had entered a public library.

Urvi was sitting at her study table, flipping the pages of a book (economics), clearly pretending to read. Her room was more spacious than my study room – there was a white queen size bed, and the walls were painted light pink. In one corner was a makeup table with a tall mirror. Many of her single photographs during her holidays to London and Kenya, along with family photos were fixed on the wall. A girl's room in every sense of the term in a fairy tale. She was still in the phase of Hannah Montana.

"Sorrrrry…"I said, literally pleading. No response. She turned her back towards me. In normal circumstances I could have thought of hugging her from behind, but not today!

"Still upset with me?"I asked and bowed to look at her face. She turned to the other side and continued to gaze at the book. I immediately placed the greeting card on the table. I had hidden it in my notebook, but she took no notice of the card.

"Nice interiors. Your mom is like a professional interior designer," I again tried to flatter her, but in vain.

"Mom is downstairs, you can give her the compliments yourself," she said, throwing her book on the card. She gawked at the card and opened the envelope in excitement. Her expression changed, and she smiled. She smiled even more widely after reading the card. And what happened after that was dramatic.

"You geeky accountant!" she said, jumping from her seat and hugging me.

I was stunned. Was this the reason that boys lie to girls? And thanks to the inventor of the greeting card. For the first time I was so close to her. I didn't want to let her go; her mild perfume was overwhelming.

"If you lie again, I will kill you!" she said and smacked my stomach, as she sat on the bed, still looking at the card. I sat on the chair where a little while ago she had been pretending to study the book-*Economics in One Lesson*: How little sleep can make a big difference!

"If you hug me like this, I will never speak the truth," I said and smirked.

"Oh! Don't try to be smart now, you naughty fellow," she said, and threw a pillow at me.

I repeated the entire conversation with Parthivbhai and told her that the deal had been finalised. I got worried as I spoke about the deal. She took my hand in her soft hands. I felt better.

"Don't worry; even Papa said that the property market is booming in Ahmedabad. Many people are taking loans from private financiers like your father to invest in properties," she said, caressing my hand softly. I felt my body tingle.

"Thanks Urvi, I am feeling better now," I said, looking into her eyes like never before. She hit my leg and turned her gaze to the card and kissed the puppy. I was jealous of the puppy, but she went further and tacked the greeting card on the mirror. I imagined the puppy winking at me. I wish I could have been the puppy. I understood today why dogs are liked by women. Dogs are lovable as a buddy because they are straight forward and honestly wag their tail like accountants; they don't use any marketing tricks like marketing executives. I hope you understand my drift.

We discussed about studies and went down when her mother called us to have sandwiches.

The situation looked under control. Uncle was isolated from the dining table. I could sense that the men had lost to women again.

"Uncle, are you joining us?" I asked. Aunty winked. Urvi pursed up her lips.

He gave me a filthy look.

"Where were you?" Bapuji asked when I came home.

"What happened today? Did you finalise the deal?" I counter-questioned.

"Yes, it is done. I paid 20 lakhs to the developer," he replied, without showing any signs of worry.

"When will they return the money?" I asked.

"They went to Mehsana to sell the land," Bapuji said and walked towards his room. "Roopa, I have talked a lot today, give me a head massage."

"What happened? Did you receive the money or not?" Ba pounced on Bapuji as she opened the door, rolling pin in her hand.

I had already phoned him a hundred times, but Bapuji had not been in his office the entire day.

"They are still in Mehsana. I tried to call them on the cell, but was not able to reach them," he said, heaving a sigh, as he took a sip of water from the glass lying on the table.

"So nothing happened today as well?" I almost scolded him.

"Tomorrow, I will go to Mehra's house after the parade," he replied, but his voice was quiet, as a week had already passed since the date of the payment.

The next day was Republic Day. I could not understand human philosophy and common man's blinkered thinking; our life was at stake, but our devotion to the nation remained unchanged. I didn't know whether Mehra Sahib was going to celebrate Republic Day or not, but for sure, we being the true representatives of patriotic India were going to watch the parade.

"Are you sure he will pay you tomorrow?" Ba questioned Bapuji.

"*Haan baba*! More than Mehra and Purshotambhai, I'm finding it difficult to handle the two of you," Bapuji said, exasperated.

Silence prevailed for a while and it seemed scarier than our ranting. Bapuji sensed that.

"I have informed Purshotambhai about the delay. He has agreed for two days' extension. It happens sometimes," he said, more to himself than to us.

Ba ran to the kitchen, as the pressure cooker's whistle blew for the fifth time. At least she could save the daal for us.

"Can you serve me the food? I am hungry," Bapuji said a little frustrated, and walked to the washroom.

We sat at the dining table and ate silently. Bapuji did not have answers to our hard-hitting questions.

"Laxmanbhai had called again early morning. His son, Krishna, will be visiting next week. We need to help him," Bapuji said, changing the topic.

"Why not? We are running the Red Cross society," Ba ranted from the kitchen.

Bapuji and I ate in silence.

"What do you have in *mukhawas*?" Bapuji asked. Ba didn't reply for almost thirty frightening seconds. I knew it was done deliberately. The tension was almost unbearable.

Ba came out from the kitchen and flung a plate on the table, as if it was a Frisbee.

"*Adadiya*!"

Life Slaps You

"Papa, do you want me to come with you?" I offered, waiting for the sizzling puri to cool down a bit. Ba had served breakfast, *tameta-batata nu shaak* and puri. Everything seemed under control in the morning. Thank goodness!

"No, it's not required, you focus on studies," Bapuji replied, tapping the hot puri with his fist.

We were watching the 26th January 2001 Republic Day parade while eating breakfast. It was 8:00 am. Ba served *shrikhand*, a thick yogurt-based sweet dessert garnished with ground nuts, cardamom, and saffron. Her mood was better now; she looked at us and smiled.

"Why did you give Papa more sweets?" I asked in surprise. We both had already gobbled five puris each.

"Don't worry, let him eat the sweets. It's an auspicious day today, he is free to eat whatever he likes. Also, it is good to eat in the morning as you can digest your food during the whole day," she smiled and went to the kitchen again.

"Why not give me *adadiya* in the morning?" I asked, while eating *shrikhand*. Bapuji gave me a dirty look.

"Finished! I gave all the remaining *adadiya* to Ghanshambhai Kaka today morning," Ba said from the kitchen.

Ghanshambhai Kaka was our neighbour. He was a retired banker, now an insurance agent and part-time bookkeeper. He kept himself busy, not to earn money, but to keep his mind away from worry as his only son had left him after marriage. He lived with his wife on the first floor in our building and also lived in the hope that one day his son would return. And just because his name was the same as my nana's, Ba treated him like her father and he got half the food and *adadiya* from our quota. That was Ba's secret to win the hearts of people. She could have been a good human resource manager.

I noticed that Bapuji was watching the parade very seriously; he had worn a white kurta-pajama and looked like a freedom fighter. Soldiers were standing in an attentive position. I could see true patriotism on their faces. Bapuji did not seem too worried about Mehra Sahib returning the money; he was still very positive.

Ba served us cups of masala chai. We never have to ask her for chai. I don't remember a single day when she has not fed us. Even if she was sick, she had managed her duties without fail. I think all mothers are like that – consistent and they never have any break from work. We should all salute our mothers. I think I am the worst number cruncher, because I cannot figure out how much a mother is worth.

"Roopa, I am leaving," Bapuji said and walked towards the door. Ba came out from the kitchen.

"What time will you come for lunch? I will make *dahi kuri, alu-guwar* and *pulao*," she said and gave the the keys of the scooty to Bapuji. She walked along with him to see him off, as she always did. I don't know why I was noticing their every move that day; maybe Urvi's touch had changed something in me. I imagined Urvi throwing the keys to me and I catching them like a puppy.

I was feeling groggy, as I had devoured too many *puris* and too much of *shrikhand*.

"Ba, I am going out for a walk, I will come soon," I said, pinching her cheeks as she came back inside, and stepped out without waiting for her reply.

"Happy Republic Day, Manav Beta," Ghanshambhai Kaka said, walking in the compound of the building. I wished him too.

He was wearing a traditional white kurta-pyjama. He was tall, with a heavy body and a bald head, and resembled Sardar Vallabhbhai Patel.

"*Hai preet jahan ki reet sada...bharat ka rahne wala hun,*" a patriotic song was blaring through the loudspeakers placed all over the colony.

"Why are you taking a morning walk so late today? You didn't wake up early today?" I asked, stopping for a while.

"Na Beta, you know we old people are like owls, we hardly sleep at night. And this is my second morning walk today. I had *adadiya* for breakfast and now I have to burn it to eat more for lunch. I have to go out to collect a cheque," he smirked at his pitiful joke.

"Kaka, don't work so hard. Now you are retired, take some rest today," I suggested.

"Beta, my body wants rest, but my soul doesn't want any. Hence, I will rest when my soul leaves this body," he said. I looked in his eyes; they held pain. He strolled past me.

I continued walking. Patriotic songs were blaring all around. The atmosphere outside was different. People were walking around, looking happy. On this day, we were not strangers. We were all Indians.

I stopped as I heard a patriotic song by Lata Mangeshkar. I became emotional, as the song hit my ears, mind and head. I became numb.

Aye mere vatan ke logon
Zara aankh mein bhar lo paani
Jo shaheed hue hain unki
Zara yaad karo qurbaani
Jai Hind...Jai Hind...Jai Hind

I had planned to have a thirty-minute break before starting studying at 9:00 am, but the heavy meal and patriotic songs changed my serious mood to a patriotic one. I thought deeply. I began to talk to myself:

"I will be an honest Chartered Accountant and never run after money and compromise on my ethics and principles. I will make Ba and Bapuji proud. I will never indulge in corruption and will strongly pursue clients to pay tax and contribute to the development of our country. I will make Gujarat and India proud," I promised myself a hundred times until some dust hit my face.

There was a loud sound and more dust. The ground beneath my feet was trembling. What was happening?

I opened my eyes to see electric polls shaking. And I saw the building to my right collapse. I could not stop coughing as I was enveloped in a cloud of dust.

I felt more tremors and there was a terrifying noise all around. A crowd gathered on the street. We all stopped and looked around. Many people were running out of their homes.

"Help! Help! Earthquake!" A family was howling from the second floor of the building next to me. Suddenly the building collapsed in a fraction of a second, leaving everyone inside crushed under its weight, most likely dead.

"Ba!" a man among the crowd shouted out. But what was I doing? "Oh my god… Ba!" I yelled. I realised that Ba was at home and I ran towards my house.

A horrible sight awaited me; all three floors of our building were tilted at a 45 degree angle, like the Titanic, and was going to collapse at any moment. However, the ground floor where we lived was still intact. But the building next to ours had collapsed and the entrance to our building was blocked.

I thought of Ba. Her face loomed before my face. I had to do something. It was a horrible scene, as people around me were crying and screaming. I felt like joining them, but that would not help.

I thought of jumping over the building, but people stopped me. I was helpless, and stood watching. I could not do anything for Ba and tears appeared in my eyes.

I saw some dead bodies outside the building. I recognised Ghanshambhai Kaka's dead body.

"A big water tank hit his head," a stranger on the road said, pointing at the water tank lying next to Kaka's body.

"*Roopa! Manuda!*" I heard Bapuji's voice in the crowd. I navigated towards his voice. I found him standing a few feet away, looking very anxious.

"*Ba…*"I said and hugged him, pointing at the debris.

"*Roo...Pa?*" he yelled again. Tears rolled down his cheeks. Even I couldn't hold them in, though I tried hard.

The atmosphere resembled a refugee camp. Rumours hovered all around for the next 24 hours.

Urvi's father said, "The epicentre of earthquake was about nine kilometres south-southwest of the village of Chobari in Bhachau Taluka of the Kutch District."

"Many buildings have been damaged and thousands of people are dead or homeless," Urvi said, gasping for air. We were homeless I realised.

After 48 hours, we lost hope of Ba's survival. But Bapuji's faith in Ashapura Ma was intact. He kept sitting beside the debris. He was broken, internally and externally. I had never seen him cry before. Watching a father cry is most hurting for a son of any age.

"The lady is alive, but she is unconscious," a rescuer shouted from the window after 48 hours. Finally, we got some hope, as the rescuer asked for help when he found Ba under the debris. I saw Ba lying on the floor, the red blood on her head had turned black. I was stopped from going any further.

We immediately rushed to the ambulance and drove to the government hospital. Every room was full of injured patients. Many volunteers were working like doctors. Patients were holding their own glucose bottles. Very soon, a team of doctors took Ba away.

In the evening, almost ten hours after being trapped, Ba moved and showed signs of improvement. Doctors confirmed that she was out of danger. Bapuji, Manu Mama and I sat next to her. Bapuji closed his eyes and offered prayers.

"Manu…da," Ba said, her voice low. I hugged her tight.

"*Baaaa*!" I sobbed as I held her.

Agent Vinod

"Babby, after the earthquake in Gujarat, the insurance business in Mumbai has also increased. People are realising the importance of insurance. It protects one from catastrophes. All my agents are selling life policies like hot cakes," Manu Mama said, as he sat next to Ba. He still addressed Ba with her nickname.

Manu Mama was younger than Ba and she loved him more than Bapuji. Mama's features resembled Ba, except that his eyes were green like Aishwarya Rai's. Another difference between them was that Mama was infamously selfish as per Bapuji, while Ba was a big hearted Robin Hood.

Anyway, there are always two sides of the same coin, and so it was with the earthquake; it brought opportunities for the insurance businesses while real estate businesses dwindled. Once upon a time, high rise apartment buildings were the pride of the city, but now they turned out to be a curse.

Two weeks had passed since the earthquake. We had moved to our uncle's house in Navrangpura. Though we Modis don't have big houses, we have big hearts, as ten of us stayed in a two bedroom apartment. Mehra Sahib had defaulted and had run away to Delhi after the earthquake. His excuse was that the deal had not clicked as the buyer for the farm house in Mehsana had died in the earthquake. And this resulted in the developer forfeiting our twenty lakhs advance and Mehra refusing to return the money, as he had suffered a huge loss. As the MoU had not been signed (Bapuji had lied to us for he had never prepared the MoU), we could not do anything.

However, Ba didn't blame Bapuji for *Kamorta*. There were two reasons:

a) She was happy that we were safe and alive, so money was not important, b) She thought we had been punished for the deal during Kamorta. But why were other innocent people in the city punished?

We were given one month's time to repay the loan, thanks to Parthivbhai. We were devastated and I only thought about the repayment of the loan. I had to earn something to support Bapuji. I was not even sure if I wanted to study and appear for the 12th standard exams.

Two more weeks passed by. The property market had crashed due to the earthquake. Bapuji tried to sell the office to repay the loan but there were no buyers. He was frustrated. We moved to a rented apartment in Maninagar. Bapuji used his goodwill and the landlord agreed that we would pay the rent after three months. Ushaben visited our home with Urvi to meet Ba. She encouraged me to focus on my studies as soon as possible, but she was not aware of the loss in business as well. Urvi visited a couple of times. She also convinced me to focus on my studies, but my mind was somewhere else. Only two weeks were left for the exams to begin.

My dreams of studying further seemed impossible. I wondered if I should drop out.

"Mama, I want to support Papa. Can you help me earn money? I also want to be able to continue my studies," I asked Mama. Ba's eyes filled with tears as soon as I said my last words. When women cry, you feel weaker.

"Why not? That's a very good decision! I started earning at the age of sixteen," Mama boomed, turning towards Ba, "Babby, you should feel proud of Manav."

Ba cried even more loudly. Mama kept his hand on Ba's shoulder, assuring her that everything would be all right. He was lying; I could see that.

"Babby if you convince Jijaji, he can also do good insurance business; he has good contacts and a good reputation in the market. Many of my agents are not even graduates, but they earn more than bank managers or any government officer," Mama said, putting his arm around Ba's shoulders.

"When can I start, Mama?" I asked.

"Yesterday," Mama said and giggled, "You are already late by one day!"

I went to the kitchen to make some chai for Mama. I had learned some basic cooking as well. Urvi and Ba had taught me how to make *dal-chawal*, *bhinda* and *sev-tomota*. I tried really hard, but my chapattis were always shaped like the map of India, so I used a round plate to cut the dough.

"Let Babby become my agent, you and Jijaji can sell the policies," Mama replied and dipped a biscuit into the chai. Ba walked towards the kitchen. Both her hands were plastered, and some of my cousins told Ba she walked like Thakur in *Sholay* to make her laugh.

The doorbell rang. I opened the door. It was Bapuji. He looked burned out. We had only a few days left to return the loan.

"*Banchot*! People are selfish! They promised to help me, but now they make up stories to say no," he exclaimed and walked straight to the bathroom.

Ba came out from the kitchen. Her eyebrows shot up and she looked at me in surprise. I shrugged my shoulders. Mama gestured at me to keep quiet.

Bapuji came out quickly from the bathroom.

"Roopa, get me some chai!" he exclaimed in frustration. He was habituated to call out to Ba for everything.

I went along with Ba to help her to make the tea.

"I helped many people, without any expectations, but today, when I need some help, these *kutra* are showing me their back!" he said and turned towards Ba as she came out of the kitchen.

"Laxmanbhai had taken the right decision; he left this city of morons, and he has minted money in the desert!" He was talking to himself, "Everybody is selfish!"

Mama shifted in his chair.

"Jijaji, cool down and be practical. Nobody is selfish or running a charity, it's business. If the property market is down, focus on the insurance business," Mama said, finishing his chai.

Bapuji gave him a look that clearly said: *you-insurance-people-are-also-selfish*.

"Don't be trapped by development officers," Bapuji said and turned his gaze from Mama to Ba and then to me. Mama winked.

We discussed the LIC agency proposition with Bapuji. He didn't like it. But beggars cannot be choosers. That is the bitter truth of life! We do many things in life even though we don't like it, or even when we don't want to do it.

"You don't trust me, fine! As you wish! But you must think before you start selling insurance policies to dead people of Ahmedabad. It's a luckless city!" he exclaimed, finishing his chai.

"Don't be so sceptical. Have faith in Ashapura Ma," Ba said for the first time. Nowadays, she spoke little. She was dejected and was at an all time low because (a) Bapuji was in tension, as the time to return the loan was close, and (b) I was not focusing on my studies, and my chances to become a CA looked bleak.

"Mama, I am good at accounts, but not good at sales. How will I start selling policies?" I asked.

"Manav, there is always a way to approach problems. The world is like an ocean; you cannot drink the whole ocean at one time. Always break the big problem into smaller problems. You need to come up with a strategy or without a strategy you will fail. You should first approach your relatives, friends, then neighbours," Mama said, looking into my eyes.

Good idea, I thought.

He continued, "You can also sell policies through CAs like Parthivbhai. They can refer clients to you, as many taxpayers don't have policies to get income tax rebates and you can share some of your commission with the CAs," he whispered and winked at me, "CA – Commission Agent."

You are kans, Mama! I hate you! I hate Deepak and his father, too, I thought.

We finished dinner. I changed into my pyjamas and went to bed early. Mama and I were sharing the same room and the same blanket.

"But Mama, don't you think there is big competition in the insurance business?" I interrogated like future journalist Urvi.

"Good questions, Manav. You have become more mature now," Mama said. Yeah, but after I was slapped by life. And from a Chartered Accountant I was now a wannabe Insurance Agent.

"Tell me, which business or profession doesn't have competition? Competition brings out the best in you," he said, looking into my eyes.

He continued, "Serve your client well. Collect the cheque from them. Don't let them come to you. Do that extra bit to establish yourself in the industry and that will keep you ahead of your competitors. This is the USP of not only insurance agency business, but is the key to success in life," he said, smiling.

Unique Selling Point – I saved it in my memory.

"But how will I manage studies and work together?" I asked.

Mama smiled slyly.

"Dont try to sail in two boats at the same time," Mamaji said looking at me, "you will reach nowhere."

"But...mama?" I asked, almost crying.

"Manav beta, you have enjoyed life on your father's income till now. Now you are entering a new phase, which is donkey's phase. You have to work and earn for the dependants until you get retired and then enter another phase, which is monkey's phase. You move from one house to another like old man does," Mama said, and turning back towards me. "Don't worry! In the beginning you will find it challenging but slowly you will get used to it,"

We didn't speak thereafter. Mama fell asleep, but I was still wide-awake and thinking, twisting on the bed. The more I thought, the more I got chaotic. I was tossing questions upon questions in my head. But no answers soothed me. Was Mama trying to fool me? I sat on the bed, more confused. A few days ago I was confident and wanted to pursue CA, but now insurance?

What about Urvi? What would she think about me? What will Ushaben think? What about my parents? And what about my challenge to Deepak? He will become an MBA and then a CEO and I would be an LIC agent? No! No!

My head was throbbing, my heart ached. I stood up and went to the window. The streets were eerily silent. I looked at the sky. It was a full moon night. I closed my eyes and offered prayers.

Bapuji's face flashed in my head. I heard him saying, "I need to give you and your Ba a good life...My intentions are not wrong...I am an honest person..."

Tears rolling down my cheeks, I decided to drop out!

"She is a very free type of girl," Ba said. Bapuji was feeding her *theplas*.

Urvi had called and forced me to meet at Shambu. Mama had heard this and now he was teasing Ba to cheer her up.

"Mama, I want to start today itself," I said to change the topic, "How should I start?"

"But what about your studies?" Bapuji asked.

"I can pass the exam," I lied. "I don't need to read a lot."

Lying is helpful to maintain peace at home at any cost. Even future.

Bapuji read my face and continued feeding Ba with a grim face.

"Good! Prepare a list of potential clients and don't call before visiting the parties," he said and winked.

"Why?" I asked, shocked.

He smiled. I was puzzled further.

"And if at all you have to call them, don't tell them the purpose of calling over the phone."

I looked at him anxiously.

"People avoid insurance agents so just drop in to their home or office. And try to convince women, as they are emotional and are easier targets," Mama winked, and Ba smiled as she came out of the kitchen. Bapuji gave him a stern look and went to his room.

"Why do people not like insurance agents? Insurance is good for them, right?" I asked, puzzled.

"Mentality, Manav, mentality. Everybody likes junk food and *chaat*, but they don't like healthy food like apples. People don't know what is good for them and what is bad for them so we need to guide them. Selling insurance is social work," Mama replied, as he put on his shoes.

Mama continued. "Contact all of your cousins and bhabis first. If their husbands don't support them, advise them to pay in installments from their savings, as their husbands will not feel the burden then," he said, and touched Ba's feet.

"God bless you," Ba said, tears filled her eyes. Mama hugged her tight.

"Jai Jinendra," I said to Mama.

"Jai Jinendra," Mama reciprocated, folded his hands and bowed to Ba in respect.

Mama came out and screeched, "All the best, Agent Vinod!"

I felt like my eardrums had ruptured.

◎

"Neelu, its Money Back Policy, you have to pay the premium only for the first five years and thereafter LIC will pay," I said, as I shifted on the sofa. I was at my cousin Neelam's home in Asarva, taking sips of the sixth cup of chai of the day. This was my fifth visit to my cousin's home. I was chasing the first victim and as I pushed them for the policy, they forced me to have chai and *dhokla-fafda-samosa*. I hadn't cracked the deal so far and it was already 5:00 pm.

I was eager to crack the first deal, but I was being tossed around like a football. Some relatives took digs at me, as finally I had become an insurance agent and settled down to lower Modi standards. I hated Deepak and Mehra with all my heart! I had cursed them a million times since the past one month.

"Really? I have to pay for only five years?" Neelam asked, as she sat on the sofa, facing me. She was skinny and ran sewing coaching classes. Her financial condition was run-of-the-mill.

"Yes, you will get the money back every five years and you could use it for personal purposes or you can pay the instalment out of it," I asserted.

"Wow! I will call Ishu and ask her to take one policy," she said and dialled a number on the telephone beside her.

"Hello Ishu, Manav, my brother is here. I told you, no, he was studying CA; now he has become an insurance agent. He has a very good insurance policy, money back... OK... Haan... Yes... Haan," she said and hung up the phone.

"Who is Ishu?" I asked, "Where is she from?" Closing my eyes, I gulped down the chai, as if it was a bitter cough syrup.

"Ishwariben Nathani is Sindhi," she said, "She is from Dadu, Sindh in Pakistan."

I fumbled, as I placed the cup on the table. I hadn't wanted her to be so precise about her friend.

"Stupid, before Partition!" Neelu giggled. Pushing her specs up her nose she added, "Now they don't have a state, no. She lives in the next lane."

In less than five minutes, the doorbell rang. Neelu opened the door and a lady with a black shawl around her entered the room. She closely resembled Jayalalithaa, the Chief Minister of Tamil Nadu in size. You can locate her from Mars.

"Namaste," she said and both sank on the sofa. I reciprocated.

Like a tape recorder, I repeated the Money Back Policy terms and conditions for the ninth time that day. I took sips of water as my stomach felt acidic.

"How much commission will you share with us?"Ishwariben asked straightaway. She was a Sindhi; they will give you water to drink and squeeze oil from you.

"You have to pay the first instalment fully. I will give you half the instalment as commission after you pay three instalments," I tried to entice her, because (a) I wanted to crack the deal, (b) I could not win in a bargain with a Sindhi or a woman, (c) I could crack a double deal, Neelu and Ishu, without drinking one more cup of chai.

"Will you give personal service and collect the premium every quarter from our home?" She smiled smugly at me, as if to proclaim that she understood business as well.

"I will not give you false promises, Ishuben, but if you ever have some problem, I can help you in that quarter, as you are also my sister," I said, looking at her with confidence.

She softened like jelly.

"Neelu, your brother is very honest. I will take one policy from him," Ishuben said, and asked me to fill up the form.

I filled up the forms for both of them and looked at Neelu, expecting the money.

"Ishu, do you want me to pay him or you have money in your store room?" Neelu said, smiling and signalled at her shawl. It was secret code, I guessed.

"Wait let me see," Ishuben said, and raised her left elbow and inserted her right hand inside the tent sized body straight into store room and slowly pulled out (a) set of keys (b) a pen (c) a Kit Kat (d) tissue paper (e) a Swiss army knife and finally (f) a wad of notes.

Ishuben started counting the notes and finally I managed to collect Rs 10,000 each, the first instalment from both. I started to leave.

"You called me sister, now come home for some chai," Ishuben invited me over.

"Next time, I had enough chai today," I said as I stood up.

"Fine, have this Kit Kat," she said extending her arm.

"What is this stupid insurance business? Are you sick?" Urvi boomed and gazed at me with resentment. We had reached Shambu Café. I ordered some juice for me, thanks to acidity, and coffee for Urvi.

"Urvi I want to tell you...," I said nervously. But she cut me off.

"I don't want to listen to anything. Don't get distracted from your vision. You have to become a CA," she said, sounding pissed off.

"Urvi, I want to tell you something else. Please don't get upset and stressed. Promise me first," I said, looking into her beautiful eyes.

"What is it? I can't promise. I will try," she replied, looking deep into my eyes.

"Mehra has ditched us. He hasn't repaid the money," I said quietly and hung my head down, as if I had defaulted and not Mehra.

"What? Really! But how will you pay now?" Her eyes widened. I knew Indian women hate loans more than Indian cricket fans hate India losing to the Pakistani cricket team.

"I don't know. Bapuji tried to sell his office but there are no buyers. We have borrowed some time to repay the loan," I said.

The waiter served us.

"I want to tell you more," I said, taking her hand in my hand, "I...I...will drop out."

"WHAT!" She yelled, removing her hand quickly and controlling her ire. "Who gave you this stupid idea, your mama?"

"No, it's my decision," I said, "I want to earn money. Quick money."

"But how much money can you make from this insurance business to support your family?" she asked again.

"I sold two policies today. I earned ten thousand rupees," I replied, but felt awkward at the same time.

"Why don't you focus on your studies until you finish your exams? Anyway you will not receive any commission until the next three months or so," she said.

Women are born accountants. She had a valid point. I hadn't calculated things that way.

"Can I talk...to...Bapuji?" she asked, her voice breaking. I became more edgy.

"Please be strong. I need your support," I said keeping my hand on her hand, but she moved her hand away. She was making me restless.

"Are you going out to sell policies tomorrow?" she queried and gazed in my eyes, almost ready to cry.

I nodded, looking down as I had a list of the relatives I wanted to visit in my pocket.

Her eyes filled up with more tears, and soon they rolled down her cheeks.

"Don't worry Urvi, I will appear next year..." I said, lying to myself, but I was not sure what I would do.

"Don't lie to me, it's not easy. Once you start earning, your focus will change," she said, recovering quickly.

Few seconds passed in silence, and I thought it was the right time to change the subject of our conversation.

"How is your preparation going on?" I asked. But she didn't reply. She was thinking.

"Why don't you talk to Parthivbhai, your CA? He can advise you about how to deal with the problem. Papa had also given up on CA due to financial problems and now he regrets it. I don't want you to repeat the same mistake," she said, looking at me. Why do girls always compare guys with their fathers?

"Good suggestion, I will call him tomorrow itself and make an appointment," I said readily. I had to meet Parthivbhai regarding the insurance policies as well.

"I will also come with you," she said, almost looking her normal self.

I took the coffee cup and held it to her lips, like Bapuji used to feed Ba. I could feed her for life. She looked so beautiful in the pink salwar-kurta. I felt an urge to hug her and kiss her.

"Are you insured?" I asked, smirking.

"Shut up, you Agent Vinod!"

We are Puppets – Entry of God

"How much longer will it take?" I asked, trying to control my frustration, irritation and pee.

"Sir is having urgent meeting with a client from London, it will take some more time," Parthivbhai's eyesore of a secretary said, and asked for the umpteenth time, "Would you like to have some chai or water?"

Urvi and I had been waiting for more than an hour outside Parthivbhai's chamber at Parthiv, Indrajit and Ashish & Co (PIA), CG Road. I had quaffed a tank of water to extinguish the fire in my stomach and scorching throat due to acidity. And now Bhakra Nangal dam was sloshing around my bladder. I had gone to the toilet ten times in the past hour. I had promised myself that I would not drink chai that day, or maybe the whole year, or my whole life.

I had briefed Parthivbhai over the phone about my purpose for visiting him and he had given me an appointment for 11:00 am. I got an impression that Parthivbhai was deliberately making me wait, as he was not interested in me or my career. I wanted to go back and take another appointment, but Urvi shushed me and asked me to have patience.

But the big question was: Why would Parthivbhai help me? Why would he care?

Urvi noticed my nervousness. She put her hand on my hand, as we were sitting next to each other. I felt better.

"You are a victim of goal displacement. I know many brilliant CA students, who have similar problems in life and when they were at the crossroads of life, they had taken the wrong decision and lost their goals and career," Parthivbhai said, pitching management jargon at me, 'Goal displacement', and kept looking at his watch, as if indicating that he wanted to end the meeting (before it even started) or he wanted to say to us, *My time is precious, get lost you morons.*

"His *Mama* has misguided him," Urvi said sarcastically. Why do all Mamas have an image of Shakuni or Kans?

"Beta, being an insurance agent is not a bad idea, but since you have only two weeks left for your exams, you must focus on your studies at the moment, as you need to score enough marks to be eligible for the CA foundation," Parthivbhai said, looking seriously into my face and into his watch *again*.

"Sir, can we come some other time, if you have to go somewhere?"I asked finally.

"Noooo, we can continue. I am not in a hurry," Parthivbhai said, smiling. "Why don't you at least appear for the exams? You might pass."

"Um, but both...Yeah, I can try..." I said nervously.

"But again after two to three months, you have to focus on CA. And after a few months, you'll have to go to college and simultaneously join articleship training and slog seven to eight hours for three years. You think you'll manage all that and work? Are you a moron? You will go crazy!" Urvi boomed, her eyes were red with anger. I lowered my gaze.

"Okay, okay! Wait young lady," Parthivbhai said, "Tell me, you took the decision to earn money, because of the loan that your father had taken, correct?"

Parthivbhai asked a meaningless question. I thought he must have been sleeping when I had told him my failed story.

No sir, I started the insurance business to beat Mukesh Ambani, I thought.

I nodded. Urvi didn't, because she had already started sobbing.

"Look at the broader picture..."

The intercom phone rang.

"Oh wait, good news," he said, smiling at me and Urvi. "Excuse me, I understood your problem, if you don't mind can you come some other day to discuss this further?"

I felt disgraced. But nodded, looking at Urvi as we stood up.

"Ask Arvindbhai to meet me for coffee. It has been long since I met him," he said smiling.

"When shall we come again?" Urvi asked looking back as we reached at the door of his chamber.

"Um, you can call my office and fix a meeting any time."

"Your Bapuji says his chest is hurting," Ba exclaimed as I entered home dog-tired in the evening

"What!!" I rushed to him.

Bapuji was sitting on the edge of the bed, sweating. His left hand was on his chest. He looked out of breath.

"When did this happen?" I asked Bapuji but he could not utter a word.

"He was fine when he received a call from Laxmanbhai from Dubai," Ba said hastily, "But soon after, he received a call from Parthivbhai also. And immediately after that he complained of pain in the chest."

We hurried to Navjivan Hospital and very soon doctor put him under the observation with an oxygen mask on and asked us to wait outside in the waiting room. Ba and I started praying.

Suddenly Bapuji's mobile rang. I snatched the mobile from Ba's hand and answered it quickly.

"Manav, why is no one answering your phone at home?" Urvi interrogated, "Did you fix up a meeting again or not?"

I told her about Bapuji and she was with me in ten minutes. She sat down beside Ba.

As the doctors were doing their job I wondered what Parthivbhai might have said to Bapuji. He might have hard-pressed Bapuji for the return of the loan. I cursed Prithivibhai.

Suddenly, a musky perfume filled the room. I stood up, looking towards the door and saw a young boy of my age and height with a dusky complexion. He was wearing blue jeans and a black T-shirt. He entered the waiting room and touched Ba's feet. Ba kept both her hands on his head, almost surprised. I was awestruck with his charismatic look. Ba and Urvi stood up.

"*Ba, Jai Shri Krishna,*" he said smiling.

"*Kaun...?*" Ba said, still confused and nervous.

"Krishna," he said, smiling.

I was stunned and felt as if an electric current was running through my spinal cord. I was motionless; I could not find any suitable words to utter. I felt inferior due to my impoverished state, somewhat like what Sudama felt when he was welcomed by Lord Krishna. My eyes filled up with tears and I thought of Lord Krishna as I hugged him tight.

"Hi Maaa...nav," he drawled and hugged me tightly. "Good to see you after a long time," he said, still continuing to embrace me, "Don't worry, everything will be all right."

"Good...to see... you as well," I said quietly, controlling my tears.

"Thank God that you all are safe. I had postponed my travel due to the earthquake."Krishna said, looking at Urvi.

"Hi I am Urvashi," she said, smiling.

"Hey Urvi," he said, offering his hand to Urvi, "Urvashi sounds like a foreign name."

"Wow! You still remember me. You have changed completely. When did you come from Dubai?" she asked.

"Yesterday..." he replied.

My cell rang before Krishna could finish his sentence.

"*Parthivbhai CA*" flashed on the screen. It was already 9 pm.

I answered nervously.

"He...llo"

"Who... Arvindbhai?"

"Ma...nav, Sir."

I said and strolled outside the waiting room. I didn't want Krishna to hear the conversation. He had come at the wrong time, I thought.

"I would like to talk to Arvindbhai about the loan," Prithivibhai said.

"Sir we are in... the hospital," I said and told him about Bapuji.

"Oh my god," he said, "This is bad news. I will come right now."

I could not figure out whether he was more concerned about the repayment of the loan or about Bapuji's health.

"Manav," Ba's voice startled me as I hung up.

I turned around to see Ba, Urvi and Krishna running out of the waiting room along with the doctor.

"How is Papa?" I exclaimed.

"He is all right," Krishna said, smiling, "He is out of danger."

"The pain was due to acidity and gastritis," doctor said. "Palpitations are feelings or sensations that make your heart pound or race. And the reason was gastrointestinal distress. You can see him now."

Krishna kept his arm around my shoulder. I looked into his eyes. Was he really our lucky mascot?

I fought to control my tears. But failed.

We walked to see Bapuji lying on his bed. He was staring at us. He smiled and turned his eyes at Krishna.

"Krishna,"Ba said, "Kalpanaben's son."

He smiled and tears rolled out of his eyes. He raised his right hand to bless him. Krishna touched his feet.

Suddenly I heard footsteps and a strong but pleasant perfume wafted through the door mixing with the combined smell of phenyl, disinfectant, and sickness in the room.

I saw a tall old man with a fair complexion and charismatic face, wearing black shoes and a light grey suit walk into the room along with Parthivbhai. He wore gold plated spectacles tied with a golden strap hanging loosely around his neck. He may have been a banker or an NRI or even an auctioneer.

"How is Arvindbhai?" Parthivbhai asked.

"He is fine sir," I replied. Ba's eyes were wet again, so were Urvi's.

"Thank goodness," he said looking at Bapuji.

"Manav, meet Mr Yogi Bhardwaj from London," Parthivbhai said, looking at me.

I was numb. Urvi and Krishna looked at me in confusion.

I folded my hands in a namaste but instead he offered his hand.

"Mr. Bhardwaj deals in property business in London. He is here to invest in property. After the earthquake, he says it is the right time to invest in Ahmedabad."

I got worried again. Parthivbhai may ask us to sell our property to him at a throwaway price and repay the loan.

Parthivbhai continued, "And he is a big businessman, educationist, social activist and he is founder of the Ayanna & Anamika Foundation Ltd in London."

"No sir, no please don't praise me. I am just an ordinary mortal," he said bowing to Parthivbhai. He continued, "Mr Patel, I am highly obliged and I hope to do something for the people of this tragic city,"

Parthivbhai looked at me.

"I was feeling guilty since I became a part of the property deal between Arvindbhai and Mehra sahib. I could have advised your Bapuji not to take the risk and stay away from unethical people like Ranjit Mehra," Parthivbhai said, folding both his hands towards Ba and Bapuji. "But thank goodness I got the chance to correct my mistake. Your father is a gem of a man."

Ba looked at me in surprise, and so did Krishna and Urvi.

"I am sorry I cut short our meeting but I did it intentionally as I wanted to give you an unforgettable surprise!" Parthivbhai said and looked at Mr Bhardwaj.

I don't know what the hell he was trying to say.

"But now I have... good news for... you," Parthivbhai said with tears in his eyes.

"Good news..?" I said, in shock.

"The good news is that Arvindbhai's entire loan has been repaid," Parthivbhai said, "You just focus on your studies."

There was momentary silence.

"Really?" Urvi almost yelled.

"How is that possible? I mean, who paid it?"I asked, still confused.

"Lord Krishna," Parthivbhai said, looking skywards. I was even more confused and looked at Krishna beside me. He shrugged, looked more confused than me. Ba 's eyes filled with tears.

Parthivbhai looked at Mr Bhardwaj who then spoke.

"My son, every year our foundation selects one brilliant student and supports that student until he becomes independent and successful. And this year, on recommendation of Parthivbhai, we have selected you," he said and placed his hand on my shoulder.

"But we cannot pay you as well. It's a burden on...' I said.

"You don't have to repay, my son. I have lost my daughter and my granddaughter due to financial and family problems and I don't want any young man to lose in the battle of life," he said and continued further, "And don't feel obliged. God is everywhere and in every person. He is omnipresent. Remember, God always tests the followers he loves the most."

I imagined lightning all around and felt goosebumps all over my body. I looked at him in awe and admiration. It seemed as if Lord Krishna had appeared and was talking to me. He was smiling. His face was shining and I felt as if he was getting bigger and bigger. My body shivered.

"And remember there are bad people who will discourage you and there are good people, who will encourage you; but be humble. You have to face both, accept the criticism and keep striding towards your goal. You are lucky as you are on this earth to do a special task. Recognise the opportunity and grab those opportunities to be a successful person in life. You have to serve your loved ones and society at large. Life is like a journey, and the road to success is always zigzag. If you are misdirected by evil, don't worry, angels will show you the right path and will bring a U-turn in your life. Your life has taken a U-turn today. My son, I bestow my blessings upon you."

I closed my eyes, folded my hands and thought of Lord Krishna's effigy in my room. Tears rolled down my cheeks. Krishna kept his hand on my shoulder. I looked up with moist eyes to thank Mr Bhardwaj, but he was gone and so was Parthivbhai.

I looked at Ba and she was sobbing. My eyes were moist. Everything was happening very fast. My destiny had changed since Krishna's arrival in my life. Was he really our lucky mascot? Bapuji was right. Tears rolled out from my eyes.

I couldn't believe that destiny could change like that; it was a miracle!

Yes, miracles do happen.

Was it the first U-turn in my life? Yes, it was.

Pain in the Ass

"Meet our partner, Mr Indrajit Singh. He is in-charge of the audit department and income tax matters," Parthivbhai said smiling as we entered Singh Sahib's chamber.

He was in his mid-forties with a pot belly. He was an FCA, a fellow chartered accountant, a senior member of the institute.

I had passed my 12th standard exams. I was excited and nervous at the same time when I reached PIA& Co. to submit the articleship form no 102. It's a three years training for a stipend of 750 rupees under a practicing CA firm as per the Institute's guidelines based on the city's cost of living and population.

Meanwhile, I was helping Bapuji in his office in my free time. He was a part-time real estate broker and had turned into a full-time insurance broker. Ba teasingly called him Agent Vinod many times, but he liked that better than Sheikh Chilli. The future of the property market looked bleak, so the insurance business kept Bapuji busy. We had shifted to our home. Ba redid the old interiors – the pink distemper and the picture of the Modi Circus. Onions, potatoes and the ceramic pickles jars were stored in my room. And of course; Lord Krishna's effigy was there as well.

Ba gave me a surprise gift. She had saved some money from the insurance commission and had bought a new scooty for me. As the insurance agency was in her name, all the commission cheques were received in her name. She was even signing cheques for Bapuji's pocket expenses.

In between, Urvi had been travelling frequently to Mumbai to find out about journalism courses. She finally announced that she would pursue journalism. Urvi's father was promoted to branch manager and they moved to Sunrise Bungalows, a new posh locality on SG Road. They travelled to London, Dubai, and Kenya for holidays; obviously, it was sponsored by the bank.

And last, but not the least, Deepak returned from London and apologised to Urvi on behalf of his father. He convinced her that neither was he involved nor was he concerned with his father's business. Urvi had accepted his apology but I hadn't, and never would. I told myself that a million times. I stayed focused as there was only one way to reach Urvi. And that was by becoming a CA.

Singh Sahib interviewed me for the next ten minutes and finally took me to be introduced to his other colleagues.

We entered Mr AK Fuliya's chamber, one of the partners and an ACA, Associate Chartered Accountant, meaning that he had not completed five years' membership with the institute.

"Oye, AK Forty-Seven, meet Manav Modi. He has joined us for the articleship," Singh Sahib said and chucked.

'You will never change," Fuliya Sir said.

"Sorry Ashishbhai, I was kidding," Singh said and chuckled again.

"Manav,this is Mr. Ashish K Fuliya, CA and MBA.He is in charge of company audits, client relations and liaising," Singh Sahib said looking towards me. I offered my hand. He reciprocated.

Mr Ashish was in his early thirties. He was wearing a slim-fitted suit. He looked like a fish out of water, maybe because he was an MBA, trying to look different from the CAs.

"Welcome Manav, and just to let you know that we have a dress code. A white shirt and a tie is a must," he said sarcastically, looking at me from top to bottom.

"Thank you, sir, I will take care in the future," I said nervously.

"He is very strict about the dress code. We all should look the same like in school,"Singh chuckled. Ashish gave him a stern look.

"Singh *Sahib*, we should have a corporate look and atmosphere in our office if we want to target big corporate clients. We have to make this company grow, so we have to think big,"Ashish said, annoyed by Singh's remarks.

"Oh sorry ji, I was kidding with the young man," Singh Sahib said and signalled me to come out.

Singh took me to the farthest room – the one allocated to auditors. He pushed the door gently. There was spine-chilling silence in the room. I was agape to see the dingy room. It was a shabby work place covered in dust and was filled with clusters of files wrapped in red cloth dumped on the wooden cupboards, unsteady staff tables and on the floor. And the ceiling fan's blades were moving slower than the hour hand of the clock. Calendars from Dena Bank, Jumbo Shipping, Mehsana Milk Dairy and Gujarati *panchang* with gods and goddess' pictures were fixed on the wall. A strong fragrance of incense sticks and human moisture made the room more suffocating. I felt like throwing up and exhaled.

"This room is a meditation room. You can enjoy the silence and also practice to breathe. Nobody chats in this room," Singh Sahib said in hushed voice and winked. Everybody looked haggard and tired.

"Meet Manav Modi, another victim of Parthivbhai," Singh said and everyone tittered. This time I was the only one who was confused.

"Welcome, we were kidding," Singh said trying to suppress his laughter.

I sighed as Singh left, but had to hold my breath.

"Hi, I am CA Bhavesh Shah, Audit Manager and in-charge of the audit team," a man stepped forward and introduced me to the other articles standing in the queue – Manoj Desai, Rajesh Soni, Sonal Shah and Kalpana Parekh. I was feeling proud to be a part of this team. Finally I had joined CA. I saluted them one by one as a president salutes soldiers in a parade.

I noticed that all the male audit staff wore white shirts and ties, like medical representatives or salesmen. There was no dress code for the female staff; both girls looked like butterflies.

"Mehul and Jignesh are outside in the field," Bhavesh said, pressing the bell.

A boy entered quickly.

"Gopi, get some chai and biscuits for us," he yelled, signalling to me to sit on a chair next to Manoj and Rajesh.

Manoj had a magnifying lens and was gawking at vouchers like a PI. Rajesh had a moustache thicker than the hair on his head; he had removed his shoes, and the smell of his socks wafted into the stuffy room. Bhavesh wore a cookie cutter fit-for-all hair wig; it was slapped on his scalp and moved as he moved his neck. Sonal was ultra-thin and wore a plain salwar-kurta with long sleeves like a nurse. She had waist-length braided hair, and looked like a brand ambassador for a hair oil brand. Kalpana wore heavy glasses and wore a mask to avoid the filthy smell. She was a new article.

"Will you be appearing for one group or both groups of Inter CA?" Bhavesh asked after gulping water from a bottle.

"Both groups. I want to pass CA in three years itself," I said with pride in my voice.

"Why are you in a hurry? Look at Rajesh," Bhavesh smiled smugly pointing at Rajesh, who looked self-conscious.

"He has been trying to pass the CA exam since the last eight years, but he's only passed the Inter CA. Don't rush; even our planning commission formulates five-years plans," he said and sniggered.

We heard a knock on the door. Gopi entered with chai and a plate of biscuits on a tray. He threw the cups and plates on the table and left.

"Singh sahib says try try till you succeed," Rajesh said and stood up. He took a biscuit, dunked it in Bhavesh's chai and gulped it down.

"Idiot, what are you doing? This is my chai!" Bhavesh said, feigning an angry look.

"Why didn't you order some chai for me? I am senior to you," Rajesh said and quickly went to his seat.

"Don't drink too much chai, you suffer from acidity all the time," Bhavesh said and smirked. I coughed as a reaction to that remark as I was about to sip the chai.

The intercom phone rang. Kalpana picked it up and quickly hung up.

"Bhaveshbhai, the boss is calling us," she said to Bhavesh, and both the girls left.

"Singh will squeeze them both," Manoj said looking at us.

"Hey sherlock holmes, finish vouching… and get me the draft report in the evening," Bhavesh said to Manoj, as he noticed he was staring at me and Bhavesh.

A few more awkward seconds passed in silence.

"Bhaveshbhai, one minute," Manoj said and walked to Bhavesh with a voucher in his hand.

"Yes, informer, what did you discover this time? It's headache to train articles!" Bhavesh said, looking at the voucher. I felt like he had just lampooned me.

"Which account should be charged for the director's honeymoon expenses and lingerie for the wife?" Manoj asked with a straight face.

"What…?" Bhavesh almost jumped up from his seat. Everyone laughed; I tried to control myself but failed.

"Stupid, don't waste time on petty issues. Focus on materiality. Get me the draft audit report quickly!" Bhavesh said in frustration.

Manoj walked to his seat quietly.

Sonal and Kalpana returned. Both looked pissed off.

"What happened?"Rajesh asked, as he untied the rubber band from around a Paan Parag sachet, poured a little in his mouth, and once again tied it and kept it on the table.

"Singh Sahib asked us why we went home from the client's place by rickshaw, and why we did not take a bus," Kalpana said, looking dismayed.

"If we had taken a bus, we would not have been able to reach home before 8:00 pm. When will we get the time to study?" Sonal said, expecting sympathy in return.

"Shhh... Let's get back to work and follow the company policy. The client doesn't pay us much so company cannot spend lavishly," Bhavesh said and stood up, adjusting his hairwig with both the hands.

"You must see USA," Bhavesh said to me after few seconds, stretching his hands.

"USA?" I said in confusion.

"Umesh Sundarbhai Acharya was a born mugger; he qualified as a CA recently. He is the son of our client, Sundarbhai," Bhavesh said and passed on his number to me on a paper.

"Thanks Bhaveshbhai," I said, taking the paper from him.

"Don't be so formal. But I will not spare you from the work. I am very strict. No leave and absence," Bhavesh said, gazing into my eyes.

"Sure. I will not give you a chance to complain," I said and stood up to leave the depressing place, inhabited by people of a primitive lifestyle.

As I rode home, I wondered where to start. How I would manage going to office daily, my CA studies and the lectures in college. On top of it, the atmosphere at PIA was discouraging. I was to work with losers. My heart began to throb.

The company's name should be changed from Parthiv, Indrajit, Ashish & Co. to Pain-In-The-Ass and that was the first step, I thought.

4Ds – Formula 4D

"Jai Shree Krishna, Aunty," I said to Umesh's grand mother (or great grandmother) and sat on the sofa.

I was at Umesh's house; Victoria Heights Apartment on SG Road. She was intently watching the *Mahabbharata* on television. Abhimanyu had entered the chakravyuh, but as we all know he would not able to get out of it.

Umesh's grandmother (or great grandmother) looked very old, older than the pyramids. I think she might have seen Abhimanyu alive. She had short hair. Women look pretty with short hair, particularly in old age. I think there are three major reasons why old ladies prefer short hair, a) convenience, b) self service, c) they give a damn to their beau after a certain age.

"Jai Shree Krishna, *beta,*" she said looking at me, and resumed watching the scene as Abhimanyu was being stabbed brutally.

I was impressed with the apartment. *Umesh S Acharya, Associate Chartered Accountant,* was inscribed on a metallic nameplate outside their apartment. It was a beautiful duplex apartment. *I should meet only successful people like Umesh*, I reminded myself again.

I wondered when I could earn enough money and buy such a beautiful home for my parents (and of course for Urvi). *Maybe after I become a qualified* CA, I thought. I had held my breath form the time I had entered the house. I imagined Umesh to be a good-looking, smart chap.

"Hello, Manav, how are you? I am Umesh Acharya," the emaciated-looking guy said as he entered the room. I was stumped!

If I ended looking like him, even if I qualify CA, Urvi and her mother would give me the boot, regardless of whether I became a CA or not. How can these unkempt CAs compete with dashing MBAs? Anyway I greeted him.

"So, you want to pursue CA?" Umesh asked sitting on the sofa next to me.

I nodded.

"Good."

For the next five minutes I told him all there was about me.

A manservant entered the hall carrying a glass of water on a tray. He kept the glass of water on the table and left.

"I need your guidance to select the books and if you share any of your experiences, it will be great," I said, looking at him. I stretched my hand to take the glass of water and thought of pouring it on my head to regain my senses. I took a sip instead.

"Sure," he said and signalled at me to follow him.

"Chai?" he asked. I nodded.

"Kaka, bring two chais and snacks upstairs," Umesh exclaimed.

We went to his study room. It was a miniature library. There were bottles of Kayam Churna – Ayurvedic medicines for constipation – on the side table.

"Don't get scared, you don't have to read all these books. I had made the mistake of reading too many books and didn't consult anyone like you are doing. And coaching classes were also confusing. You are smart and proactive. Before preparation, planning is a must," he said and asked me to sit on the chair (actually I wanted to rest on the bed).

Our CA course is a correspondence course, and the institute couriered study material to students. Unlike MBAs, who have classes in high-tech buildings, we CAs have to ramble like camels in the desert for tuition at private coaching classes in most cities. And we receive the CA degree certificate by mail, unlike the convocation ceremony held by MBA colleges.

Umesh went through his things and handed over some books, booklets of suggested papers, questions and answers for the last ten years. We discussed how to beat the institute for the next ten minutes, and I felt like running away.

Kaka brought the chai with *chakri*, *mathri*, and *gathia* in three small bowls and left. I took a *mathri* and thought about stopping at a pharmacy on my way home to buy a few bottles of Kayam Churna.

"How can I schedule college, articleship, CA, and B.Com?"I asked, taking a sip of the chai.

Umesh took the *gathia* bowl and emptied it into his left hand. I followed him as I wanted to be like him. Of course, only until I pass the CA exam, and with that thought I took as many *chakri* and *mathri* as I could hold in one hand. He started wolfing down the *gathia*.

"First step, wake up early by 5:00 am and sleep early by 10:00 pm." He paused and ate some more *gathia*. I hadn't tasted it yet.

"And boss, prepare and strictly follow the timetable. Have a fixed time for studying, sleeping, entertainment, and everything else, including daily chores. Just imagine that you are on the border with a gun in your hand and are facing your enemies. If you lose your focus even for a fraction of a second, a bullet will hit you and you are finished," he said seriously.

I was scared. I stopped eating.

"But how, I mean where should I live then? At home or at a spiritual place, like saints live?"I asked anxiously. He laughed.

"You have to go underground," he said and stood up to pull out a book (Economics) size of Oxfod Dictionary, from the drawer. He pulled out a paper from it.

I stared at the paper; it said RTS-Roadmap to Success. I felt dozy as I looked at the Economics book and RTS plan.

It looked like a grid plan to reach the gold mine of ICAI. It stated:

(a) From morning 5:00 am to 9:00 am – mugging for CA,
(b) From 10:00 am to 6:00 pm – articleship,
(c) At 7:00 pm, dinner,
(d) From 7:30 to 9:30 pm – mugging for B.Com.

Note:

1. Attend college alternative days.
2. Keep flashlight ready all the time(with extra batteries)
3. Pls don't forget to take-before going college – Kayam Churna (MUST MUST MUST).

And on Sundays, 16 hours of mugging – from 5:00 am onwards with few breaks for breakfast, lunch, dinner, and to go to the bathroom.

I looked at him in annoyance, thought bad words for him, Mehras and...the institute.

We discussed for some more time, and finally I dumped the tomes into the bag. For the next three years, I would have to sit, stand, and sleep with them.

We walked down the stairs. Umesh's grandmother (or great grandmother) was still watching the serial. She was sobbing, watching Abhimanyu's death scene. His body was on the funeral pyre and everybody was mourning his death.

Don't worry Aunty, I wanted to say, *I am the new Abhimanyu of the 21st century. I am caught in the chakravyuh of ICAI*-Institue of Cold-Blooded Accountants of India.

"Jai Jinendra, Aunty," I said, looking at her.

She looked at me, then turned her gaze to the bags in my hands.

"Have some food, *beta*," she offered, wiping her eyes with her sari.

"Aunty, Ba and Bapuji must be waiting for me. Next time for sure," I said.

She raised her hands to bless me. I needed that from every mother on earth.

Umesh came out to see me off and pressed the lift button for me.

"The road to success is always bumpy, but you can overcome all the hiccups if you remember Formula 4D," Umesh said, as the lift arrived.

I hopped into the lift puzzled. "4Ds?"

"*Discipline, Devotion, Determination,* and *Dedication,*" he said as the door closed.

I thought, *it should be Formula 5D. Deepak.*

Guantanamo Bay or GB

"What are you doing at 5 am? Are you not well?" Bapuji asked.

"Study," I said briskly and rushed to the bathroom.

The next morning, I jumped out of bed at 5:00 am and articulated the RTS. I wondered if the roadmap would lead to success, but success without Urvi would be hell.

I had allotted just one hour in a week for Urvi, only on Sunday or would meet her at college. I could call her during breaks to boost me. She was my Bournvita, the secret of my energy. I missed those beautiful moments in the past that I had spent with her without worrying about time.

I was nervous about sharing the RTS with Ba, but finally I announced that for the next three years there will not be any celebration of any festival, and she had to cut out the jamborees at home so that I could focus on mugging.

Although she mourned for weeks, but finally accepted it.

That's life and that's CA articleship. Both suck.

I spent the next two years, six months, ninety days, twenty hours, ten seconds and equal nanoseconds of my life in a Guantanamo Bay-like jail.

By the time I reached the CA final and my final year of B.Com, I had lost a lot of weight and looked gaunt. By now, most of the seniors were having best of their time and fun in sunbathing in the quad rather than taking classes.

RTS – Articleship Sucks!

"You are a very quick learner, just like Umesh. I will recommend Singh Sahib to get a big client, Continental Real Estate, Bengaluru." I had heard this a hundred times; yes, I swear, the hundredth time from Bhavesh since I had joined articleship.

He dropped me outside my home and left. But finally, he had gotten convinced to allocate big corporate clients after more than two years of slogging along with him and slogging all over the villages of Gujarat.

PIA soon discarded the dress code due to the articles' demand to raise the stipend allowance, and we all began wearing jeans, T-shirts and some even wore kurta pyjamas with sneakers.

During the articleship, I was tortured by the vouching and verification of petty cash, journal vouchers, bank payments, purchases, sales, fixed assets, and inventory. Vouching means inspection of documentary evidence supporting and substantiating a transaction. It was considered a trivial job, but for me it was new-fangled and stimulating as it helped me understand the business and the internal controls of the client's business. I became famous and a master of vouching and my red tick marks were famed like the legendry John Hancock's signature.

I was mugging auditing and income tax subjects at home for the final year exams, so it became very easy to grasp and implement the procedures at the client's house. Preparation does help. But it also sucks! I visited college like visiting doctors pay flying visits to hundreds of patients.

I was bushed as I started walking towards my home. Bhavesh's killer car vanished into the distance.

"Jai Shri Krishna," I said to Mohan Kaka, an old neighbour. He was out on his evening walk (after dinner at 5 pm). He didn't respond. I realised that I looked unkempt, as I hadn't shaved since a week and my shirt was untucked. A stray dog stopped and growled at me; I imagined he was Deepak and scared him.

I pressed the bell and Ba opened the door.

"Kaun...?" She looked at me in surprise; she took some time to recognise me.

I was bamboozled at her reaction. Was I looking so weird and doleful... like Umesh? How would I face Urvi the next day? Hell, I had lost tons of weight! I was surviving on tea, *mathri-gathia-chakri*. Of course, Kayam Churna as well.

"Manav Arvindbhai Modi," I said, pinching her cheeks as I entered.

"You don't have time to even shave during your articleship?" Ba chided.

I smiled and sat on the sofa.

"*Gando thai jaise. Tamari* institute *gandi che*?" she said (You will go mad. Your Institute is mad) and banged the door hard.

I removed my shoes, and didn't reply.

"You are smelling! Go and take a shower!" Ba yelled, holding her sari pallu to her nose.

She ran to the kitchen without waiting for my reply. I realised that she was frustrated, as she hadn't met any relatives for a long time and Bapuji was in Mumbai since the past three days (Agent Vinod's felicitation). She needed to talk to someone. I smiled at her reaction, said sorry to her in my head, and went to the washroom.

After changing I rang up Urvi's residence, but got no response. I tried ten more times, but the result was the same.

"Are you calling your institute's helpline at this time?" Ba asked sulking.

I didn't reply.

"Sanjay and Kavita from your college called many times," Ba exclaimed from the kitchen while making chai for me.

"Who?" I asked coming out from the washroom. I had to meet Urvi the next day; only a few days were left for the college vacation to start. I could focus more on RTS then so I could afford some time off.

"I don't know. They wanted your advice for CA," Ba yelled from the kitchen.

"So what did you say?" I asked.

"I told them to join MBA instead."

"Welcome, *Eid ke chand*," Krishna said, hugging me. He introduced me to a girl named Beena Zaveri. She was as thin as a pencil. She was wearing a yellow salwar-kurta while Krishna was wearing black jeans and an orange T-shirt.

I was at HM College near Navrangpura, after hitting the books for two hours in the morning. I had shaved and sported new blue jeans and a black T shirt, as I had come out from the world of Stone Age and re-entered the cultured world. I was happy to be in the company of lively and enthusiastic people.

"Hi," Beena said softly, offering her minuscule hand to me.

I reciprocated; her hand was very soft, like jelly pudding.

"Dude, she is my *habibi*," Krishna said and winked at me. I started looking for my belle.

I heard Urvi's scooty's horn. Deepak was following her on his bike. Both stopped near the entrance gate of the college where we were waiting. Deepak parked his bike next to me.

"Dude, what's up?" he said and patted me on the shoulder. Idiot!

"Not too bad. You tell me, how are things with you?" I asked casually.

"Just killing time, I have to wait for my MBA till college is over," he said and snickered, "But don't worry, I will catch up with you."

He had grown his hair up to his shoulders. As usual his appearance was above reproach.

"You both are always talking about yourselves, without worrying about others and their careers," Urvi said, clasping my right hand.

I felt like my breath had been knocked out. There was something special about a women's touch. I think God created girls with extra care. She was wearing my favourite – a white salwar-pink kurta.

"Sorry Urvi, I am almost there…just last final exam. Little extra push and I will be through," I said and once again chanted the 5Ds in my head.

"Okay fine! Can you give a bit of extra time to your old friends at least during the vacations and before I go to Mumbai?" Urvi asked looking into my eyes.

I will have to check my RTS, I thought to myself. But looking into her eyes, I nodded.

"How is your insurance business?" Deepak asked and smiled smugly.

I don't like this question. He touched my wounds.

"As usual, your welfare is our responsibility," I chanted LIC's slogan and laughed. Urvi joined me.

Krishna made a farting noise with his mouth and laughed even louder. Beena was already deeply immersed in her favourite book *Ayurvedic Cooking for Self-Healing* by Vasant Lad and Usha Lad.

Deepak was knocked out for a six.

"Which policy do you sell the most?" Deepak asked again, looking pissed off.

"The Money Back policy twenty years plan is very popular, especially if the client has difficulty in paying the premium after five years," I replied, emphasising last words, "You get cash back. And good thing is that *LIC doesn't cheat.*"

Urvi was shocked. Krishna looked at me and smiled while Beena stared at her nails.

"Oh, I see. You are a smart insurance agent. I think you should continue this as a full time career. Just forget CA," Deepak replied angrily. I felt even more anger.

"Yeah, it doesn't make any difference to me if I'm an insurance agent, CA, or an MBA," I replied but couldn't control my last words "I will just be happy if I don't cheat anyone *like your father.*"

"Excuse me," Deepak exclaimed, "Mind your…"

"Just shut up, and accept the truth," I said interrupting both.

"You shut up! Do you want to know the truth?" Deepak exclaimed and paused abruptly. He hesitated, scanning me from top to bottom, "Business...is not... your cup of tea, so don't try to be a know-it-all!"

"You both are jerks...total jerks," Urvi shrieked, her eyes red, glaring at me and then at Deepak. I kept quiet. Krishna shushed Beena.

"Excuse me," a male voice called out from behind.

I turned around and saw a boy with a homely looking girl. He was unshaved and was wearing an un-tucked loose shirt. I thought that the peon had come to catch me due to my regular absence. I became sober instantly.

"I am Sanjay Joshi and she is Kavita Dahiya. We had called you at home a couple of times," the guy said in a low voice.

"We both are pursuing CA," the girl said. I was back in Stone Age era.

"First do welfare for your CA fraternity," Deepak said mockingly, glancing at Sanjay and Kavita. Sanjay and I overlooked his comments, but Kavita stored this insult in her memory permanently, and glared at Deepak with the same expression on her face which Shikhandi would have had while facing Bhishma in the epic battle of *Mahabharata*. Women can trace their roots back by a hundred generations and spend their entire lives chasing for their revenge.

"How are your articleship and studies going on?"I asked and walked them away from the group to avoid mockery of my profession any further.

"We are dummy articles. We don't go to the office," Sanjay said.

"We did our schooling in Gujarati medium, now we have to study hard for 14 hours a day to prepare for the CA examinations in English," the girl said. "We want your help in Accounts subject."

A siren rang out. All the lovebirds started walking towards the classrooms.

"Let's go," Krishna said, tugging Beena's hand and started to walk away. All of us followed them.

"Can we go to the canteen?" Beena asked, "Krish, I am hungry!"

Krishna stopped. We walked past both of them.

Modi Massage – Knowledge is Power

"Don't worry; the new income tax officer is trying to create an impression that he is very strict. He had sent a similar notice to many people. Send me a copy of the notice. And get ready for the Bengaluru audit next week," Singh said and hung up the phone.

A few days remained of the college holidays. Urvi had gone to Mumbai, Krishna to Dubai, and Deepak to London while I was busy with PIA, and GB. I mean the 5Ds.

I had come to the office, Modi Investment Broker, which had merged into Modi Insurance Broker. Bapuji had received an income tax notice under section 139, asking for some more information. However, I was not yet trained to handle income tax matters at our office. And Bhavesh said that only partners handled such matters, neither articles nor even paid staff like Bhavesh. And the official reason was its highly complex and confidential nature. But in fact, partners and the ITO negotiate for a cut. They twist income tax rules, which would cause the partners embarrassment in front of the articles. What hypocrites!

"Papa, send a copy of the notice to Sir. I am going straight to the client for an audit," I said.

"Why have you not shaved?" Bapuji asked. But my mobile rang before I could answer him. I guessed that Urvi had returned from Mumbai. College started the next week.

"Hello, when did you come back?" I asked, as soon as I picked up the call.

"Today morning. Where are you, wonk?"She asked.

"With Agent Vinod," I said. Bapuji gave me a dirty look. I winked, and turned my back to him.

"Come home; we have not met for a long time," she ordered.

I recollected my RTS and modified it immediately (guys, sometime you must listen to your heart).

"Everything okay?" I asked as I came out from the office and walked towards the scooty.

"My back hurts and am feeling low. I am upset with Deepak. He had called me from London and said that he was coming back early. I cut short my trip and returned from Mumbai, but he hasn't come back," she complained, "He never keeps his word."

"Why do you trust him? He is like his father, they never keep their word," I smirked.

"Stupid, don't laugh. I am alone. Mom and Dad have gone to Baroda," she said, "Coming, no?"

I was in a dilemma: Urvi or the client? In other words, follow my heart or my mind?

I went with my crazy heart because after all I am a guy. I hadn't met her since the past three weeks; so she had a credit of three hours, according to the RTS.

I jumped ten traffic signals and drove on the pavement and between the electric poles and reached Bhuvi in excitement.

◎

"It's a bob cut," Urvi said, sniffling for virginally girly reasons. Why was she so different? What was wrong with this girl?

Already five minutes had passed. She was sitting on the sofa next to me; the door was sealed. And before that, we had hugged each other like never before.

And the girly reasons were : (a) Deepak had ditched her (We had already discussed this, but she didn't care for my advice), (b) I was ignoring her as well (It was difficult to make her understand that the institute demanded utmost devotion from all students), (c) Her back hurt due to her periods (This was something new for me).

She was wearing black Bermuda shorts and a pink loose sleeveless striped top. Green veins were visible on her neck. She had a pearl necklace and matching earrings. She looked strikingly hot in her new look.

As we sat on the sofa, she signalled for me to support her head on my lap. I followed her instruction like a slave and she put my hand on her head. I started moving my fingers slowly through her hair. Here we go again.

"Stupid, why have you not shaved?" she asked.

"It's a weekly job now. It takes five minutes daily, so I save thirty minutes in a week," I said and smirked.

"Oh, then am I wasting your time?" she asked.

"Yeah, but I will cover it. I will not shave for the next one month," I replied and grinned at my lame joke.

"You are a real nerd," she laughed, and held her stomach in pain.

"Mumbai is a beautiful city," she said, looking up at my face. I looked down at her face.

"Don't be biased against Ahmedabad. We have everything that Mumbai has," I said and started massaging her head. She closed her eyes. Her shorts slid down as she bent her legs. I turned my gaze to her head and pressed her forehead.

"Ah, I am feeling better..."

My fingers were moving gently on her head.

"Mumbai offers more opportunities for a career and people are more forward. They only talk about career and business," she said, her eyes still closed and legs straight. But we Ahmedabadis are smarter at milking an opportunity than Mumbai people; I continued my massage more energetically.

"Am I pressing too hard?" I asked, as I pushed hard with both my hands on her forehead.

"No, it's nice. Can you massage my legs?" she asked, her eyes still closed, "They hurt."

I stood up; she slid upwards on the sofa and loosely widened her legs. I bent down on my knees and pressed her left thigh with both my palms. I have been massaging Ba's and Bapuji's legs since I was a kid. Experience and knowledge are never wasted.

"Yeah, very good.Do it a bit slowly, don't put so much pressure, stupid…" she said smiling. My soul felt rejuvenated.

"But I have heard that people are selfish in Mumbai. Our city still cares about relationships and friends," I continued.

"It's not true. No one cares about relationships and friends, whether in Ahmedabad or Mumbai," she said. I looked at her eyes. Tears rolled out from her closed eyes. I was surprised at the way in which her mood was swinging; it was unpredictable, and I didn't know if she was sad about me, Deepak, or her period.

"Once I become a CA, then I will always be with you," I said, continuing to massage her right leg.

"I don't know that, but if you both have your careers, then I will also focus on my career," she said, and sat on the sofa, tears rolling down her cheeks.

Now here is the thing about women, I just don't get them!

I took out a hankie from my jeans pocket and sat beside her to wipe the tears on her cheeks. I had seen Bapuji doing the same when Ba used to get upset; after all, we Modis know how to love our women.

"Urvi, I need your support. I have to focus on my career," I said to change the mood, "Trust me, I will support you once I become a CA."

She raised her head, looking into my eyes, she slowly kissed my right cheek. I gave her my other cheek. She threw a pillow at me.

Mahatma Gandhi had said that if someone slaps you, you should turn your other cheek to him. Why can't we use the same credo for the kiss? It's win-win situation for both the parties concerned!

"How is your articleship training going on?" she asked. I wanted to vomit my anger on the notice issued by the ITO.

"Our firm has these primitive ideas about articleship training. We are not exposed to important matters of income tax hearings and most of the time we are slogging and doing vouching of small firms in villages and bank audits," I vented.

"Yeah, but then how do students learn to handle income tax matters?" she asked.

"By reading books and by trial and error methods," I smiled. "I learnt massage by watching my grandfather and practiced on my grandmother and now on you."

She laughed, holding her stomach.

I felt hungry after the massage. We went to the kitchen to make a sandwich.

"Good, now you look like the original confident Urvi. Why were you so nervous?" I asked and touched her hair, while she was cutting the bread.

"Leave it; I don't want to talk about that. Why should I waste my life in Ahmedabad? I want to be a journalist and I will have to go to Mumbai for that," she said and opened the fridge. She took out a cucumber, a tomato, some boiled potato, and some butter.

"Fine, you focus on your journalism. I have to go Bengaluru for an audit for a couple of weeks," I said and turned on the gas with the lighter.

"See, how passionate you are about your career!" she said, "No one has time for me."

"I wish I could always be with you," I said and went close to her. She took two pieces of cucumber and tossed one into her mouth, and one into mine.

"Why is Deepak not like you? Straightforward?" she said and looked into my eyes. I suddenly went back to the past.

"Deepak has ditched my birthday party two years in a row. Why is he not like you – honest and trustworthy?" she said, looking at me with tearful eyes, "Deepak will not understand a girl. Maybe his father didn't teach him anything after his mother's death."

"His father ditched his mother for another woman, and she committed suicide along with her daughter after suffering from depression for more than three years," she had said.

"I think you know him better than me. Like father, like son." I replied, coming back from the past.

"I don't know," she said and continued to chop the onion, with tears in her eyes. Why do girls contradict what they believe? It's so confusing.

"It's yummy," I said, as she fed me the sandwich. We were sitting on the sofa again.

"Are you coming to college next week?" Urvi asked.

"I will check the RTS,"I said and snickered. She laughed, holding her stomach in pain again.

"Let's start the audit of CRL, Continental Realty Ltd, in Bengaluru. It will take a month. We chose you, because you are good in FEMA matters," Singh said as I entered his chamber, "Mr Banerjee, the CFO of the company is disciplined, unlike other CAs."

I wondered if that was a compliment or criticism of CAs.

Anyway, I had read the Foreign Exchange Management Act (FEMA) ten times; it was covered in the CA final syllabus.

"Okay but when are we starting?" I asked, "Also, I have only theoretical knowledge of FEMA, not practical."

"Even I don't have practical experience because we don't have clients in Ahmedabad who have offices abroad. I tried to look for associates in Mumbai but couldn't find suitable ones. But don't worry, you just be sincere, we will take care of the rest," Singh said casually.

"Sir, what about our income tax hearing?" I asked.

"You focus on Bengaluru and enjoy 4Ds – *dance, disco, drink, and dinner*," Singh said and chuckled. "I will take care of Tripathi Sahib and his dog."

I ran out of the office and pumped my fist in the air to celebrate.

Yesss! At last, I got a the chance to handle a big client.

Invitation to White House

"Good morning, Manav. I am impressed. You are punctual and sincere," Ramesh Kamadolli, the chief accountant said, as I sat on the chair facing him in his chamber. He was an old man with grey whiskers under his chin. His face was almost mahogany coloured. I was the first one to reach office and had collected the newspaper at the doorstep of the office.

I had reached Bengaluru at 6:00 am (after a 40 million hours train journey) and quickly, after dumping my baggage in the 'flophouse', I gobbled twenty tiny idlis. Our flophouse was just behind the Royal Orchid Central Hotel on Ulsoor Road, adjacent to Mahatma Gandhi Road. The head office was walking distance at Ulsoor Road, near Ulsoor Lake.

"Sir, I always give my 100 percent," I said.

"Manav, you have to verify the sales of local projects. I will introduce you to Chandrashekar Yadwad, senior accountant, he will explain the details," Ramesh said.

"Fine, Sir," I nodded. A boy brought in some chai. They both had a brief chat in Kannada and giggled. I guessed that the boy must have mentioned to him that this was my fourth cup of chai.

"Later, we need to work out some FEMA issues before Mr Talwar, chairman and Mr Pankaj, CFO return from their trip abroad," he said in an indistinct voice and took a sip of the chai.

"Sir, what is the problem?" I asked.

He looked into my face and replied feebly, "We want to sell our properties to Non-Resident Indians in the Gulf and in western countries. But we don't know any advisor abroad who can help us to form a wholly-owned-subsidiary company in the Gulf and in Europe under FEMA guidelines," he said taking a sip of the chai, "And Mr Talwar wants to start selling in the Gulf region urgently, before our competitor starts selling there."

"So, you need an advisor in the Gulf?" I asked.

"Desperately, and another problem is, how do we receive remittance from NRIs under FEMA? They want to remit funds through official channels only, as NRI clients want home loans against the property, otherwise we will not be able to start the sale of the project," he said holding the cup to his lips until the last droplet of chai dripped into his mouth.

"I also drink a lot of chai," he said, and winked.

"No, real estate activity is not allowed in the freezones in Dubai," Manish Jain said over the phone.

I had returned from office to the flophouse and had called Krishna's advisor, JCA Business Advisors in Dubai.

"You mean there is no solution?" I asked.

"Did I say that?"

"Sorry Sir, please tell me," I said in excitement, "It's urgent."

"Why are you people in India always in a hurry?" he said. Silence prevailed again for a few tongue-tied seconds.

After a pause, he continued to explain how a real estate company can operate in Dubai through representative offices.

He continued further.

"Indians in Dubai can remit money through money exchanges in Dubai to their account in India, or pay directly to the developer in India, that is, the parent company of the representative office in Dubai."

"But, I have to form a company as per FEMA guidelines..."

"For Indian tax issues, contact Mr Bharat, our associate in Mumbai," he said, paused, "But he will charge you for his advice unlike us in Dubai."

"Sure, we will pay him and you as well."

"Good and listen, ask Krishna to settle last year's audit fees as well,"

"Sure Sir, I will tell him."

"And last," he said.

"What?"

"Give him my regards."

"Well done, Manav!" Pankaj Banerjee, the chief financial officer said in fluent English. I had met him for the first time.

We were all in the conference room and I had finished my presentation about setting up the company in Dubai after consulting the associate in Mumbai (and of course after the payment of fees).

Banerjee Sir was an ex-NRI from USA, but originally from Kolkata. He had returned as India was growing, and he was now settled in Bengaluru. He had some grey hair, mainly at his temples, and he had a charming face. He was wearing black pants, a white shirt, and a slim red tie. He looked fit in his slim-fit suit. He was a fitness freak.

"Pankaj, he will be an entrepreneur one day," Vimal Talwar said in a hoarse voice and lit a cigar in style and walked to the window to blow the cancerous smoke outside.

Vimal Talwar had a potbelly. He was wearing an off-white safari suit. He was six feet tall, and in his early sixties, I guessed. His face and arms glistened as if he had just come from a massage centre in Thailand.

"Sir, can we appoint him as our tax advisor after he completes CA?" Ramesh proposed.

"No, we can offer him a job in our Mumbai office on the Powai project," Vimal Talwar said in a husky voice. "Maybe Siddharth can also learn from him. He is spoiling his life in the USA."

Siddharth was the only and spoilt son of Vimal Talwar. He loved his son, like Spike dog loved his son Tyke in Tom and Jerry. Siddharth was in the USA pursuing an MBA degree. Senior Talwar wanted to retire, but junior was not ready to take over as yet.

"Sir, I think I should take a call after my final exams," I said, vanity creeping into my voice.

"Keep it up my boy," Vimal Talwar roared and left from the conference room.

"Good decision," Pankaj said as we all walked out from the room.

"Young man, what are your hobbies?" Pankaj asked.

"Sir, I am focusing on studies at the moment," I said quietly. He further interrogated me about my hobbies and the future and finally came to the point.

"Are you free on Sunday?"

I bobbed my head up and down.

My New Birth – Hats off to Bengaluru

"Hi, I am Riya," she said in a sweet girlish tone, "Please come in."

When a guy meets a girl for the first time, she will present herself like a cute and polite Alice in Wonderland but once they become close, she will become the athletic and sexy Lara Croft: Tomb Raider. Anyway, I entered slowly, carrying a huge bouquet of roses in my hand.

The nameplate outside the villa whispered "White House".

"*Jhuki jhuki si nazar...beqarar hai ki nahi...*" Jagjit Singh's ghazal made the atmosphere of the hall warmer. I was feeling nervous and heartsick.

"The music is fine?" she asked again in her melodious voice of Alice in Wonderland. I nodded. Riya was tall and slim, with shoulder length hair. She had a slightly wheatish complexion. And she was beautiful, rather hot, to be precise. She was wearing a black mini skirt that ended three fingers above the knees and a blouse that showed off a lot of cleavage. But she was Pankaj Banerjee's daughter. It was Banerjee Sir's 21st wedding anniversary. I was the only invitee at the White House (*Why did they invite only me? Why are we auditors always wary? Let's enjoy the moment*, I scolded myself).

The sofa, walls and floor were all white. The dim silver-light in the hall and at the entrance created a very relaxing ambience. There were photographs of rivers, birds, animals and plants on the walls and in the hallway. All the furniture looked new. I think if women's love for furniture and interior decoration is not prohibited immediately by The Ministry of Environment and Forests, the world will not have any more forests left.

As I walked in, a manservant scurried behind me and dusted my footprints. He was in a white uniform too.

I sat on the sofa (white) and inhaled deeply as Riya's mother entered the hall. She was a high-tech advanced version of Riya. She looked ultra-modern and was wearing a full length red skirt with slits up above the knee on both sides and displayed more cleavage than her daughter. I gazed only once at her to respect the designer for his or her creativity, and for the expensive investment made by Banerjee Sir, and lastly for the sake of all the hot women in the universe.

"Congratulations, Madam," I said and stood up.

"Thanks. Don't be so formal. I am Sonica. But you can call me Sony," she said and offered her hand. I reciprocated and handed over the red rose bouquet nervously. I was told not to bring a gift, because Banerjee Sir told me that I was like a 'family member'.

"Wow! Lovely roses!" she exclaimed and passed the bouquet to Riya.

Can I breathe now? I asked myself and exhaled as I saw Banerjee Sir entering the room with a glass of red wine in his hand. He wore blue jeans and a black T-shirt.

"Hey young man! Good to see you," Banerjee Sir said and stuck out his hand. I congratulated him and offered him my hand. All the members of the family were clearly fitness freaks.

I was wearing blue jeans, a grey T-shirt and grey-black sports shoes. I thought I looked cool. I thought of Deepak; he would have been a perfect fit in this scenario.

"*Tumko dekha to yeh khayal aya...*" another ghazal changed Banerjee Sir's mood and he cheerfully raised his hands and moved slowly to match the ghazal's rhythm.

Aunty gave him a tolerant gaze.

"Sony darling, I can't believe it. We have completed 21 years of marriage!" Banerjee Sir said looking at Sony and turning towards me, "What would you like to drink, Manav?"

But before I could reply, Aunty said, "Riya, can you change the music please? Otherwise Pankaj will bore us today," she threw a fake smile at us.

"Dad, we will have booze at the disco," Riya said and walked towards the music system. She played *Jane kyo log pyar karte hai* from *Dil Chahata Hai*.

"Okayyyy, let's cut the cake first," Banerjee Sir said.

"Say something. Why are you so quiet?" Riya asked, as we walked towards Kito's Garden Pub on 80 Feet Road, Koramangala. Aunty drove the car to the parking lot.

Young couples were standing around the place.

"What you studying?" I asked, looking at her slowly. She laughed. I joined her in nervousness.

"You will be a really cool CA," she said and held my hand.

I felt nervous. My heart was pounding!

"I will be going to the USA to be a Certified Public Accountant," she replied and let go of my hand. I exhaled.

"I thought you must be pursuing fashion or modelling," I said (now I felt better, as we were from the same nerdy accounting fraternity. I imagined a high-five with her).

"Why... can't accounting professionals dress well and put on makeup?" she said and stopped.

After a few nervous seconds, we continued walking, she continued talking and my heart continued pounding.

"People should change their mentality. After office hours, everybody is the same," she said, looking into my eyes. "We should live a normal life. My dad is great. He balances his personal and professional life very well."

"Even I have a similar mentality," I said.

"Don't worry; you will change if you stay in Bengaluru," she said with a big smile on her face, "Can you dance with me today?"

"Um, do you know the *garba*?" I asked once again, feeling nervous.

She laughed again and once again she held my hand. I felt a strong urge to... pee.

"Do you watch movies?" Riya asked as we walked through the garden. I thought this was easy to answer.

"*Titanic*," I said.

She stopped, looked at me and burst into laughter. I gazed into her eyes. She held her gaze for a long time. I felt trapped.

"You are so sweet," she said and looked flirtatiously at me. I knew that I was in danger. My instincts warned that there will be stirring times ahead.

We went inside the pub. The passage was dark. Riya held my hand and navigated us towards the stage, where couples were dancing to "Beautiful Stranger" by Madonna on ear-piercing music. On the big TV screen Madonna was dancing and teasing the crowd. Banerjee Sir and Aunty were already waiting inside at a table. They looked tranquil. They had parked the car in the parking lot behind the pub and had entered through the back door. I felt like slipping away from the back door, but Riya was still holding my hand.

One thing was good about the pub; you cannot chat much due to the insanely loud music. I wanted to avoid talking. I looked around, most of the families and couples (young college students) sitting at tables were swaying their bodies to the music. I was worried about losing my study time; I would have to make up for the lost time next week (RTS, dude!).

After we had settled down, drinks were served. I had ordered a glass of orange juice. Banerjee Sir and Aunty had ordered a red wine bottle. And Riya had asked for a martini garnished with olives. She forced me to share it. I picked up the toothpick with the olive and gulped it. She beamed and patted my lap. Anyway I sipped it; it tasted sweet.

"*Do you like this place*?" Riya yelled in my ear, coming very close. Her soft touch erected the sleeping man in me. I jiggled.

"*Do you like the music*?" she asked again.

I gestured 'okay'.

And suddenly the music changed – a song from the movie *Koi Mil Gaya*.

It's magic, it's magic.

It's magic, it's magic... Parde ke girte hi, parde ke uthte hi...

Riya held my hand and yanked me towards the floor. Our bodies moved with the music and I forgot where I was, with whom I was, and what I was. Our bodies touched a thousand times, as I tried to copy Hrithik Roshan's steps. One young guy went further; he lay down on the floor and started to roll his body on both his hands. I thought he was drunk or was having convulsions. But to my surprise, others followed him as well.

I can tell you, my body and my mind were not in my control and I felt as if telekinetic Riya with her magical touch, like *Jadoo* the alien, had enhanced my brain and nervous system and shattered my inner soul. I felt as if I had been born again on that day!

Cup of Joe–I Owe Her

"You danced superbly!" Riya said when we met for coffee at Café Coffee Day at Windsor House, Brigade Road.

She wore blue jeans and a red turtleneck T-shirt. I thought she looked adorable. I had gone directly from office and was wearing black pants, a white shirt, and a purple tie.

"Nice tie," she remarked when I met her.

You might think that I was not mugging and that I had lost focus, but Urvi and Riya were the secret of my energy. I started my day at 4:00 am. We had a five-day working week at office, so I spent more time with my tomes over the weekends just so I could take out time to be in the company of the magical girl. I thought that in her company I could become cool like Deepak. Was I being selfish or practical?

"It's because of you," I replied.

I mean your magical touch, I thought to myself.

"No, it's because you don't know your strength. You spend your energy on mugging all the time. You should have some hobbies – some passion other than your career. If you have an edge, you will stand out from the crowd or else there are a million CAs, MBAs or other professionals, who are struggling in the market," she said, raising her hands and moving her thin fingers slowly, hypnotising me once again.

A waitress came to take our order.

I wanted a coffee. However, Riya studied the menu for a full five minutes and asked the waitress the amount of calories in each item. After calculating the additional workout she'd have to do the next day, she ordered.

"Two cups of joe and one veg sandwich," Riya said, pointing at the picture of the coffee and sandwich in the menu.

The waitress gazed intently at the coffee cup picture that Riya was pointing to. At last understanding what Riya meant, she ambled off.

"What do you mean by 'edge'?" I continued

"If your body language is good, you look stylish and sharp, and if you have a positive attitude, you will have an edge over others in the same industry. Knowledge alone will not help you be successful," she said, tapping my hand.

"But I am a CA. How will being stylish and my body language help me in my career? I have to deal with only files 24x7," I said gently.

"Why? You can't be a CFO or CEO?" she asked and paused, continuing to smash my slumbering soul.

"Today's leaders should be physically fit to be able to work long hours, travel around the globe, and to direct different departments of a business corporation," she said, taking a sip from the glass of the water.

I was awestruck at her knowledge and felt a strong urge to give her a bear hug. I had thought that the being a CEO was only the birth right of MBAs; I mean, I had never imagined that a CA could be a CEO.

The waitress placed the coffee and sandwich on the table.

"You are very bold, like your mom," I said.

"You mean to say that she is also hot and sexy?" she said seductively.

"Not like that! You're crazy!"

"You mean mom is not sexy?"

I grew very nervous. She laughed uncontrollably and kept her hand on my hand.

My heartbeat skipped. I looked at her but Urvi's face flickered before my eyes. I could not think beyond Urvi, CA, and Deepak! How could I focus on my look and body at the same time?

"I am here for a purpose. I have to be successful and focus on CA," I said sternly.

"You should be sombre, but not sad. Take it easy, man!" she said looking into my eyes.

"Riya, you are lucky; you have everything in life. I have yet to earn money. This society is phony and respects only money and status. I can't relax. For me, life is a race. I have to work hard to be successful in life," I replied and banged my fist on the table as thoughts of Mehra's broken deal, Deepak's abusing CAs, and Ba lying under the building during the earthquake circled in my head.

"Wow! You are a warrior!" she said in excitement and held my hand firmly; I melted like soft snow.

"Dad said that you like reading and you want to improve your presentation and looks," she said after a few seconds of silence.

Did she want to write a thesis on me?

"I don't know, I had said it just like that," I said, taking a sip of the coffee and thinking deeply.

"Okay, I will tell you the secret," she said in a steady voice and paused, "Do you know that most people who focus on their looks, fitness, and diet have longer life expectancies and they are always enthusiastic and successful in their careers?"

I shook my head in confusion. She leaned forward. She had beautiful eyes.

"See, looking good makes you feel good. And feeling good motivates you," she said looking into my eyes intently, "And motivated people are enthusiastic about success. They think big. They think positive and think different."

I had never thought of it that way. So my goal to reach Urvi and to outplay MBA, I mean Deepak, was interlinked with CA *and* appearance along with style?

Yeah, she was right. I was awestruck. I looked at her intently.

"A leader, whether a CFO or a CEO, or the head of the organisation, should be physically energetic, who can inspire the team to achieve greater productivity levels, enjoy work, as well as life," she said and winked, "And the ability to deal with stress, conflicts, and crises is a major requirement for a successful professional in any field, whether you are a CA or an MBA or entrepreneur."

She was dominating my thoughts like Peter Drucker, management consultant and author (yawn). Before I could recover, she offered me the sandwich.

"Now, that was from me. Tell me more about yourself," she asked curiously, "Do you have a girlfriend?"

And here we go again! I poured out everything about my past, about Urvi, Deepak, Krishna (including PIA and the Modi circus) and of course about Mr Yogi Bhardwaj, who changed my life. I thought it might help her to write a more effective thesis on me. But she went into depression. Silence prevailed.

"Friends..." she said in a low voice, and finally offered her hand with moist eyes.

Hey! I am not selfish; I am transparent in my relations.

Why do Chicks love Sugar?

"What do you want?" I asked Riya over the phone one day before her 20th Birthday. I had reached flophouse from office.

I had only two more days left in Bengaluru.

"Give me some sugar on my birthday," she said after a pause.

"Sugar? But you don't eat sweet stuff," I said. She explained that sugar also meant a kiss. It seems I had invited new problems into my life.

"No, forget it," I announced.

"Why? Lips never get defiled," she said, still maintaining calm.

"Crazy…" I said, "I made a mistake by asking you what you want. I will bring a beautiful gift for the beautiful magical girl."

"Wow! Then give me your heart. I need your heart on my birthday. Just for one day… 24 hours?"she said slowly. Oops! *Why was I playing with fire?*

"Hello…Riya?" But she had hung up the phone.

My phone beeped; Riya had texted me:

"Can you give me your heart… please?"

One full day! Well, I had to study, sleep, work along with the daily chores. And my heart was already with Urvi, so I texted her:

"First option looks okay to me."

"Thanks. I am waiting for the moment...Gud night and sweet dreams."

◎

"I will be flying to the USA next month," Riya said, as we sat in the garden at the Polo Club restaurant at the Oberoi Hotel and Resorts on MG Road.

An hour earlier we had been at White House.

Riya was wearing a light yellow full length skirt. A real pearl necklace around her neck and pearl earrings made her look stunning. Her lips were shining with lip gloss. She had used a bronzer and had a light golden glow on her face to match her dress. I wondered if the kiss would be possible as no girl in the world would like to spoil her makeup for the sake of a kiss. Why do chicks love sugar, I mean kisses?

At the last minute, Banerjee sir had gone to Dubai for the new venture and to meet KCA Consultancy. I had a new spikey haircut and had gelled my hair. I was dressed completely in black. The manservant brought the cake. It was a tiny brown pastry-sized cake with 'negative calories balance' made at White House. She cut it in the presence of Aunty. I didn't recognise Aunty at first, she had a severe cold hence she had covered her head and face with shawl and wore a polo-neck T-shirt with full-sleeves like a nun and hadn't put on any make-up. White house had turned into St Paul's Cathedral. Aunty planned to stay at home as she was missing Banerjee sir. It's so hard that when husbands and wives are together, they squabble but when they are apart, they miss each other a lot. Life is a challenge with or without a spouse!

After we left White House, Riya turned into the sexy Lara Croft and robbed some sugar from me in the car. She pulled me to her and we embraced. We locked our lips and indulged in some tongue wrestling. I think she had done a PhD in kissing. For the first time, I came to know that a car could be used for other purposes, apart from commuting, and as a status symbol.

Soon we were sitting in the restaurant garden.

"That's very good. Focus on CPA instead of sugar," I said and winked.

"Have you given some sugar to Urvi?" she asked, a naughty smile on her face, still looking at menu.

"Not yet, maybe after I buy a car," I smirked. She hit my hand and laughed as well.

"Will you miss me?" she asked, looking into my eyes.

And suddenly, before I could reply, a male waiter with a big walrus moustache appeared like a hangman to take the last order of life.

She placed the order as usual (taking her own time, enquiring calories and planning work out for the next day) and hangman left.

"Why do you ask this question?" I asked and kept my hand on her hand. She went even further and pushed her leg against mine.

She didn't reply. Her eyes were wet. I felt nervous.

"I will miss every single moment I spent in Bengaluru. At flophouse. At CRL. At White House. At the disco and in the car," I said.

"Urvi is lucky… to have… you," she said, fighting her tears.

"I promise that we will remain friends. So let's celebrate and make this moment the happiest moment of our life," I said and I pressed her shoulders gently with the palms of my hands using my Modi massaging skills.

She smiled again. But all good things must end. The hangman came and placed the food on the table.

"You have a very nice big moustache," I said looking at the hangman.

"Sir, this is my identity. I got a job here because of my moustache. Our foreign customers like it. I get a lot of gifts, chocolates, and sweets from them," he said. *So his moustache was like a tourist spot.*

"Do you like sweets... sugar?" I asked. Riya hit my leg.

"No sir, my wife likes a lot of sugar. I can't as I am a pre-diabetic," he said shyly.

Riya laughed loudly. I laughed in silence.

Dandi March

"Jai Shri Krishna," I touched Ba's and Bapuji's feet as I entered our house.

The camel train, Ahmedabad Bengaluru Express–16501, had travelled 40 hours, had had 25 halts and crossed 234 intermediate stations. Most of the passengers turned from co-passengers to almost family. And apart from sharing meals, everyone started sharing blankets and combs. It was a mysterious world in itself. One kid was crying loudly making all passengers nervous. I gave him Economics book to play with, and he slept like Kumbhkarna. I think if our ruling government travelled with the opposition party in this train, there would be no dissent on any political agenda in the parliament.

"Did you put coal tar in your hair? Why is it so hard?" Ba asked, as she kept her hands on my head to bless me.

"Ba, it's gel," I said, irritated and looked into the mirror. I was aghast to see my face. After travelling for 40 million hours in the train, my face looked befouled and hair was erect like cables, as the gel had indeed turned into coal tar.

"We need to pay Rs 10,000 to the income tax officer to close the case," Bapuji stated. After an hour of my arrival and after catching up on everything, we were sitting on the sofa and waiting for Ba to serve dinner.

"What?!" I exclaimed. "Why do we have to bribe him if our accounts are perfect?"

"Singh Sahib said that Tripathi Sahib is not ready to close the matter, he wants money. It's more practical to pay up, otherwise unnecessarily he will drag the matter and harass us," Bapuji replied.

Once again a 'practical' approach. I hated it!

"When do we have to pay him?" I asked and shifted to the dining table. Ba had prepared dal, rice, chapatti and bhindi. I had sorely missed her food in Bengaluru.

"Tomorrow, I will give the money to Singh Sahib," Babuji said and sat on the table. He closed his eyes and folded his hands to pray to God.

"I will deliver the money to ITO," I announced.

"Some Riya called many times. Who is she?" Ba asked, as she brought more out chapattis.

"Banerjee Sir's daughter," I said and gazed at my mobile phone lying on the centre table, its battery dead.

I told *Ba* about White House, the disco and the shopping.

"Urvi called many times," Ba said and went into the kitchen, her voice fading away, but clear. "She said you must go to college tomorrow. Sounds bossy."

I kept quiet. "How is Riya? Is she modern and bossy like Urvi or a simple girl?" Ba asked, coming out of the kitchen with some shrikhand.

"*Java de ne*, why are you asking unnecessary questions? Let him first focus on his studies," Bapuji said and signalled to me to serve him *some shrikhand*. But he had to pay the price for intervening.

"Naaaa, no sweets! We both have to stop having so much sugar!" Ba exclaimed, "Only Manav will have as much sugar as he wants."

"Ugly duckling!" Urvi smirked, as I reached the college campus. I was wearing blue jeans, a black T-shirt and had applied gel in my hair.

The whole night I had been restless. I had an experience similar to astronauts having to resettle to life on earth after their space shuttle returned from planet Mars. I felt jolts, as if I was sleeping in the train. I felt lurches even while sitting in the toilet. I even fell off the loo once and the sign 'Please avoid using the toilet at stations' flashed in my head.

"Man, I think you chilled a lot with chicks in Bengaluru," Deepak said, and winked. Urvi looked at him and turned towards me.

"Yeah, Riya Banerjee," Urvi announced. She had spoken to Ba that morning.

"Really? I am sure you CAs can give stiff competition to MBAs if your institute starts hiring chicks as trainers," Krishna said and winked.

"No way man, MBAs directly contribute to the growth of the organisation. Their contribution is visible unlike CAs, who do secondary jobs or are best for support jobs; they don't come forward and lead from the front. Their inputs are not visible," Deepak said and kept his arm on Krishna's shoulder, "Therefore, MBAs are the leaders and entrepreneurs of the future."

"My dad is not even a graduate but he is a successful businessman," Krishna said, jerking his shoulder lightly to displace Deepak's arm.

"I think your father is not an MBA, am I right?" I said and winked at Urvi.

Deepak burst into deep hearty laughter.

"I am not talking about traders and shopkeepers. They employ slaves and rule their staff like a *munimji*." Deepak said and smiled smugly, "I am talking about CEOs of big corporate and MNCs. You will see one day, I will head thousands of people."

"Wow! I will surely interview you in my magazine, Sir," Urvi giggled. Deepak bowed to her.

"Why not?" Deepak said instantly, "You are smart and can be more successful in Mumbai than here in Gujarat."

"Really, you think so?" Urvi said with glittering eyes. But Kavita, waiting for her chance ever since she had met Deepak, interrupted immediately.

"But don't forget Deepak, even Dhirubhai Ambani was not an MBA. In fact, he was a school dropout, but still he headed a big corporation." Kavita boomed, showing expressions of bitterness at him the way Shikhandi had thrown at Bhishma before his fall. She finally felt relieved of the resentment ever since Deepak had taunted her on her clothing. I felt elevated.

"And man, leadership or entrepreneurship is not a monopoly of MBAs. Success is about taking calculated risks, taking timely decisions and actions. It's about discipline and commitment and thinking out of the box," I announced. I recalled Riya and my high-five with her.

Beena clapped who until then had been deeply engrossed in her cookery book-*Art of the Grill*.

All memories of Bengaluru were expunged from my memories as I finished the last sentence. I don't know why, but Deepak always brought out fear within me, like a cat facing a dog.

And from that day until the exams, I started the Dandi March.

Beware of Dogs

"Beta, would you like to have some chai?" An old peon asked me as I sat on the sofa. I had a packet in my pocket, and without the support of a belt, my pants were slipping down my waist. I nodded in confusion.

I had reached the income tax officer, Tripathi's old bungalow at Ashram Road. A 'Beware of Dog' signboard was fixed at the entrance. But I was more scared of the ITO than a dog. An old hammock hung from the ceiling on the porch. Most of the plants in the garden were dead. I wondered if the dog was alive or dead. I wondered if there were any human beings living in the house, as there was an eerie silence. I was dripping with sweat.

I looked around at the pictures of freedom fighters, including Mahatma Gandhi and Subhash Chandra Bose mounted on the wall. I would have admired him for his patriotism, but I reminded myself that I was there to grease his hand and mine as well. I looked at some magazines lying on the centre table. I picked one up; it was a CA journal from our institute. He was a CA!

I heard footsteps. I stood up.

Tripathi entered the room. He was wearing a white pyjama-kurta and looked like he was in his mid-fifties.

"Sir, I am Manav Modi from Modi Investment," I said, offering my hand to shake. He reciprocated and signalled to me to sit.

"Young man, what do you do?" He asked as we sat on the sofa.

"Sir, I am a CA final year student," I said.

"Very good, I am also a CA, qualified in 1990,"he said sketchily. I corrected my calculation; he must have been in his early forties but looked ten years older. He had screwed his health for the sake of wealth.

"Sir, are you patriotic?" I asked, pointing at the pictures on the wall.

"Yes I was, in the beginning of my career. I had a lot of dreams about India and a lot of ideals. But today, with a bunged judiciary and badly bunged environment, those dreams lie shattered," he said miserably, looking at the pictures.

I remained silent as the old peon strolled in with a tray laden with a glass of water, two cups of chai and a plate of rusk biscuits.

"Sir, this is for you," I said, placing the packet on the centre table. He ignored me.

"Jujo!" he cried out. A dog with a long snout appeared and sat near his feet.

"Are you hungry, Jujo?" he asked, kissing him and patting his head gently. Jujo looked at him and turned towards me. He growled at me; I winced.

"Don't worry, I have trained him," Tripathi said proudly, as if Jujo was his article. Yeah, we articles lead a dog's life as well.

Jujo gazed at the packet and leaned forward to sniff it. The dog had a better sense olfactory than us. He liked the smell and picked up the packet in his jaws and slowly left the room. I heaved a sigh of relief on facing another big dog.

Tripathi's cell phone rang and he left the room.

The old peon walked in to collect the cups.

"You are from Modi Investment, no?" he asked, and then looked behind nervously.

"Yes," I said in surprise.

"Don't tell anyone, Singh Sahib had asked our Sahib to issue the notice and asked for Rs 10,000. Sahib will share 50% with him," he said and left the room quickly.

I was aghast! I understood the 'practical' approach that day and for the first time I felt bad, sorry, I felt disgusted about my profession.

I hoisted myself up and trudged outside without waiting for Tripathi to return.

I sat on my scooty. The 'Beware of Dog' signboard mocked me.

I don't know whether to beware of dogs or crooked humans? I thought to myself, pressing the ignition button hard.

I, thus, tossed the idea of having my own practice and made up my mind to join the industry where my future was waiting for me.

And I became a real monk as I buried myself in the tomes like a mad mugger.

A Dream Come True

21 January 2004.

"Well done! Keep it up buddy," SMS from Krishna.

"My Manav is inching towards glory. I am always with you, my sweet puppy," Urvi's SMS (I had read it ten times).

"Gratz man! Still a long way to go," Deepak's SMS. I wondered if I should delete his SMS.

"You are next big D of Gujarat," SMS from Sanjay and Kavita. I was confused, but he meant Dhirubhai Ambani, I guessed.

"Well done brother," from Manoj and the whole PIA family.

"We are proud of you," Banerjee Sir and Sony.Congratulatory messages were pouring in. I had become a CA. I was on cloud nine.

"Amazing! You have done it!" Umesh said over the phone again.

"*Baa*! I passed the CA exam!" I said as I reached home and touched her feet. Bapuji hugged me and kissed me.

"Neelam, don't come alone. Come with Vijay and kids," Ba was inviting all Modis over the phone to come and celebrate my success.

"Wow! Let's have a party tonight at my home," Krishna said over the phone.

"Hey Dude! I will bring a bottle of champagne to celebrate your results and my enrolling in the MBA institute next week," Deepak announced, reminding me that it was a new beginning.

"Manavvvv, I am so glad... I am so glad... I can't tell you!" Riya told me ten times. She was back from the USA.

"Thanks, Riya, for your support," I said, my voice breaking.

"But just thanks is not enough. Let's have a party," she said with excitement.

◎

"I am at the airport. Can you give the address to the driver?" Riya asked.

"Whatttt? You are here?" I yelled, startling everybody. My face turned a kaleidoscope of colours.

We were preparing for the bash at Krishna's home at Royal Galaxy apartments on SG Road. Krishna and Beena were busy with the decorations and lights. Urvi, Deepak, and I were busy burning CDs. Sanjay and Kavita had arranged the food from outside with a little help from Manoj. Umesh had promised to join if his grandmother (or great grandmother) gave him permission. Bhavesh was in Mehsana for an audit, but he said that he would try to come but I was not confident about his killer car making it on time.

"Hey guys! This is Riya Banerjee from Bengaluru. She is studying CPA in USA," I introduced Riya as she entered the hall so that someone else could take over and I could focus on my one and only Urvi. She looked stunning in a tight black dress that covered her knees. She was wearing a spotted scarf and black link chain drop earrings. She was also wearing a black bracelet with a gold chain

"Hi!"All the boys said in unison and offered their cheeks. Deepak went a step further as he bowed to her, "Welcome Ms Riya Banerjee, a beautiful lady and an angel from heaven." The girls offered their hands unenthusiastically, green-eyed. Soon she was bombarded with questions.

"Do you have any special order?" Manoj asked with a notepad in his hand.

"Have you visited Dubai? I can get you a visit visa," Krishna offered (Beena looked daggers at him).

"My uncle lives in New Jersey," Sanjay said.

"Wow! You came from the USA to celebrate?" Urvi asked mockingly and sat on the chair next to Riya.

"Have you read the diet book-*Skinny Bitch* by Rory Freedman?" Beena asked. Riya smiled at her.

There was one hour to go before the party started. But I felt like the party was over after Riya's arrival. Manoj messaged Bhavesh, "If you want to settle down in USA come with a passport now". And he promised to come... in a taxi.

"Can I help you guys?" Riya asked, ignoring their remarks and realising that she had brought in a hurricane to the party.

"Yeahhhhh!" all roared in unison. Umesh and Bhavesh also made it. Both had planned to stay for an hour but hung around till early morning. I think they changed their minds because (a) they had three bottles of thumbs up mixed with booze, (b) the party was rocking, as everybody was dancing to the music,(c) Riya hugged them when they announced that they were also CAs. After all, accountants belong to the same extended family.

Everybody's mood picked up further when Deepak brought out the champagne. After the third failed attempt, Riya helped me to open the champagne bottle. I hated Deepak for embarrassing me in front of Urvi and Riya.

The party got started. The guys convinced the girls to booze and the girls without any arguments nodded. I managed with Pepsi though Krishna had mixed some Black Label in it, he told me later on.

The mood picked up. Everybody was dancing. Manoj raised the volume of the music and the song from *Kal Ho Na Ho*, 'It's the time to disco' began playing.

Deepak danced swaying his body, then crouched towards the foot-knee bent in rock 'n' roll style of Elvis Presley, and asked Riya to dance with him and she agreed. Urvi and I were dancing together like never before. Krishna had drunk a lot. He took Beena in his arms and danced with her. Sanjay and Kavita were dancing-garba style.Manoj was dancing alone in the middle. Umesh and Bhavesh were clapping. The flickering lights reminded me of the pub in Bengaluru where I had danced for the first time with Riya.

Manoj, Umesh, and Bhavesh started dancing in circles on the side, their hands over each other's shoulders and slowly everybody joined them, making a train. Urvi and I were dancing in the centre. Everybody was hooting, dancing and running around in a circle. Our human train finally stopped at 4:00 am when the watchmen threw us out.

But my train kept running between Bengaluru-Delhi-Ahmedabad and finally stopped in Mumbai in 2007.

Life in Mumbai

Three years later - August 2007.

"Good morning, Sir, am I speaking to Arvind... Harish... Modi?" an unfamiliar male voice from a call centre called.

He is my father, idiot! He doesn't know my name I thought and disconnected the phone. It was my first morning in Mumbai and I had just come out from the gym in the building at 7:00 am after a heavy one hour workout session. I was following a strict diet with lots of protein shakes. And with my buff body and six packs, I looked pretty cool-Riya said over the BBM.

I had been transferred as a Financial Controller for the Powai Marina project in Mumbai. I had acquired a new Hyundai Accent GLE car and a one bedroom flat in Darshan Apartments in Powai.

Krishna had gone back to Dubai to join his father's business. He had decided to marry Beena once he settled down. He had asked Beena to study further until then and she had agreed picking Home Science.

Deepak had gone to London to complete his MBA. I tried to erase him from my memory, but it was not possible.

Urvi was living in Dhamji Khengarbhai Lohana Kanya Hostel in Worli. I had met Urvi sporadically during these three years. As time went by, she got more and more obsessed with her career.

I didn't know about the whereabouts of Manoj, Bhavesh, Sanjay and Kavita. I used to see their faces only on Facebook, otherwise I didn't even think about them; I guess this happens to all of us. We move on, life is a journey after all. I only thought of Umesh, Riya, Krishna and Mr Yogi, a noble man wearing gold plated spectacles, as they played significant parts in my life. And of course Pankaj Banerjee; I still work under him, hence I can't forget him. He was the one who inspired me to remain disciplined, fit and healthy. Top leaders should be smart and dynamic; his lovely daughter had also told me that. Young India was knocking at the door for its identity, for a better quality of life, leaving behind issues like food, clothing and housing. But, housing was the reason why I was in Mumbai – to sell houses to the middle class, which to me was the most powerful population of India. I was working on the PMIGC (Professional Middle Income Group City) project.

"Sir, do you need a credit card?" a chirpy voice asked.

I said, "No", and entered the lift. I pressed the level ten button.

Once again the phone rang as I came out of the lift. A new number flashed on the screen this time.

"Sir, we offer holiday packages and hotel stays in Goa with family..." the voice of a young boy said. The last word 'family' startled me. I cursed the foreign companies for spoiling young India's talent- who have been overpaid by them for outsourcing- to harass innocent people. I cursed my luck; I had everything – a car, a nice house, good job, fit body, handsome salary, and lovely Ba – except for a family of my own.

The phone rang again. I picked up at the last ring as I entered home.

"You should answer your phone sooner," a familiar voice alarmed me, "Bad phone etiquette!"

"Urvi, so early! And have you changed your mobile number?" I said and sat on the sofa.

"No man, this is my Reliance phone number. I have three mobile phones now, but yes, I have changed the company," she said.

"Why are you changing jobs? Stick to one company. You will have benefit in the long run," I preached and turned on the television. Suddenly Riya's face flashed in my head when I saw Fox News channel. I had been chatting with Riya on Blackberry Messenger the night before and got to know that the company she worked for, Lehman Brothers had closed its BNC mortgage arm and had laid off 1,200 employees, announcing the arrival of recession in USA. However, Riya's job was still safe.

I picked up the newspaper.

The newspaper headline said: "As per the Gujarat elections poll survey Narendra Modi to cruise for the 2nd consecutive term as Chief Minister". I tried to memorise the headlines – I wanted to be a successful Modi as well.

"Babe, you are new in Mumbai. You need money, position, and quick success here. And for that you need to take risks," she said like a young ambitious and career-oriented Mumbai girl.

"So what's the new job like?" I asked.

"Our Gemini PR agency is very old and has had long relations with corporates and politicians. I am in-charge of creating media images of leaders in the real estate sector. I am organising interviews of CEOs. I can call any big fish any time," she giggled.

The word 'CEO' reminded me of Deepak.

I flipped the news channel in disgust. A young lady reporter had invited experts Mahesh Bhatt, Archana Puran Singh, author Vikram Seth and Lalu Prasad Yadav to debate on implications of gender-nuetral marriages in society.

I understood today why there are a countless number of MBA institutes swarming all over, like chain of Goli Vada Pav restaurants. Because MBA institute are formed on the principles of Marriage Institutes. They are promoting themselves in all tier 3 cities in India and among everybody, yes literally anybody irrespective of caste, age, gender, degree and any creature of nature can enroll online.

Hold on guys, I am talking about Marriage Institutes. MBA Institutes have a wide network up to tier 6 cities in India, including Kutch.

I flipped through the channels again. Another channel was showing a recorded interview of a young CEO and an MBA qualified from an unknown transoceanic institute, who was charitably advising the viewers on how to invest (or dump) money in the right mutual fund. Marketing people's job is to create tricky names "Mutual funds", "Hedge funds" instead of "Wager fund" or "Vegas funds". And why they call it tag lines like "Citi never sleeps" instead of trick lines such as "Give us your cents we will remove your pants!" or the tagline of a bank saying "Where every individual is committed" instead of "Where every individual is criminal!" I think marketing people's motto should be "When life gives you lemons, invest in mutual funds".

I switched off the television and decided to focus on Urvi.

"There is one surprise for you," Urvi said. I was already shocked by her over-ambitious thoughts, the annoying calls, and the marketing tricks on television.

"What is it?" I said and stood up to have protein shake supplements.

"Deepak has returned from London and has joined Landmark Realty Ltd in Mumbai," she announced.

"What the? Oh... fuck!" I said and stumbled. I hit the corner of the centre table and my toe became red like a tomato.

"What happened? Are you all right?" she screamed.

"I stubbed my toe but I'm fine," I said in pain.

"Watch your steps and language," she said and giggled.

"Yeah, send me a manual on how to answer the phone and what to talk about over the phone," I said quietly.

"Stupid, I am joking," she said and chuckled. "Let's meet for coffee today. I am going to be near your office today."

She ordered. I obeyed.

◎

"Sir, your coffee without sugar," Raghu Kharche, the tiny office boy said volubly; he weighed less than a penny but could speak faster than a rap music artist.

"Thanks," I said, but he had already left.

"Manav Sir, this is your first day here. Are you going to work the whole night? You should enjoy life," Rita Shinde, my secretary said, as she entered my chamber and dumped a few more files on my table – commissions for the sales and marketing team. I kissed the files and continued to work.

"I enjoy working," I smiled and buried my head into the files to search for the formula "How to succeed in love, life and race".

"My brother Manoj is also a CA. He works for a bank and is also a workaholic," she said casually. Work was a CA's second wife but my first wife as of now.

"His wife must be complaining," I said, taking a sip of the coffee.

"He is separated," she said and left, leaving me stumped.

The cell phone rang. I was expecting call from Bengaluru office.

"Good evening, Sir."

"I have convinced junior and senior Talwar to curtail advertisement and marketing costs and focus on the People Middle Income Group Project," Banerjee Sir said.

He paused. I remained silent. Siddharth's face flashed in my head, and I got goosebumps. I don't want to generalize but beware of the Gemini zodiac sign. I will tell you later about him.

"We don't want any Bollywood actor or cricketer to be associated with our project. But we need to work out alternatives and an aggressive marketing plan, otherwise the directors and management will reject our proposal," Banerjee Sir said worriedly.

"Don't worry, sir, our customers are our brand ambassadors. We will not waste money on marketing and advertisement. I am working on the project report. We have enough time as well."

"No, do it sooner, before Siddharth changes his mind. And once you organise a meeting with the banker, do let me know. Siddharth would like to meet the bankers."

"Okay, Sir. I will do that at once," I said and disconnected the phone.

◎

"Manav Beta, did the banker call you?" Mama called to ask when I was just leaving office to meet Urvi. I had asked him to introduce me to senior bankers to finance our new project.

"Na Mama, it's urgent. Ask him not to call, but to come directly for the meeting at the office tomorrow. If they agree, I can call the CEO," I exclaimed, "And ask them to come with a senior person."

"*Wah* Manav Beta, it's your first day and you have picked up Mumbai's speed," Mama said and chuckled. "When we will have a party at your house?"

"Mama not now. We will discuss this after office hours," I said in a hushed voice.

"Okay, Sir. Do you have beer…"

I disconnected the phone. Sorry Shakuni Mama, I don't have any phone etiquette.

◎

"People are crazy here!" I said to Urvi, opening the door of the car for her.

She looked spectacular in a green kurti and off-white salwar and dupatta around her neck. Her hair was cut up to her shoulders. I loved that. I was sporting black jeans and a slim-fit black T-shirt with a V-neck.

"Don't worry, life in Mumbai is like a one-way road. Even if you want to stop, you can't. People will push you to move forward," she said, looking at me as I sat in the car. "Nice car!"

A good car or a good home without a woman is not praiseworthy. Soon we thundered our way to CCD at Jheel Darshan Apartments, Hiranandani Garden, Powai. It was 7:00 pm by the time we reached.

"Two cups of coffee," I said to the waitress.

"You know, Deepak has hired our PR agency and he is spending a lot of money for interviews in all our publications and newspapers," she proclaimed as we settled down. "My boss, Abhiraj, is very happy. I am expecting a promotion."

"He is over-ambitious," I said as Urvi finished. But she ignored my remarks.

"Also, we have arranged for interviews of Deepak and his boss, Baweja, in various magazines and television channels to promote all the projects of their company, Landmark Real Estate. He wants to promote himself and his company quickly," she said excitedly, moving her head. Her long earrings moved together, as did the chemicals in my head.

"I haven't heard about Landmark Real Estate," I said.

"Correct, and media wants something relevant to hook them and their target audiences or readers. They need something newsworthy, otherwise without the media hook their story will not get good coverage as there are already established developers on the scene," she said.

We CAs are so shallow when it comes to media and marketing. I never thought of the media hook. She continued further.

"Deepak wants quick results and our PR agency will give him just that," she said and snapped her fingers in the air.

She looked beautiful, but her ambitions were worrying me.

"It's a marketing trick. I don't like creating artificial demand," I said and peeked at the reception to see if our coffee was ready and to divert Urvi's attention from the topic.

"Only one year, and then all the media and magazines will cover him without any PR agency. He will be a big leader and expert in the real estate sector," she said, twirling her hair around her finger. My eyes were entranced for few a seconds; she noticed and she continued twirling.

"But be careful. He may use you for his personal greed," I said.

"Why do you auditors think negative all the time?" she said, looking into my eyes a little longer.

"Maybe I am a sceptic," I said, looking into her eyes even more intently, "But you must keep your eyes open."

"Don't worry. I know many clients like him, even celebrities, Bollywood actors, businessmen and politicians; they use the same tricks. I can handle such clients," she said and tapped my hand.

The waitress strolled to our table with a tray, placed the coffee on the table and drifted away. And we drifted away from our subject as well. As the coffee's aroma reached my nostrils, I felt better. I leaned forward and bent over the cup to further inhale the aroma.

"What are you doing, crazy?" she asked and snickered.

"I love the smell," I said, closing my eyes.

"You learned this in Bengaluru?" she asked and put some sugar in her coffee and picked up a sachet to put into my coffee. Earlier Deepak and now Riya, I don't know why she was hanging on to taboo topics.

"No sugar," I said holding her hand.

"You have changed a lot... after your Bengaluru training," she said finally, taking a sip of the coffee and slowly looking into my eyes.

"Yeah, but that change was the need of the hour so that I could be successful in this profession. However, I am still the same for you and my friends," I said diplomatically, taking a sip of the coffee.

"Who else is in your friends' list?" she asked, opening Pandora's Box.

"Not many," I said, smiling.

"Not even Riya?" she asked, taking a sip of the coffee. Finally she asked me about her directly.

"She and Banerjee Sir have a special place in my life. I don't know where to place them," I said.

"Wow! Special place! Sounds cool," she chuckled, "Where is she now?"

"She is in New York. And if you stop interrogating me, we can talk about our life, Mumbai and maybe your generous boss Abhiraj or even your marketing maniac client Deepak," I said, irritated.

She smirked.

"Why do you still dislike Deepak?" Urvi asked. "He just doesn't like your profession."

I looked into her eyes intently.

I don't care about Deepak. But I enjoy your company when he is not around, I thought.

Gemini – The Most Complicated Zodiac Sign

"When will these stupid people come?" Siddharth exclaimed about the bankers for the umpteenth time on the intercom from his cabin. He hated waiting.

I was waiting in my cabin and praying for the bankers to arrive quickly before Siddharth became completely crazy. Guys, I will tell you about this eccentric man with a dual personality.

His Excellency, Siddharth Talwar, an MBA dropout from the USA, and the son of Chairman Vimal Talwar, had joined as the CEO of the company recently. He was a very impersonal and rude man. If you visited his chamber, he would never ask you to sit, and he would completely ignore you like you are a scum. When talking to you he would either stare at the computer screen, while you sat facing him, or he will play games on his phone. He would even watch the Discovery channel, the news or Tom and Jerry instead of looking at you.

But you think that's not enough to label him rude, here's some more information about him: he hated the people below his rank. If any of the staff didn't submit reports on time or made mistakes he'd say, "I wish there was a separate world for CEOs. Only CEOs and no other minions in the world!"

One time, I was in his Ferrari. He was driving, and as usual he was in a hurry. A small car was blocking his way. He had murmured, "People who drive small cars have small brains."

Ratan Tata will sue you! I thought to myself.

Hc always complained and was never satisfied. He had unique ways to differentiate between honourable people and stupid people. Those he deemed really honourable, he addressed respectfully with a 'Sir'. People he did not respect were addressed as 'Sirrrr' with a slow drawling out of the last syllable "r", acting very respectfully, but he didn't mean it. But sometime threatening (and he meant it), with a slow drawling out of the last syllable "r". This was mainly directed at his junior staff, those who made mistakes or didn't perform well or didn't like him.

He was a restless soul; he wanted everything 'right now'! He paid attention to minute details, which was highly stressful for the people around him. He was clearly a case of Obsessive Compulsive Personality Disorder. He was rigid and perfectionist like one famous Bollywood actor. I hope you understand my drift.

Someone had said that his zodiac sign was Gemini, the most complicated zodiac sign on earth! He was in his early thirties and like most Geminis, he looked younger than his age. His customary attire comprised of a turtleneck T-shirt and a tweed jacket. He was divorced twice in America. He changed his watches, Patek Philippe or Rolex to match his cars, Bentley or Ferrari. He was full of arrogance and loved speed. Here we go again.

"They messaged me; they are in the lift," I said.

Finally, the two bankers, wearing suits and carrying black bags came at 4:00 pm along with Raghu and he took them to the conference room.

I hurried to Siddharth's cabin to discuss the agenda of the meeting. I entered his cabin.

"God damm it!" Siddharth exclaimed, looking at his laptop, "Microsoft Outlook is not working!"

He ignored me as usual.

"I think there's some problem with the network. I will ask Suresh to look into your laptop," I said.

"Sometimes it is a virus! Sometimes the network! Rubbish! Why has Bill Gates retired and doing charity work when there is so much to do in IT itself?" he grumbled, "It's so unreliable! I hate IT!"

I kept quiet.

"It's a useless spam box," he said, slamming his laptop shut.

He dialled intercom and kept the phone on speaker.

"Yes, sir," Vasant's voice echoed. He was in-charge of travel, insurance and vehicle registration.

"Did you book my flight and hotel?' he asked and walked to pick his blazer hanging on the stand.

"Um, I am waiting for the agent's reply," he said hesitantly.

"And hotel?"

Siddharth walked back and sat on the chair, fastening shoelace.

"Um, I...am calling...them now,"

"Sirrr, am I your secretary to remind you and follow up?"

"No sir, I called twice but the concerned person is not..."

Siddharth cut him off. "I don't want reasons; I want results!"

Siddharth looked pissed off. It was not a good time to take him to the meeting, I thought.

"Sir, give me an hour. It will be done,"

"And what about car..."

But Vasant hung up the phone. Siddharth got angry. He dialled again.

"Yes, sir."

"Sirrr, it was me who had called you, so I should be the one who should disconnect the phone and not you!"

"Sorry, sir."

"GET MY BENTLEY NOW!" He said and hung up. He took a sip from the glass kept on the table and stood up.

There was a knock on the door. James Peter Chikala, dark-complexioned, middle-aged man, just about 4'6" tall entered the room. He was a cashier.

"Sir, you had called me earlier?"

Siddharth walked towards him, towering like a coconut tree. Peter frowned.

"Sirrr, I had called you at 12.15 pm and it's 4.10 pm now," Siddharth said head-down and signalling at the wall clock.

"Sir, I had gone to my daughter's school. It was parent's day today,"

"But Mr. Chikala, even yesterday you were absent?"

Peter flinched. He doesn't like to be called Chikala even if pronounced with a prefix.

"Sir, yesterday I had visited my son's school."

"I think we are running this company for the staff only. We are an employee of the employees," Siddarth said controlling his ire and stood up, "Just leave now. I forgot why I had called you."

He left and Siddarth rushed to the washroom.

"Sorry gentlemen, I have run out of my cards," Siddharth said and thrust the bankers' business cards at me, as we settled in the conference room. He didn't like sharing his cards or keeping the cards of every Tom, Dick and Banker, he had said a few seconds before we entered the conference room. I had asked him to carry some business cards. But on the way to the meeting he tried to recall why had he called Chickala.

"Are you an MBA, Sir?" one guy asked me and gave me his business card.

"No, I am a CA," I said and gave my business cards to both of them.

"I am sorry," he said with a moronic expression. "Sir, you look very smart like an MBA."

I felt an urge to slap him for saying 'sorry'.

"How is Mumbai's property market?" I asked, as I glanced at their cards; both were MBAs. Do MBAs get suits along with their degree? Maybe to cover their flaws.

"Who are your target customers?" Ashok Nambiar, the senior one asked, taking a sip from the glass of water.

"Mostly middle class people," I said. "How is the market for small budget apartments?"

"It's good. Nowadays, joint families are becoming nuclear families. There is a consistent demand among lower middle class...," the junior banker replied.

But Siddharth cut him off. "Sir, I think profit is in luxury lifestyle schemes. It's an important niche market," Siddharth said restlessly, smiling.

The banker grew nervous. He stretched out his hand to take the glass of water, but it was empty. I had forgotten to offer them tea. I dialled pantry and asked Raghu to bring chai and coffee along with dry fruits, samosas, and biscuits, using Mehra sahib's trick.

Siddharth dialled intercom. After about the tenth ring, his phone was answered by James Peter Chikala.

"Why did you take so long to answer the phone?"

He must have been in the washroom. He suffered from Kidney stone and drank a lot of beer and water. It helped flush the kidney and bladder perhaps.

"Sir, I had called you earlier for ten thousand dollars."

"Then arrange quickly!...ok...it's fine..yes...No...check with Vasant...yeah...good...thank you Mr.Chikala," he said and hung up.

"I am sorry, please carry on," he said.

"Sir, luxury lifestyle requires big investments and you should be ready to take some risk as well," junior banker, Santosh Joshi, said excitedly.

"Sir, the Mumbai market is flooded with luxury properties, the yields are screwed up. It's out of reach of the service and middle class people," Ashok said to support his colleague. "A luxury project's demand is not stable..."

'No, we don't want to make more shanty towns in an already saturated Mumbai. *We want to build dream homes*," Siddharth said raising his voice loudly and deliberately, keeping both his hands on the table vehemently, looking into the banker's eyes.

He does this calculatingly to dominate morons.

Both were taken aback. Siddharth began bragging; our company had land in Powai and that location was good for lower and middle class communities. I was sure he would mess up the meeting, so I tried to change the topic.

"When can we have a meeting with your manager?" I asked.

Raghu entered with a trolley and placed the various things on the table. He stopped to ask Siddharth in a single breath.

"Sir, we don't have American coffee. Can I bring cappuccino?"

Siddharth looked at him, took some time to catch what he had heard, and his face changed from white to pale then orange, red and finally green – angry like HULK.

"Sirrrr, you want me to give it you in writing? Do that *quicklyyyy*!" Siddharth said firmly and deviously. The bankers grew nervous.

I signalled to the bankers to continue.

"I can ask him to visit your office any time," the senior banker said and leaned towards the plate of samosas.

"Good," I said and shushed Siddharth, hoping that he would listen to me.

"Sir, we know your company has successfully finished a project in Mumbai. We will be happy if you are on board," the junior guy said and cornered a few biscuits before the senior could reach them.

Raghu brought the cappuccino quickly. Siddharth gave him a dirty look, but Raghu ignored him and darted away. The bankers looked sideways.

"We need a 500 crore loan. We can mortgage the Powai land, and if you give us the assurance, we will not approach other banks," I said and looked into the senior banker's eyes.

"No problem, Sir," both said in unison and dipped their biscuits into their chai. "Once you submit the project report, we will arrange a meeting with our manager."

"Sirrrr, if you don't mind, can I leave? I have another meeting," Siddharth said looking at the watch. "I don't want to be late."

◎

"Sir, I am enclosing the feasibility study report for PMIG City and I had also discussed with our sales and marketing teams about the customers' test and market trends," I said to Banerjee Sir over the phone and clicked the send button of my email.

I wish I could solve life's problems or at least Vimal Talwar's and Banerjee Sir's problems with one click of the mouse. However, it doesn't work like that; life sucks and nobody is immune, it doesn't give a damn about your wealth and position, and we have to live with the problems. And I was not superman for I had my own problems as well.

Anyway, I had worked hard to prepare the feasibility report for the Professional Middle Income Group City project. There were a few reasons to take this as a priority. Number one, Siddharth was intent on a luxury project and some directors were backing him, but our limited resources did not allow us to borrow beyond our paying capacity and to take a risk further. Secondly, Banerjee Sir requested or rather demanded that I present the proposal for the PMIGC project to the board of directors and the chairman as soon as possible. Third, I could not meet Urvi for long as she was busy promoting Deepak and his properties.

And I think, no, I am sure Deepak was insane. Every crappy magazine, newspaper, television channel had Deepak's pictures and the Landmark group's project. They had offered many prizes and introduced promotional schemes from cars to Europe holidays to attract customers. They had tied up with banks and were offering a studio at a flat price on opening a bank account, and 1 BHK and 2 BHK apartments for opening fixed deposit accounts.

"Very good. But I am worried as Siddharth is making it difficult for even the chairman. Once he is back from America he wants to be stationed in Mumbai permanently," Banerjee said, his voice low.

"Sir, don't worry. We need to be patient with him. I can manage him," I said to give him and myself some confidence.

"Very good," Banerjee said, and again in an irritated tone, "Who are the owners of the Landmark group? Is he gone crazy or what?"

"Yeah, Sir. I know Deepak Mehra, the COO of the company. We studied together in school. He is using the media. He wants to become a big name quickly," I said the last word loudly and abused Deepak in my mind.

"He will be in big trouble. Keep your distance from him," he said and hung up.

His last words went from my ears to my head and moved back and forth through my whole body. I thought of Urvi, and shivered.

The phone rang. Urvi was calling.

"Manav, did Deepak call you?"

"No, my phone was busy," I said in a low voice.

"Why don't you have one more mobile phone? Don't save too much money. You CAs are really closefisted accountants," she giggled. "Fine, listen baby, he wants to celebrate. This Sunday he wants to have dinner with both of us as he is very happy with the media coverage."

Urvi had hung up. I collapsed in the chair like a pricked balloon.

The intercom rang. I pressed the speaker button. A voice echoed.

"Sir-can-I-bring-the-coffee?"

Return of the Devil-Abracadabra

"Man, you have become a hero in no time," I said to Deepak, holding up the magazine which had his face on the cover along with his boss Savinder Singh Baweja. They had announced many luxury projects worth Rs. 2,500 crore within two years.

I had picked up Urvi at around 8:00 pm from Joggers' Park opposite her hostel. We had gone to Mahesh Lunch Home, near Fountain in the Fort area. I had to drive from north-east to south Mumbai, and it took me two hours to reach due to ridiculous traffic. Deepak always troubled me, but Urvi's company motivated me to drive. The restaurant was jam-packed with people. It was famous for its sea food.

After the long drive, we both were ravenous. We waited on the mezzanine floor for Deepak and he finally arrived almost an hour late.

We hugged each other and sat at the table. He looked debonair as usual.

"Yes boss, I like speed," Deepak said. "We have to project our vision – what we will be like after five years. I don't believe in showing what we are today,"he said and called to the steward to take the order. He had not changed a bit.

"Speed? But you came so late," Urvi interrupted.

"Sorry, Urvi, but thanks, you have done a wonderful job. I am receiving many calls from my friends. I have emailed the online magazine coverage to my friends in London as well,"Deepak said looking at Urvi.

"But man, are you going to invest 2,500 crore in such a short period?"I interrogated and returned the magazine to Urvi.

"They will invest 250 crore only. But media wants big figures. So they have inflated the figures to make it big," Urvi said and winked.

"Really! It's false figures!"

"Whatever you call it. This is a marketing trick man," Deepak smiled playfully; "everybody wants to project big."

I stayed numb.

"And what do you think; cricketers and Bollywood actors get such big fees for being the brand ambassador of the brands in just one year or so? And do you think these Bollywood movies make big business of crores? It's just media created figures," Urvi said.

"But will they start these luxury projects that they have announced or not?" I asked Urvi in disbelief, pointing towards the luxury project in magazine.

"That's not our look out. And media also doesn't care either," Urvi said, uncaringly.

"Abracadabra!" Deepak said, laughing and high-fived with Urvi. And both burst into laughter.

Marketing is a mirage! I felt like I was hallucinating. I ate some more peanuts in bewilderment.

"And what do you think Tata Nano car costs rupees one lakh only? It's a marketing trick, man. They will sell only a few cars at a loss for rupee one lakh. And they will incur a few crore losses on those cars, but they will get media mileage worldwide and their brand name will be elevated in the international market. And they will be noticed in the word, which is otherwise not possible even if they spent billions on the marketing," Deepak said and signalled to the steward.

I think there are only two major hurdles that make CAs short of MBAs.

1. Institute's code of ethics – not allowing members to advertise.

2. We don't get an opportunity.

The steward came to take the order.

Urvi asked for an orange juice, I decided to have a cocktail juice, and Deepak ordered Kingfisher beer, extra strong. He also ordered fish tikka and veg grilled kebabs.

The beverages arrived quickly.

"Cheers! Happy days and for our reunion," Deepak exclaimed and we all raised our glasses.

"Hey Deepak, you stupid, we are here to celebrate the media coverage, so let's toast for that too," Urvi giggled along with Deepak and both raised their glasses again. I joined them reluctantly, just for the sake of my love. After all, love is as blind as a bat.

Deepak finished half a pint of beer in one long sip. I took small sips of the juice again and then because I was starving, tossed some lung scorching fried salted peanuts in my mouth. I thought that I might have to buy Kayam Churna if Deepak's booze party dragged on any further.

Deepak's mobile rang. He didn't answer it. It kept ringing continuously; all the food lovers around us gave us dirty looks. Deepak looked at his phone and smiled, finally turning the silent mode on.

"Answer the phone, no, it's bad manners," Urvi said, looking at his cell. Urvi should be the brand ambassador of Idea network. But I think their brand ambassador is Abhishek? Or the owl? I don't know. I don't care either.

"Dad has been calling me since morning. He saw my picture in the magazine. Now he wants me to join his shop and dirty politics," Deepak said, signalling to his phone. "I will show dad that I can create an even bigger empire than him."

"How is your boss, is he happy with the PR?" Urvi asked again.

"Baweja doesn't deserve a person like me. He should have appointed some sales manager instead," Deepak said loudly and finished the remaining half of his glass in a second gulp. He signalled the steward for another one.

"Don't speak loudly, please," Urvi said to her best client, who was saying bad things about his company.

The steward brought the second beer and served the boozer sitting opposite me.

"How does beer taste?" Urvi asked like the teenage cutie Hanna Montana.

"Taste it, you will like it," Deepak said, offering his drink.

And to my disbelief, she took a big sip. My lungs burnt and the peanuts jammed in my throat. I started coughing. My eyes got wet and red at the same time. Urvi stood up in surprise.

"Easy man, easy," Deepak said and gulped down his beer quickly.

"Sorry, the peanuts were spicy," I said cursing the peanuts, and took a big sip of the juice.

We ordered the food and by the time the food arrived, Deepak had finished his third beer and he called the steward for a fourth one. His voice had started slurring.

"Anu, I gotta tell you something," Deepak said, and then quickly added, "Sorry, Urvi. I'm gonna be the CEO within six months."

"Deepak, don't create a scene. Talk properly and stop drinking if you can't handle it," Urvi said and asked the steward to take the glass away. The steward came forward.

"Nah," said Deepak looking at steward. "Whatcha doing here, man? You ain't my father!"

The steward was agape and looked at Urvi. She signalled to him to leave.

"Manav, I wanna make a lotta money. More than Baweja and my father," he said loudly and gulped down the beer. A tubby boy gawked at Deepak and his mouth remained open till his mother threw chicken tikka something into his mouth.

"And very soon you will be on the cover pages of all the business magazines in India and on all the business channels, that's it, okay?" Urvi said to Deepak, clearly annoyed. "Now for god's sake please keep quiet and let us have our food and leave."

Deepak smiled and some embarrassing seconds passed.

I was busy eating some palak paneer and daal makhani with tandoori roti when Deepak burst out again.

"Anu... sorry...sorry...um, Urvi," Deepak said and paused, looking at Urvi. "I could have never gotten any media coverage without you. One day I'll... make you...very big."

"Deepak! Stop now, eat your food," Urvi scolded him like a nursery teacher. "And who is this Anu?"

"I ain't done with beer yet," Deepak said and paused. "My sister. But she is no more."

I was shocked and so was Urvi. We stopped eating.

"You miss her today?" Urvi asked after a few nanoseconds of silence.

"I miss her every day, every moment," Deepak said, suddenly he sounded lifeless.

"Sir, how is the food?" the supervisor asked, passing by, "Would you like to have one more beer?"

"Yeap, gimme one beer," Deepak said and then looking at Urvi added, "Lemme celebrate tonight."

Urvi smiled and we resumed eating.

Deepak kept talking, but we both just nodded at him. We finished the food and stumbled to my car, parked near the Akbar Ali showroom. Urvi advised Deepak not to drive.

"Urvi, I dunno why I am very happy today. You'll have to have my single photograph on the front page when I 'll become a CEO," he said for the fifth or sixth time in the last one hour. Urvi jogged towards the car without looking at us.

"Manav, you see, I started my career after you, but I'm gonna have the double of your package. 'Cause this is the power of marketing and MBA," Deepak said.

I ignored him and opened the back door of the car. Urvi hopped in the front seat next to me. She was speechless.

"Manav, one day I'll rule the Mumbai city," he said, standing and holding the car door with his left hand. He raised his right hand in the air and waved to make circles. "I'll fly and will mint money, money, and money."

I had to force him to sit in the backseat.

I hit the ignition and stomped on the gas paddle.

"Anu, come back," Deepak said, his voice low, "I miss you a lot."

Work,work, and only work

"Talwar has liked the PMIGC project. The board has also approved. I will email it to all the directors," Banerjee Sir said over the phone,"Your three months' hard work has borne fruit finally. You will get a good increment this year."

"Thanks Sir," I said lethargically.

Siddharth had tried hard to persuade the directors and Banerjee Sir to launch the luxury project instead of the lower budget PMIGC project, but no one listened to him. I was sure that he would get pissed off once he received the email from Banerjee. I had to be careful.

"Keep it up," Banerjee Sir said and hung up the phone.

In Mumbai, time flies, especially if you have a passion to grow, and if your inamorata is a go-getter, over-trusting and emotional. She forgave Deepak's silly behaviour once again.

Finally I called Urvi and announced that I will receive an increment and also that the PMIGC project had been approved by the board. But as usual, she stunned me.

"Wow! But aren't you going to announce this in the media?" she said, "Why don't you hire us as your PR agency? Look at Deepak, how fast he is making a headway into the big league."

Goodness me! She still compared me to Deepak. Now who could explain to her that our company was bigger than Landmark Realty Ltd and we were a public listed company. We had to follow procedures, unlike Baweja's one man show private company.

"Baby, let's meet and discuss this," I said.

"Later. I am walking towards the studio. I had to bring the client in all of a sudden. Deepak is reaching the studio very soon. Watch him live."

I galloped to the conference room to watch Deepak's interview.

"The Landmark group of Mumbai is constructing an ultra-luxury project, Sunrise Luxury Tower, in Worli. The tower will have thirty stories. The prices begin at seven crores and will go on to fifteen crores..." the reporter screamed.

As soon as the background commentary was over, a replica of Sunrise Luxury Tower was screened. Apart from a private gym, swimming pool and a jacuzzi, there was a business centre, cafes, shops and restaurants. All residents would be members and could use these facilities. But outsiders and guests would have to pay to enter. I realised that I had stopped breathing. The project was awesome!

"We have with us in our studio, Mr Deepak Mehra, the young and dynamic COO of the Landmark group,"the reporter announced. The camera moved to Deepak. He was sitting in the studio. He looked spectacular in his Beau Brummell clothing – black suit, white shirt, and red bowtie. From a female's perspective he looked like a Greek God.

"Deepak, can you tell us more about this project?"

"Well, these luxury homes will be dream homes for the elite class, and we are targeting only the niche market. These are houses for people who are not just looking for a home, but a place to live and feel better. It will be a fantasy home for families, especially women."

"When will you start selling the properties to the buyers?" the journalist asked.

"From next week. However, we have a press conference and we are launching the tower this evening at Trident Oberoi to celebrate the 25th anniversary of the Landmark Group. We have invited the honourable minister Mr Ramesh Dattatraya Dixit to be the chief guest."

The interview ended and I became nervous. Deepak always made me feel mediocre. The intercom rang.

"Sirrrr," a rude voice said slowly, "I would like to see you right now."

The Worst Day of my Life

"Manav, you sent me the email for the PMIGC shanty project just now. Shame on us! I saw an interview of Landmark Realty's COO; the guy spoke fantastically. They are launching Sunrise luxury towers this evening. It's amazing! I want a project like this!" Siddharth said excitedly. Marketing deceives people like Siddharth and depresses people like me, for sure. He had just received twin blows – my email and Deepak's dream home project.

I was sitting in front of His Excellency Siddharth's chamber. I was dog-tired and feeling blue.

"It's a really good ambitious project. And they are targeting higher middle class, but our target…" I started calmly.

"Thank you very much, I will ask for your advice, if I need it," he said sarcastically, looking at the television.

Silence. After careful thought, I said, "I know Deepak Mehra. We had studied together since school. He did his MBA from London."

"Good. For the first time you have said something sensible and positive. Can you arrange a meeting with Deepak this week?" Siddharth said and lit up a cigar. I get nervous if someone smokes in a closed room.

"But our Powai project will take three years to complete. I think we should first complete this project," I said quietly and held my breath.

"Three years? Its hooey! I don't like to wait, man. You CAs have no foresight!" he exclaimed, blowing smoke rings in the air.

"But it's already approved..."

"No, it's too long a period to wait. Look, look at Deepak. He is an MBA and he is so smart and dynamic," Siddharth exclaimed and blew some more smoke rings.

"But our financial figures don't support such luxury projects," I said straightforward. And I had to pay the price.

"I don't understand why we have appointed clowns who are just happy fabricating cabanas like the way CAs fabricate figures and financial reports on the computer?"

Rascal!

"Manav, sorry to say that you might look fit, but you don't have the brains of an MBA!" Siddarth said sarcastically,"You cut off a dog's tail; he will still be a dog because of his DNA."

"Siddharth, watch your language, please. It's not that Banerjee Sir or I are conservative. It's the board's decision," I said and stood up.

Sidhharth's chin shot up. He stoodup, looking even more pissed off.

"You know, this Baweja was a salesman when dad started his real estate business in Delhi. And today he is selling luxury dream homes and we are selling camps for refugees. And this is because of you and your sick Banerjee Sir. And I think daddy is gone sick as well, because he listens to both of you computer jockies in our office!" Siddharth yelled and threw a paper weight on the floor so hard that it ricocheted and broke the window. I was stunned.

Was I a computer jocky? I think I deserved this new title. I was sorry to the institute for letting our profession down. I felt like crying or at least mourning the death of my self-respect. I felt weak as water.

Instantly Ba's face flashed in my head; she signalled to me to be patient. *But why can't I cry Ba? I will feel better.*

I stood up slowly and meandered towards the door.

"Sirrrr... If you don't mind, can you give me Deepak's contact number?" Siddharth asked as I reached the door.

◎

"No, I can't," I screamed, "Hell!"

Not because I was lifting an eighty-pound dumbbell for the first time, but because I was feeling low. I hadn't slept the whole night and because of my habit of working out daily, I was in the gym at 6:00 am.

"Focus... Focus... grab it tight... get angry with it," Victor, the trainer scolded me. "One hour daily in the gym is hell but it makes your whole day and whole life heaven."

"I am sorry. I didn't sleep well last night," I said and sat on the bench table, wheezing.

"Why didn't you tell me before? We can reduce the weight," he said, looking at me.

We CAs don't express our feelings, even if we are in pain. We like pain and anyone can screw us.

We finished the workout with lesser weights but did more repetitions, it was hard and painful.

"Do some cardio now. You will feel better," he said and winked.

"Can I skip cardio today?" I asked after the workout, still puffing.

"Noooo. Challenge. Challenge. Feel the pressure!" he cried out and left me alone with some fleshy aunties, chatting and walking on the treadmill.

I touched 30 minutes on the treadmill, 350 calories burnt. I was sweating like a pig but felt better. I reached home and picked up the newspaper. I was stunned as I saw a full page advertisement of Sunrise Luxury Tower in the newspaper. The heading howled:

LANDMARK celebrates Silver Jubilee.

Buy an apartment in the fantasy building and get a chance to win a Rolls Royce with every duplex apartment.

My stomach ached. I sprang up from the sofa, took a towel and ran to the...toilet.

◎

"Ritaaaaa, give me all the newspapers and can you call Suresh urgently?" I yelled like Siddharth.

I was upset due to a lot of reasons – my body was sore because of the workout. I was sleep deprived, my laptop was not working and to top it all, the humiliation heaped on me by Siddharth. Finally, I had lost my temper and yelled at the subordinates like all bosses do. All bosses are assholes. Total assholes. Period!

Rita entered and dumped the newspapers on the table. I didn't even say thanks.

"Where is Raghu? Do I need to beg him for coffee?" I chided again.

"I will make coffee for you," she said, looking at me quietly, "Raghu is absent. His mother has been admitted to the hospital."

My eyes became moist and suddenly Ba's face flashed in front of my face. I felt feverish.

"Manav, you look so tired," she said in a straightforward manner.

I remained silent, still thinking of all my kith and kin.

"Yesterday, you left late?" she asked.

How did she know? I think a woman's brain has magnet which produces powerful invisible magnetic fields and pulls on the information. They don't have to go out and get information. They sit anywhere and it comes to them.

I looked at her puzzled.

"Suresh told me," she said and turned to leave. Suresh Denageri from Bengaluru was head of IT and Security division. He must have seen me on the CCTV camera.

"Why is the office so quiet?" I asked, softening.

"Siddharth is not in office," Rita smiled. "He has a meeting with Mr Deepak Mehra."

"Hey wonk where were you? I have been calling you since long," Urvi said peevishly. "I am so happy today; my project is over."

It was around 7:00 pm. I had had a terrible day. I had come home early and called Ba and asked her about all the Modis. All were fine, except for me.

I was drowning in my sorrows with the help of Jagjit Singh's sad ghazals. I rewound "*Chithi na koi sandesh*", "*Jhuki jhuki si nazar bekarar hai ki nahi*" and "*Tere khat aaj mai Ganga me baha*" ten times.

Urvi's phone had startled me while I was resting on the sofa. My body still hurt and my eyes were red. I had turned off the lights.

"Manav, I want to celebrate now!" Urvi exclaimed, "Let's celebrate the weekend today."

Urvi, I am not feeling well. Why don't you celebrate with your client, Deepak? I thought. Could I say this? *No, you dumbass. Hold on. Think of a second option.*

Celebrate what? Deepak's advertisement? My foot! No, even this would not do.

"Okay, I am at home. But I am too tired, baby. I don't want to go out," I said.

My mind became clear as the CD had stopped. I felt relieved; I had been hypnotized by the ghazals.

I sprang to the music system and ejected the CD.

"No problem, I will come over,"she said.

The doorbell rang soon after. I wondered how Urvi had managed to reach so quickly. I opened the door to find a figure covered from head to toe in a wet raincoat? It was Manu Mama!

"Jai Shri Krishna!" we greeted each other in unison. I hadn't realised that it was drizzling outside.

I tossed a box of tissues to Mama to dry off.

"At least give me a towel," Mama said, irked.

I threw the towel at him.

"You've been in Mumbai for four months and we have not met! Roopa shouted at me today," Mama said, placing two bags on the centre table.

"Mama, I have been busy at office," I said softly.

"The weather is beautiful outside; why are you sitting alone at home? You CAs are really deadhead and don't know how to enjoy life," Mama said, covering his head with the towel.

Hey Mama, my life is coming right now, I wanted to tell him.

"What is in the bags?" I asked.

"*Adadiya* and *gathia-mathri-chakri*. Roopa sent them by courier today. Half for you and half for me. But you can keep all if you want," Mama said and winked.

"You keep all the *adadiya*. I will keep all the *gathia-mathri-chakri*," I said, "What about the other plastic bag?"

"Kingfisher strong beer," Mama said pulling out two bottles of beer from the bag and raising his hands, "Your Mami had gone to her mother's home. I was missing her."

I turned on the television to watch CNN news.

"What is this news?" Mama said, piqued again.

"Play some nice romantic music. You CAs have poor taste in everything, and please don't play sad ghazals," Mama said and strolled to the kitchen.

The doorbell rang after an hour. I was alone.

Mama had gulped down the two chilled beers, as Attaullah Khan's ghazals,"*Idher zindagi ka Janaza uthega, udher zindagi meri dulhan banegi*" hovered in the room, on his mind, and in his heart. He moaned, boohooed and ululated like a wolf. Finally I bundled him into a cab as it had started raining heavily. Fortunately Mama had left four bottles of beer behind.

"Oh my goodness, you are wet!" I said, as I saw Urvi standing at the door wearing black jeans and white transparent kurti, stuck to her wet body.

"The weather outside is really cool! Mumbai's first rains are always beautiful," she said excitedly stepping inside and raising her hands shoulder-high.

I bolted the door and turned around.My eyeballs nearly fell out from the socket when my eyes followed her wet footsteps and became stuck to her transparent bosom. She looked at me and nervously turned around. She was still trying to cover her bosom with her tiny and thin hands.

"Wow! Nice house!" she said, looking around. And like the CBI conducting a raid, she marched into the kitchen, examined the fridge and cupboards, and returned to stand beside me cautiously.

"This is only a house, not a home. Men can only make a house, only women can transform a house into a home," I said eloquently.

She laughed uncontrollably, keeping one hand on her bosom and one hand on her mouth. She looked sexy at that moment.

"So finally, you accepted that without women, men are incomplete," she said, looking into my eyes as she kept her hands on my shoulder. Her touch, her wet body and the loud thunder outside were making the room atmosphere cosy, sensual, and awkward at the same time.

Before I could say anything there was a bout of loud thunder outside. A window opened in the wind and banged against the wall.

Urvi hugged me tight. I felt the warmth of her body as she pressed her bosom hard against me. I placed my hands on her head and she buried her head in my arms. Her wet hair and the aroma of her body rejuvenated my body and soul. My pain was gone.

"Oh Manav, I was really missing this," she whispered, still holding me tight.

"We both have missed a lot because of our careers," I said, looking into her eyes as she released her grip softly, "And your clients."

"You are responsible for that. Since you started your CA, you have ignored me completely," she said, and feigning a furious look, punched my chest lightly.

"But you wanted me to be a CA, no? I was happy being Agent Vinod with minimal work and a few simple clients." I grinned. "Unlike your demanding clients."

She was feeling cold; I gave her a towel instantly.

She bent her head to a side and dried her hair with the towel and then, turning her shoulder to the other side, repeated the process. Water droplets from her hair fell all over my body. I felt a deep desire to hug her.

"Yeah, some clients like Deepak who are too demanding," she said, still wiping her arms, "Times are changing; we women should first think about our career. That's what I learnt from both of you guys."

"So, Deepak is just a client for you?" I asked.

"Yeah, of course, client and friend as well. He has supported me," she said, smiling and added sarcastically, "In fact, he has a special place in my life, like you have for Riya."

"Deepak is wooing you and wasting his boss' money," I said. I ignored her subsequent remark.

"I don't want to discuss my clients and...and...my business," She said looking up, controlling a sneeze but failed, "AAAKCHEEE".

She sneezed with the force of a tsunami.

"Stupid, leave it, no. Get me some clothes," she said, throwing the towel at me. It smelt nice.

I walked towards the cupboard, and she shadowed me. After jumbling through all my clothes, she pulled out a pair of black shorts and a pink sleeveless T-shirt. She went to the washroom to change.

My eyes were transfixed as Urvi walked in slowly and cautiously, wearing the black shorts. My gaze swept up her exposed fair legs and glossy thighs. She looked beautiful, no, she looked luscious in the pink sleeveless T-shirt. She came and slowly sat next to me, rested her head on my shoulder and held my hand firmly.

I glanced at the thousands of green tiny blood vessels on her polished thigh.

"Want some coffee?" I asked.

"You are so boring. You don't have any booze? I will inform the hostel I will be staying with my aunty in Powai," she said and resting on the sofa, she put both her legs on my lap.

"And what is your aunty's name?" I ask curiously.

"Manavi aunty," she said, laughing.

"Sounds cool, but what if your parents call the hostel?"

"They always call me on my cell, so I will tell them that I am in the hostel," she said and winked. "Now don't worry about me. I handle many clients and politicians. Mom and the hostel in-charge are nothing in comparison."

"Mama left behind some beer," I said and gestured at the bag.

"Wow! Beer!"she yelled and ran to the bag.

"Can I order a pizza?"

"Yes, please...I love pizza, beer and rain!" she said excitedly. I ordered a pizza.

"Don't drink, you won't be able to handle it," I said, as she returned to the sofa and sat next to me. The pink T-shirt was loose and without a bra, her bosom was drawing all my attention.

"I wanna fly!" she said, chuckled and took out a bottle. A sudden breeze blew open the window and I stood up to close it.

"Let me close the window. I heard that you cannot enjoy your beer in cold weather,"I said coolly looking into her eyes. She hit me on the hand.

"Don't worry when the heater is with you,"she said and winked. She asked me to get two glasses.

Urvi turned on the television. A song from *Aaja Nachle* began playing on one of the channels. It changed the atmosphere in the room.

Is Pal mein hoon ya tum bhi ho
Ya dono hoke bhi na hain
Kyun ho kya ho
Ho bhi ki na ho
Ya kehna sunna mana hain...

Urvi started moving and dancing holding my hand. We both were on cloud nine. I did't need to drink the beer, I was already feeling tipsy. I wanted to stay like that, forever and ever.

But Urvi was in a perfect bossy and naughty mood. She tilted a glass and slowly poured the beer like a professional bartender.

"We will drink from one glass," she said.

"Is it strong?" I asked like a teenager.

"Women are stronger than any booze in the world," she winked and laughed wildly. She looked lovely and fearless.

"Cheers!" she announced, raising the glass. I picked up the beer bottle and clinked it with the glass. She took a sip and offered it to me; it was really bitter, but I took in a big sip for the sake of my love.

She grabbed the glass from me and took a big sip; I had to forcibly pull it away from her. And very soon, we had knocked back two full bottles of Kingfisher beer. With the evil spirit inside my little head, I felt tipsy.

There was a knock on the door; it was our pizza.

She opened the pizza box, pulled one piece and fed me like a baby. It tasted delicious. I wanted to have a full portion but she hit me on my lap signalling for me to feed her. I instantly followed her command.

"I am very happy today. My boss, Abhiraj Chaturvedi, is happy with my performance," she announced. "He wants me to handle a big portfolio, and deal with ministers and the big fish only."

"What does a PR agency have to do with ministers?" I asked, feeding her the pizza.

"This is a big game. My boss is a shrewd businessman. He is lobbying to influence the decisions of the ministers in the allotment of big projects. He creates a platform between corporates and ministers for the allotment of big government projects," she said, looking into my eyes. Her pretty eyes were turning slightly red. I felt nervous.

"I think this is a bit risky and unethical," I said, concerned.

"But that is the way the system works. You are a CA, you know it," she said. I pinched her thigh for her condescending remarks about our CA profession.

"All CAs are not the same," I said with feined anger, "Now, you eat the pizza yourself."

"Stupid," she cried and put the pizza into my mouth forcefully and then into hers.

The pizza lasted for exactly thirty seconds.

"Baby, beer please," she said, tapping my lap. I followed her command and poured the remaining beer into the glass.

"How old is your boss, Abhiraj? Is he young?"I asked. I don't know why I asked her that. She laughed and looked at me.

"Why? Are you... jealous?"She asked, keeping both her legs on my lap. I kept one hand on her leg and another on her glossy thigh, and started massaging her legs slowly.

"No I am not, but I care about you. You know this is a man's world and anyone can exploit a beautiful girl like you," I said looking at her, as my hands massaged her feet, legs and thighs.

Silence prevailed. She looked at me.

"You never said that before," she said, slowly trying to stand. I offered her support. I remained quiet; my hands and my words had done my job already.

"You CAs are such... tubelights! Why did you take so long to say this?" she asked and fell into my arms.

She sat next to me and I felt her soft touch.

"I thought you were busy in your job and career. I had promised you that I will support you once I become a CA," I said looking into her eyes deeply.

"Say it again...for me baby," she said, looking into my eyes.

I got charged up.

"You are... beautiful...Urvi," I said.

She smiled, and her eyes filled with tears.

"Do you still have a relationship with...Riya?" she demanded, looking into my eyes.

I thought to confess. It was the right time. Now or never!

Yes, I thought first, *Riya was an amazing ultra-frank and crazy friend; for her kissing was cool, like sugar in her coffee. However, since the last three years I had not touched her or had any sugar*.

I stood up and bowed like cupid, the god of love. And with that thought, announced.

"No, I gave her sugar, meaning kisses, and maybe hugged her a couple of times when she cried. I told her that I had feelings for a school friend, Urvi, and that I would wait for her until she came back to me," I said resolutely, looking into her eyes. Urvi smiled. I continued.

"I was just waiting for my turn to come... I just felt... that I am nowhere close to you and your family," my voice genuinely broke.

"Your support... gave me strength to fight with the world when... I was working as an insurance agent and had almost dropped out from school and when we had suffered after the earthquake. I may not have been with you physically, but my thoughts and my soul were always with you and you only, and I feel weak when you are not with me... Urvi... I need... you... I can't live without you...I love you, Urvi, more than my life."

I think she was struck by cupid's arrow. She looked into my eyes intently and hugged me while still sitting on the sofa.

"Oh Manav! I love you too!" she said and continued to hug me tight. I couldn't believe what had just happened. I was so close to her that I could hear her heartbeats.

Urvi came very close, our noses touched. She raised her head to kiss my forehead. She then came closer to kiss my lips.

Her breath smelled of pizza.

The worst day of my life had turned out to be the best day of my life.

She poured sugar on me just as the deserted marshy wetland of Rann of Kutch receives a sudden downpour of rain. We remained locked, our bodies hardly moving. It was a moment of bliss and liberty. I surrendered to her, physically and mentally. My stress vanished. I felt powerful like never before. That day, I understood why women are beautiful and why we men are incomplete without women.

Yes, we had become one.

All Good Things come to an End

"Sir, this is absurd! The US market is already in recession; we should be careful as it may affect us in the next six months or so!" I exclaimed to Banerjee Sir over the phone.

I was on a roll. My new life with my sweetheart Urvi had just begun. Mumbai looked beautiful like never before. And like two free birds we both flew around enjoying every moment. But all good things end, and so did our happy days when Banerjee Sir announced that Spike a.k.a Senior Talwar had bowed to Tyke a.k.a Junior Talwar and they wanted to put the PMIGC project on hold and invest in a luxury project.

"Manav, I know that we professionals always go by numbers and calculations but these but these entrepreneur calculate risks by their gut feelings and intuitions. They are real visionaries."

"But sir we are public listed..."

"No more arguments. We will discuss it in the board meeting," he instructed.

"Manav, as the management and the board of directors want to invest in luxury projects instead of investing in low return projects for middle class people, we need put the PMIG city project on hold. And for that we need to fix up a meeting with the bankers and talk to them about the items 1 and 3 on the agenda. And you have the responsibility of fixing the meeting at the earliest," Harish Shukla, company secretary narrated the scripted speech.

I had flown to Bengaluru. I sat on the chair next to Banerjee Sir. Rakesh Padukone, Sachin, Manjunath, Harish Shukla, company secretary and some directors-cum-auidance were also present. Mr Gill, one of the directors, was out of town. We all were sitting in front of Vimal Talwar and Siddharth. Corporate meetings were like carnivals, especially if the meeting was called at the instruction of the top management, because everybody, including the directors, paraded to the tune of the top management and the issues on the agenda were not decided, but declared.

I reviewed the agenda on the paper lying in front of me.

1. PMIGC project on hold.
2. Appoint consultants to prepare feasibility report for Environment-friendly luxury Hill City project, 'The Firmament' in Pune.
3. Meeting with bankers to re-negotiate finance for Hill City project.
4. Deepak Mehra to be appointed as CEO of the Hill city project.

I hated all four items on the agenda!

They decided to appoint a local consultant to liaise with the consultant in Italy to prepare the feasibility report and design to build 'The Firmament' in Pune, as proposed by Siddharth Talwar.

I looked at Banerjee Sir as Harish finished.

"But Sir, what about our land in Powai?" I catechized.

"We will sell it and if required, we can tie up with another developer or get a new investor,"Siddharth spoke, looking at the directors. They all nodded like puppets.

"Sir, a luxury project at Powai still sounds workable, but selling this land and reinvesting in Pune and finding a like-minded financing partner will require a lot of time and effort," I said concerned. "Sir, who has suggested such a big change in plans?"

"Your friend, Deepak Mehra," Siddharth said cold-heartedly. "We need to hire more MBAs. They are experts in marketing. And Hill City will be a big project. We cannot take chances and rely on CAs who are only experts at paperwork and administration."

I felt somebody had stabbed me but I kept quiet.

"Sir this is not about the marketing decision..." I said.

"Manav, don't take it personally," Banerjee Sir interrupted, sensing my pain.

"We know you are smart, but we have to think big otherwise we will be left behind," Sachin said, taking a sip of water from his glass.

"YES! And I don't want our rivals like Baweja to succeed,"Vimal Talwar said in a gratingly harsh tone and banged his fist on the table. This was the first time I saw him acting in this manner.

"Dad, cool down!" Siddharth said.

Rakesh, like a minion, offered his glass of water to Talwar. The meeting was over and Harish Shukla started preparing the minutes of the meeting. And directors started chatting and checking their emails in mobile phones.

"Manav, you and Banerjee have a big role to play. We are taking up a challenging project, and without professionals, the corporate world is incomplete... much like a house without a lady,"Manjunath said and winked, "You professionals are like wives and the businessmen are like husbands."

Everyone chuckled; I was annoyed.

"Manav, think like a businessman but act like a professional," Rakesh said. He was a fawning courtier, an ass kisser.

"But don't forget behind every successful businessman, there is a professional accountant," Banerjee Sir said.

Everyone nodded.

"Manav, the new CEO Deepak will take care of the Hill city project," Rakesh said, and smiled smugly at me. "You just focus on the accounts and finance."

"Sir, I have known Deepak since my school days; he is not straightforward and just brags," I said and looked at Banerjee Sir.

"All MBAs are like that. You CAs should learn from them. It's all about presentation, boss, show business," Siddharth said and chuckled. "Deepak is a dynamic guy."

"Manav, let's focus on the job at hand. We will go step-by-step," Banerjee Sir said to end the row.

We discussed the issues for thirty more minutes. They humiliated CAs and they labelled me Mr Negative before the meeting concluded. They decided that Banerjee Sir and I were to re-negotiate the loan with the bankers for Hill City. Rakesh Padukone would select the architect and construction firms along with Siddharth Talwar, and would also be responsible for selling the land in Powai and purchasing land in Pune. Lastly, Siddharth would appoint the new CEO, Deepak Mehra once the Hill City project was approved by the ministry and the bank loan was approved.

My heart pounded in my chest as I read the minutes of the meeting and adrenaline surged through my veins.

I am a Coward

"Good morning, Sir," I said, as I entered Vimal Talwar's chamber.

Banerjee Sir and I had organised countless meetings with the bankers, and persuaded them about the change in the plan or goal displacement, in MBA terms. And they had asked us to submit a revised proposed project report for the Hill City project in Pune.

We had sold the Powai land at a throwaway price due to the urgency. Siddharth and Rakesh had finalised another piece of land above the market price on the Mumbai-Pune Expressway near Varasgaon Lake. I came to know (from Rita) that Siddharth and Rakesh had paid huge commissions and cuts to the brokers for the sale of the Powai land and the purchase of the land on the Mumbai-Pune Expressway. But I didn't receive any documents or any vouchers. It was as if suddenly our company had started a campaign to go paper-free to reduce carbon footprint.

Rakesh hired an architect and a consultancy firm for the preparation of the design and for the preparation of the feasibility study. They submitted a feasibility report in quick time. I think they had copy-pasted it from the internet. Banerjee Sir and I had worked day and night to review the project report and loan arrangements with the bankers.

Political connections were used to get the approval for the project as many environment issues were by-passed. Senior Talwar didn't give a damn to what we had discussed and had agreed on in the meeting. We were a public listed company, but they could not care less about public and SEBI guidelines and corporate governance. Transparency and professionalism were thrown by the wayside for Junior Talwar's sake.

I slept at night in Bengaluru and woke up in the morning in Mumbai. My workout comprised mostly running at the airport to catch the flight in the morning.

Finally, we submitted the copy-pasted feasibility study report and designs to the bankers. The total project investment was Rs 3,000 crore. Our funding, including land, was Rs 1,250 crore short as per the bank's norms. But nevertheless we decided to approach the banker first instead of looking for another financing partner.

Siddharth made another quick decision; he changed his mind and even before the banks had sanctioned the loan, he appointed Deepak as the CEO of 'The Firmament' Pune project and his salary and benefits was precisely 19.99% – like Bata shoes prices – higher than my salary. Finally, a CA had lost to an MBA, or Manav had lost to Deepak, and presentation, marketing or tricks and so on had won while honesty and simplicity had lost. I felt like a loser.

Deepak joined the company. With his shrewd, smart and abracadabra approach, he became Siddharth's alter ego. They were meeting privately with the advertising companies and politicians to invite them for the launch. They had also hired Gemini PR Agency. Banerjee Sir, the other dummy directors, and I just watched from the sidelines. After a few marathon rounds of meetings with the bankers, the bankers asked to raise the equity capital equal to 50% of the project cost.

And as Siddharth was either cocky or born yesterday, he borrowed money from a private financer to fund the project to meet the banker's requirements. But Deepak proposed to increase the marketing budget to double, meaning that Talwar had to borrow more from the private lenders at an exorbitantly high rate of interest. I gave my negative opinion, I was Mr Negative afterall, on the same and emailed Deepak, Talwar, and Pankaj and the entire board of puppets.

If you ask me, corrupt corporates are like cocks and corrupt politicians are roaches. I mean, corrupt people are like unhygienic cockroaches; they kill young India along with their hopes and future. However, the bank sanctioned the loan once the project was approved by the ministry of environment. Nobody cared how the approval had been obtained. And finally I was back in Mumbai.

I received a call from Rita that Siddharth wanted to see me and was waiting for me in Vimal Talwar's chamber. *Here we go!*

"Good morning, man," Deepak said. Vimal Talwar gestured me to sit. Siddharth didn't even greet me. His eyes were transfixed on the television. I sank on the sofa next to Deepak, facing Vimal Talwar. Siddharth was sitting on the visiting chair placed near Vimal Talwar's table.

"Manav, Naresh Joshi, an ex-banker and freelancer will join us soon. I have discussed about the funds required to increase the marketing budget with him,"Deepak said as I sat next to him.

"But we can start marketing with the present budget and if the response is good, we can think of increasing the budget at a later stage,"I said, looking at Vimal Talwar and then turned towards Deepak. "And who is this new ex-banker?"

"Don't worry about the banker, Deepak has set up everything. We will have a soft launch with some stories to create curiosity in the elite class," Vimal Talwar said coolly in a hoarse tone.

"But Deepak..."

"Boss, don't worry about the response. I am damn confident. And once the marketing starts, we cannot hold or stop it," Deepak said frowning arrogantly.

"Manav, my prodigy, don't be so negative all the time. This is a dream project..." Vimal was interrupted by the intercom ringing.

Siddharth picked up the phone placed near him.

"Send that bugger quickly,"he said and hung up the phone.

A banker in his mid-fifties entered the room. He was wearing spectacles and seemed to have not shaved for ages. He wore ten rings of different coloured stones on his fingers. A white kurta-pyjama and grey sports shoes completed his outfit. He looked more like an astrologer and less like an ex-banker. He offered only four fingers of his cold sweaty hand apathetically, and distributed his business cards like he was playing a cards game. (Vimal Sir winked at Siddharth (both mocked others quite often). I glanced at the card.

Naresh Joshi, Ex-Banker and Freelance Consultant.

Services:

Private finance, real estate agent, advertisement consultant, bookkeeping, share investment, Vastu expert, and astrologer).

A *janma kundli* was printed on the reverse side.

"Sir, Naresh has good connections with big private landers as they all are his followers. He can get quick finance without much formality and paperwork," Deepak said excitedly, looking at Vimal Talwar. "He has helped Baweja many times. He has been in the market for ages."

Baweja's name caused Vimal Talwar's eyebrows to shoot up. Naresh smiled and made a gesture to indicate that it was all possible by the grace of god, and with folded hands he looked skyward.

"My friend, we are a public listed company, unlike Baweja's private limited company. The board will take a decision." I said, looking at Deepak and turned towards Vimal Talwar, "Sir, apart from that, we need to watch our cash flow as well. I have emailed Banerjee Sir, and we should wait until he replies."

Vimal Talwar remained silent, and closing his eyes, moved slowly on the chair, pretending to think like Warren Buffet.

"Your Banerjee Sir is gone to the USA on emergency leave. He called me last night," Siddharth said sarcastically. "We need other solutions to arrange for the finance for a short term, as we need to start promoting the project by next month."

I was shocked to find out that Banerjee Sir had gone to the USA. I thought of Riya; she hadn't replied to my latest emails. I hadn't chatted with her for more than a month!

I had been damn busy since the last few months. I could not keep a track of my own whereabouts, how would I know the whereabouts of others? My life was a mess!

"What about the board of directors? We should seek their approval," I asked again.

"Don't worry about the directors. Dad will take care of them," Siddharth said, looking at Vimal Talwar, who like bulldog Spike threw a 'That's my boy!' gaze at his son.

"Sir, I can arrange private finance through my client," Joshi said for the first time, moving one of the rings on his fingers.

"How much will the interest be?" Deepak asked.

"Four percent to five percent per month, but I can convince him to come down to four percent," Joshi said looking at Siddharth.

Vimal Talwar and Siddharth looked at each other in confusion.

"No, it's very high," I woofed.

"You know private financiers, Sir," Joshi said again, "They are greedy, and they will not accept anything less than four percent."

"Sir, we can inflate the price of the property to cover this extra burden of interest. We will give one bungalow to Bollywood star Shah Rukh Khan or Katrina Kaif or Sachin Tendulkar for free, and then many people will buy the property to become their neighbours," Deepak said with excitement.

"Katrina Kaif; it's a very good idea," Joshi said, looking at Deepak.

"Siddharth, Baweja had also done the same for Emerald Luxury Tower," Deepak said, looking at Siddharth.

The mention of Baweja, like a bomb, blasted Siddharth and Vimal Talwar. Both lost their remaining sense and very seriously started thinking about Deepak's suggestions. *Damn it!*

"We have already borrowed money for equity capital share!" I exclaimed, looking at Deepak, "This is a waste of money! It's suicide!"

"Oh come on, Manav; it's not a waste, its marketing *funda,*" Deepak replied sounding annoyed. Who cared! Even I was pissed off the day he had joined CRL.

"But if our product is good, then why do we need all these marketing gimmicks?" I said casually. "You are an MBA and you claim that you are smart at using resources – man, machine, and money."

"You are just talking about what you see on paper. Man, you CAs won't understand. Just try to read beyond the wall; some risk will pay off in the future," Deepak said and smiled haughtily, "And please, don't remind me about my job. I know very well how to use the resources – man, machine, money, and *munimji*,"

"And do you think we are stupid,?" Siddharth yelled, "We know our business very well!"

"Cool down Siddharth," Vimal Talwar growled softly. Looking at me, he asked, "Manav, how old are you?"

"27, sir," I said, surprised at his question.

"I am 64, and I have been working since I was 16; that means I have 48 years of experience, more then your age," Vimal Sir said and took a sip of water. "If we do not take risk and borrow, how will this economy move forward?"

Boom! He was talking like Bapuji. *No sir, don't do this*, I shivered. *Sir, 64 is the age to retire*.

"Sir, I respect your experience. I have had a bad experience before; my father borrowed money that was beyond his capacity to repay and later we were on the verge of bankruptcy," I said and once again Yogi Bhardwaj's image flashed before my eyes. Deepak looked nervous and turned his gaze to Siddharth.

Vimal Talwar looked confused, and stood up to walk towards the toilet.

Everybody turned to the television and on the screen, Spike was tossing a sandwich to Tyke and Jerry. Tom was watching them from behind a wall.

"Sir, I think we cannot attract reputed investors with such a publicity stunt. Only those who have slush funds will buy the property in our project, as everybody knows that these Bollywood actors or cricketers will not stay on the property," I said as Talwar came out of the toilet.

"It doesn't matter who buys the property," Vimal Talwar said as he zipped up his pants and sat on the chair.

I don't think he had even washed his hands. Sir, first you should clean your dirty hands before planning an environment-friendly project!

"But why, all of sudden, do we need to gift bungalows to celebrities?"I asked and looked at Deepak, "Why are you not confident about selling properties without these stunts?"

"Boss, we can sell them. But, but, but... it will be an icing on the cake and our company's brand image will be elevated. The media will be hooked and they will take this to further heights," Deepak said, pausing.

"But we should not haphazardly increase the marketing budget..." I objected. But Deepak Interrupted me.

"Let me tell you something..." Deepak said in style and stood up.

Everybody looked at him in confusion, and standing behind my chair he kept both his hands on my shoulders. I thought he might strangle me.

"Dear friends, this is just the beginning; we have to market Hill City as heaven on earth, like its mini Switzerland. Residents will feel the breeze in Hill City like they are on top of the world; Jungfraujoch in Switzerland," Deepak said.

It tickled Vimal Talwar and Siddharth; both looked at Deepak, the way Spike and Tyke gawk at a bone. I wondered why people got carried away with bizarre ideas. But then I got an idea; why not use the same technique and knowledge and heave a zombie bomb? Yes, I had read on Wikipedia.

Deepak leaned back on his chair.

"Well dear, that isn't the point," I said.

"Excuse me?" Deepak said while the others frowned.

"I got to tell you something," I said and stood up like a rocket. Everyone was stunned.

"Sir, we should not keep our project on life support and continue to borrow. We should end this zombie business style until our project becomes independent and sustains the marketing cost," I said taking a sip from the glass of water in front of me. "Until then, we should not borrow any further."

Everybody looked at me. I started to walk slowly and continued.

"If we do, we will earn money to pay the debt and interest to the banker, similar to zombie companies in Japan that are constantly being bailed out by the Japan government *since 1990,"* I said the last words loudly, looking at Siddharth and the banker.

"Really? The government has been supporting zombie companies since 1990?" Joshi's jaw dropped.

"Yes, even zombie banks have been put on life support constantly by the Japanese government, and since 1990 there has been no increase in price of real estate," I said to further shock him.

The bomb had exploded in the room and there was tension in the air.

I thought this was the right time to strike the iron while it was still hot. Joshi looked nervous. I started to walk back towards my chair.

"Sir, even I can arrange funds from a private financer at less than 3% if required. But the point is whether we really need more funds at this point?"

I didn't even know whether what I was saying made any sense but it certainly got everyone thinking seriously. Abracadabra!

Vimal Talwar closed his eyes, as if the flight was making an emergency landing from Switzerland to Mumbai.

I sat back quietly on my chair again.

"Well, Manav has a point. Why don't we wait until Banerjee returns from the USA? And meanwhile, you can liaise with celebrities," Talwar said in a husky voice looking at Deepak.

Everyone in the room looked indecisive, including me.

"We can call the banker later on or Manav can also talk to the financer if Joshi doesn't give us a competitive offer," Siddharth said, using common sense for the first time in a CA's company. He looked at the ex-banker. "Deepak, first try Katrina Kaif. What do you think, Sirrrr?"

Deepak looked gloomy, as did Joshi. I think the 'zombie' word worked like a bomb on all of them. Deepak and Joshi gave me dirty looks. I smiled smugly at both of them as we got up to to leave.

"Siddharth, I have to fix a meeting with our PR on Monday next week. Are you available?" Deepak asked, as he stood up.

"No problem, bring them anytime," Siddharth winked, and turned on the television.

Jerry was throwing bombs at Tom. Siddharth laughed loudly and I laughed silently.

◎

"Deepak, good news, Kadamb has agreed to be the chief guest at the ground breaking ceremony," Urvi announced as she entered home. She tossed her bag, *dupatta* and kissed my cheek. She was wearing a maroon tunic and tight blue stretch jeans.

"The first story on the Hill City project is ready. I will send it to you for approval. I have used a quote from minister Kadamb as well. We will run the second story next week. We will discuss it when we meet in your office next week so don't disturb me until then, I am exhausted," she said and disconnected the cell, throwing it on the sofa. She hugged me tight.

"Manav, I love you, baby," she whispered, "I can't live without you."

"How did you manage for so long without me?" I asked.

"You have spoiled me. I was not like this before," she blamed me. I sat beside her; she kept her head on my lap. I kissed her cheek in response. I crossed my leg over hers and snaked my arm around her waist. I felt entranced.

"Papa and Mom are going to Dubai as Mom's sister has shifted from Kenya to Dubai. They will be back next week," she said casually. She grabbed my hand and held it in between her thighs securely.

"When should we inform our parents?" I asked.

"Can I call Mom next week? Is that okay?"

"Why to bother them?" I said. "We can go to Ahmedabad. Ba and Bapuji will also be happy."

"But then it might take a few more days and I need to convince Abhiraj to give me leave," she said.

"Yeah, even I will have to ask Siddharth," I said.

"I have been so tired lately. These big clients are big suckers!" she said calmly. "The next few days are gonna be tough as well. You have magic in your fingers. Now give me a massage, baby."

"Hellooooo, Baweja Saab," Talwar said in a husky voice and winked at Siddharth.

Vimal Talwar had called me to discuss a confidential and important matter. But as I entered in the room, his phone rang.

Siddharth was sitting on the visitor's chair playing games on his phone. I sat beside him reluctantly.

"*Ha...Ha...* How was my shot? You like it, no?" he laughed loudly.

"Your pawn Deepak is very clever and ambitious," Talwar growled, and rotated slowly in his chair.

If Deepak was like a pawn to them, then what was I? Maybe a clown accountant, I guess. My cell buzzed. Spike and Tyke were busy. I looked at the SMS.

Urvi: *What's up?*

I replied quickly, looking at Talwar.

With boss

"Be patient, Baweja. Why are you in a hurry? You will come to know very soon about our project," Talwar said and spun on his chair, "No, my friend, I am not stupid that I would borrow at four percent from the astrologer. I have a smart finance team."

Talwar high-fived Siddharth. I felt love for both swiftly.

Another SMS from Urvi:

I have a meeting with your boss and Deepak, I am at the reception.

She sent me another quick message:

We will have coffee after meeting.

Ok.

I replied and looked straight up again.

"You want to know everything over the phone?" Talwar said and before he hung up the phone, "Let's meet for golf tomorrow morning."

"Bastard!" Talwar said and took a big sip from the glass of water.

He will play golf with his arch rival. He was really Machiavellian, one who used politics and business to his advantage to satisfy his greed.

"Manav, we have to reserve four bungalows, B-321, 322, and S-220, 221 for minister Kadamb," Talwar said and threw a green file on the table. I was aghast.

"Reserve! For what?" I asked as I read the papers. They were four allotment letters for Minister Kadamb, signed by Siddharth and Deepak. Crooked! That's what he says about CAs.

"For cleaning the dirty city," Siddharth said and smiled arrogantly. "My friend, it's a gift for speeding up the clearances and greasing the palms."

Here we go! So this was the important and confidential matter. I knew that when Deepak was involved, all such things were bound to happen.

My cell phone shook. My body shook. I focused on the latter.

"Sir, why do we need to indulge in unethical practices?"I said firmly, "We should avoid such things; after all, we are accountable to the society,"

"Manav, if we leaders think the way the common man thinks, the world would be one thousand years behind, and people would have to travel in bullock carts. There would be no planes, buildings, cars or the Hill City project," Vimal Talwar said piercingly.

Siddharth sneered still playing on his mobile.

The intercom rang.

"We are in a meeting. Ask the young lady to wait," Talwar said and winked at Siddharth.

"Yes, Manav, continue," Siddharth said, looking at his phone. I wondered if he had heard what his father had said earlier.

"We should bring this matter to the board of directors as we are a public listed company and we should keep records of important matters," I said quietly and returned the green file.

I fumbled and the file fell on the floor. Both the Talwars looked at each other. Siddharth looked mad and stopped playing the game.

"Are you really a CA? Or did you bargain for your degree? I need to check your degree certificate!" Siddharth said. My lungs burned up. He stood up and came close to me.

"Siddharth I think it's better if we talk business," I said, ignoring his remarks.

"Oh Really! Now you will teach us business...and what do you think about us? Oh come on man, I am the CEO of the company; do I need the approval from the bunch of directors or you?"

I grew nervous but collected myself. Come on Manav!

"Siddharth you may over rule the board's decision but their opinion matters," I said, "And you should have the eye to foresee the risk associated with the shortcuts. You should stick to the long term plans in the foreseeable future."

"Manav..." Talwar said.

"Dad, wait a minute," Siddharth cut him off, looking at me.

"Man, you chartered accountants are always asking a thousand questions. Have you ever been positive in your life? Never, my friend, never!" he said scornfully.

I felt embarrassed and had to respond.

"Siddharth we are a public listed company. We carry the trust and faith of many other stakeholders," I said, trying to catch my breath like an asthma patient. I had wanted to remain calm, but my temper shot up as I spoke. I continued.

"I am sorry and please don't expect me to bypass the procedure. *I will not do anything without the knowledge of the board of directors*."

Silence!

Both the Talwars looked at each other.

Siddarth snorted. He looked pissed off but controlled his ire.

"Now I understood why you CAs are not at par with the MBAs. And why you CAs are paid peanuts compared to the MBAs. You deserve this! You see, Deepak, who is an MBA draws a larger salary than you," Siddharth said and once again came close to me. "And you... you are a conformist and like a cockroach you will live a miserable life. *And that's your destiny*!"

I felt jolts in my body, as if somebody had slapped my face. I felt unbalanced and tears rolled out of my eyes. Suddenly, images of the earthquake flashed in my head. I had not felt so fragile, even on the day of the earthquake; maybe abuse from a human is heavier than the cruelty of god. I was shaking all over.

A black curtain descended in front of my eyes. I had never been humiliated like this before. My eyes grew moist as I thought of Ba and Bapuji. I wanted to ask them if any Modi had ever been insulted like this in their lives.

"S...ir, if you... have finished, I think I should leave now," I said. My voice was heavy. Both didn't reply. I shut the door slowly. My shoulders slumped, I started trudging to my chamber with moist eyes.

I felt like resigning.I felt like committing suicide. I felt like waiting for Banerjee Sir. I chose the last option. I wondered when he would be back and why he was taking so long to return.

I drank some coffee, chatted with Ba on the phone to get all the news about the Modis and felt better. I looked at my phone as I regained a sense of balance. Krishna had texted me.

My phone rang; it was an international number.

"Hello."

"Hey pal, what's up? It's Krishna. I'm calling from London. You didn't reply to my SMS,"

I controlled my emotions as I was still feeling weak.

"Sorry, I was in a meeting," I said, "What are you doing in London?"

"We have started a joint venture for investing in real estate with an old Emirati friend, Mr Mohammad Shirawi. We are mainly investing in London at the moment to take advantage of the recession. I think property prices will go down further."

My heart ached as I heard the word 'recession', but I controlled myself.

"How much are you investing?"I asked.

"USD 200 million."

"Wow! That's a lot of money. Man, you have become a big fish now!" I said proudly.

"My stake is only 20%. Mr Mohammad Shirawi, my partner, has the major stake in the company. He is property tycoon in Dubai and he invests a lot in property worldwide."

"So finally you are independent. When are you planning to marry Beena?" I asked. I wanted to gossip to change my mood. I thought of calling Bhavesh after the call with Krishna.

"Insha'Allah. Just a few more months. I'll be back to finalise things," he smiled.

"Good. It has been long since we last met," I said.

"By the way, how is real estate in India? It's very expensive in Mumbai,"

I exploded.

"Don't come to India, there's corruption everywhere. Those who abuse the system get rewards and promotions and those who follow the system are called fools. An honest person will never make money in India. This place is for crooked... people. Not people... like you and... me," I said, my voice broke as I finished.

"Man, what is wrong with you? You were a patron of India?"

I remained silent for a few seconds, but eventually blurted everything out.

"Don't worry man, you know Deepak always wanted to be successful by hook or by crook, and you know he believes in shortcuts. Just ignore what Siddharth said to you, move on and stay focused on your principles," Krishna advised me.

I remained silent.

He hung up the phone after some gossip-to flatter me-about London and Beena's growing passion for food and latest passion for furniture and onterior decoration.

"Your boss seems to be sick. I'm not surprised that he has been divorced twice," Urvi said, as we met after office hours. I briefed her about the meeting and why I had cancelled the plan to drink coffee in the office.

"But don't worry honey, I am with you," she said childishly and hugged me tight. I gently put my arms around her.

We were sitting on the sofa at home. She came closer and kissed my lower lip slowly. Every single kiss on my cheek altered my mood.

"I want a break from the job. I am fed up of dealing with politicians and their secretaries. I don't know how the common man can reach them; it was a nightmare to reach a minister!" she said, raising her neck to kiss my cheek. I felt better.

I needed to get out of my depression. I couldn't live thinking 24x7 about crazy Siddharth. Riya and Banerjee Sir were still out of reach. And I wanted to tell Urvi about how unethical corporates and politicians were abusing the system and playing with our future.

"Do you think the minister agreed because of your PR relations?" I asked rationally.

"Yes, Abhiraj informed me that he had fixed the meeting with the minister directly. And his secretary has sent him a quote," Urvi said casually and hugged me again. "But why are you talking about office and work? *Just love me, no.*"

"They have bribed the minister with four bungalows," I said, looking into her eyes.

"What!" she yelled and released me.

"These big corporates are using professionals like us," I said, "I guess Talwar is using Deepak as well; they know his weakness. He is over ambitious."

"Abhiraj and Deepak didn't tell me this. These corporates sponsor politicians for their election funds and then in return, they make the ministers dance on their fingertips," she said in disgust.

"And 'young India' like you and me have to slog the whole day and night for these corporates," I said, distressed.

She nodded in agreement and once again placed her head on my shoulder. I felt better after sharing my thoughts and venting my frustration.

"Leave it, no, focus on me," she said after a while and kissed me. I kissed her back. I stared into her eyes. She looked lovely. I felt an urge to marry her that very moment.

"My leave has been approved," she whispered, "What about yours?"

I think she had read my mind. My hand reached to her bosom and she closed her eyes.

"We will talk later..." I said, but was interrupted.

Urvi's cell rang. It was a call from her office.

"Hello," she answered, adjusting her clothing and bra. Her face expression changed and she quickly hung up the phone.

"Baby, listen I have to go. The media is criticising our client. A female patient was molested by a male doctor. She has complained to the police," she said and quickly collected her stuff. "I have to reverse the negative press and reshape the image. See you later."

She looked at the mirror, opened her bag, pulled out a lip gloss, applied it on her lips gently, and kept it back. Then she pulled out her perfume and sprayed a bit on her body, winked at me and hugged me. I felt aroused. I did not want her to leave. I craved her presence.

"Even you have molested me many times," I said.

She hit my stomach; I grabbed her in my arms.

"When will the Hill City story be out?"

"Tomorrow,"she said coming close to me. Her eyes transfixed on mine, she pressed her bosom to my chest.

I loved that!

"I had thought about giving you a special oil massage today," I said and stretched my hand to unbolt the door reluctantly.

"Don't worry, keep it for next time," she said and planted kisses on my forehead, nose, cheeks and lips. "Don't burn unnecessary calories and don't workout hard. Preserve your energy for me."

"I love you, Urvi!" I exclaimed, "Why don't you come over later today?"

She opened the door and smiled.

"See you over the weekend Manavi Aunty," she said. "I will not let you sleep."

Black Day

15 September 2008.

"Lazy bones!" I murmured as I reached home after my workout in the morning. I was annoyed that the newspaper was not outside my door.

I was already frustrated since the last evening as Urvi had left me burning with desire. I had tried to reach Banerjee Sir a thousand times in the past ten days but there was no response. His cell was switched off and I didn't get a reply to my countless emails. Riya was also out of reach.

I turned on the television in loathing and took a sip of the chocolate flavor protein shake. It tasted cool, but the news on CNN was hot as fire!

LEHMAN BROTHERS FILES FOR BANKRUPTCY

Merrill Lynch has been sold and insurance giant AIG has sought USD 40 billion from the Federal Reserve.

The future of 60,000 employees of AIG and 25,000 employees of Lehman remains unclear.

This has been the most dramatic day in the history of Wall Street. Lehman Brothers, investment bankers, will be liquidated as it has failed to get any buyers. Once-proud financial institutions have been brought down to their knees due to the loss of hundreds of billions of dollars caused by bad mortgage finance and real estate investments.

My mind was buzzing and my body felt taut when I heard the last words, "...losses caused by bad mortgage finance and real estate investments."

I understood why Banerjee Sir had been out of reach; Riya was in trouble.

There was a sharp noise at the door, the newspaper had finally landed. I fetched the newspaper, and my eyes widened when I saw the full page story of 'The Firmament', environment hill city. There were images of *Jungfraujoch* along with Deepak and Talwar's photos. There was a quote from the minister with a photograph of the replica of the Hill City project, which looked very impressive, and for sure would uplift the brand image of our company. Urvi had done a good job.

"Did you hear the bad news?" Rita asked, as I entered the office.

"Yeah, about Lehman Brothers" I said casually. I had never thought Rita would be worried about the Lehman Brothers.

"Who...who are... these Lehman Brothers?" she asked like a moron.

"Rita, it was a more than 150 year old USA Company. And sooner or later, this is going to affect the world, including India. It's bad news; Lehman Brothers have filed for bankruptcy," I said in a low voice.

"Sir, I am talking about 'The Firmament', the Hill City and how our company paid bribes to get the environment clearances,"she yelled.

I was stunned. I could not believe what I had heard!

"It's all over the news channels!" she said again as I stood frozen.

"What are you saying?" I bawled finally. Not waiting for her reply, I loped towards the conference room and switched on the television. I still could not believe it!

Continental Realty Ltd bribes ministers to get environment clearance.

Mumbai developer Siddharth Talwar and Deepak Mehra bribed minister Kadamb.

The opposition party has demanded the minister's resignation.

The luxury environment-friendly project has by-passed the environment clearance test.

Urvashi Doshi, political and corporate lobbyist coordinator between ministers and Talwar.

The channels were playing the taped conversation between Urvi, Siddharth, Deepak and minister Kadamb. They were discussing about inviting minister Kadamb for the launch, and Urvi was heard saying excitedly, "Deepak, the minister has accepted the invitation."

My heartbeats were slowing down. I was dripping with sweat. My Urvi was in trouble. She had been used by these crooks.

"Rita, can you connect me to Vimal Sir and Deepak?"I exclaimed. I wanted to avoid calling from my cell.

"Sure."

I flipped though the channels in a hurry; all the national news channels were screening only one thing – the news about our company. They began exposing Vimal Talwar and Siddharth's private lives. Siddharth's background from his school days, his affairs during his college days with ten girls, bribing cops and taking drugs in New York – it was amazing how the media had been able to find out so much. Siddharth's lavish weddings, his divorces, and his fight with the college principal were played and replayed. Only one English channel was showing a documentary on the Lehman Brothers.

"What happened?" I yelled, as Rita hadn't responded.

"Both cells have been switched off,"she said quietly,"Can I try his home?"

"Good, try quickly and after that call Urvi.Do you have her cell number?"I asked.

"Urvi?!" She asked in surprise, "You mean Urvashi Doshi?"

"Oh, yeah," I said, shocked.

My cell rang.

Bhuvi calling flashed on my phone. It was Urvi's Ahmedabad residence number.

"Hello."

"Manav, what is going on? Where...is my...Urvi?" Urvi's mother asked. Her voice was trembling, "Where is my *bacheee?* I made a mistake by listening to Raman and sending her to Mumbai."

"Aunty, wait," I said and dialled Rita on the intercom phone, "Try Urvashi first."

"Her phone is off as well," Rita said quietly.

"Hello, Manav beta, Raman here," Urvi's dad said in a firm voice."Please tell her that we are with her, and not to worry. I trust her, not the tape. She has done nothing wrong. Please, ask her to call us or else we will go there..." he said in a shaky voice; he was trying hard to control his emotions.

"Yes uncle, don't worry, give me some time. I will update you soon," I said more to myself than to him, as I was not sure whether I would be able to help her.

The intercom rang.

"Hello, Manav, there is a journalist on the line. She wants to speak to Talwar and Deepak," Rita said nervously. I had never spoken to the media. But what I will tell them?

Tell them they are in hell, I thought.

"Should I tell him to call later?"

"Okay, do that," I said and disconnected the phone.

Once again the intercom rang. Uncle was still on hold (Aunty was howling at him).

"Hello, boss's residence phone is ringing," Rita said as I was still talking to Urvi's father.

"Uncle, we will talk later,"I said and without waiting for his reply, disconnected the phone.

"Hello Sir, good morning. Manav here,"I said uneasily.

"Hello, I... Lakshmi," a housemaid lady spoke with prolonged vowels and chuckled.

"Where... Sir? From office calling, urgent,"I pleaded, trying to match her drawl and tone.

"Sir played golf... now relaxes... take massage... call later," the housemaid said.

I was damn sure that the boss did not know that Hill City had become Hell City.

"IT'S URGENT, PLEASE CONNECT ME NOW!" I yelled.

"Ok...wait...I check,"she said.

"Hello, Vimal here," Talwar's heavy voice echoed. There was some soothing music being played in the background much like the relaxing music played at a spa. The phone was on speaker.

"Sir, did you watch the news?" I asked breathless.

"Yes, I know, don't worry. I have spoken to our lawyer, Ajit Vaghle. I will go to his office around 1:00 pm. Deepak and Siddharth will meet me there. I will come to office later," he said quietly as I heard the clinking of bangles.

"Sir, open... legs," I heard Lakshmi's voice.

"Leave it now. Give me my clothes," Talwar exclaimed.

Was he not a bit worried? He knew everything and yet was getting a massage? I was worried about Urvi.

"Sir, journalists are calling our office. They were enquiring about Siddharth and Deepak," I said.

"Baweja has played a game with us. I was drunk and I told him that minister Kadamb was our chief guest. Just wait until I come to office," he said. After a pause he said, "If I am late, you handle the media smartly."

"Sure sir," I said.

"Sir this...my cloths," I heard Lakshmi chuckling in the background.

"Where are my fucking clothes?" Talwar roared loudly.

The phone was disconnected.

The Media Mania

"Ms Urvashi Doshi, you introduced your client to the minister and you were the negotiator... is that correct?" an aggressive journalist grilled Urvi.

"You were the link between minister Kadamb and your client Talwar," a male journalist probed.

I was all alone thinking about Urvi. And suddenly the news changed, Urvi was avoiding media and was taking big strides towards her office building. The reporters were chasing her like bullies to get her. Finally she stopped and turned towards them. They shoved their mics at her face.

Since the last two days, only one story dominated the news: the 'Hill City Scandal'. It seemed as though nothing else had been happening in a country of 1.2 billon people. Both the Talwars and Deepak didn't show up at the office for the next two days. The parliament session was adjourned after the opposition parties were up in arms demanding the resignation of the minister and asking for a CBI enquiry.

Media had created a hoopla by sensationalizing the news and as Deepak and Urvi had rightly said, media was habitual of extrapolating small issues as whopping issues – projecting a dog as a dinosaur. And to make it a memorable event, they will tag these issues as "Bofors Scam" or "The Fodder scam" or "9/11". Now they tagged the CRL corruption scam as the "Hill City scam". Media has tagged nicknames to famous or infamous people – "Bad boy" to Salman Khan, "King Khan" to Shah Rukh Khan and "Mr. Perfectionist" to Aamir Khan. Urvi had similarly been labeled – Corporate Lobbyist.

I received calls from the Bengaluru and Delhi offices. Ba and Bapuji were also worried. And they passed on their worries to me and the result was that I had started drinking ten cups of coffee a day. But the situation remained the same, and instead, I developed acidity. I had stopped working out. In fact, I had stopped sleeping. My body was distressed and mind in chaos. I had tried to reach Urvi but she had been thrown out of her hostel and in her office, everyone was too scared to answer the phone. Her cellphone seemed to be dead since last two days. But finally she had answered my phone last night:

"Hell..o, Urvi," I asked as she picked up the mobile. But there was long-errie-silence.

'It's me," I said again to break the silence, "Where are you?"

There was painful silence again. All I could hear was sobs. "Don't worry darling, I am with you. Everything will be all right. You are not alone. Have you spoken to you mom? I know you have not done anything wrong," I said emphatically. "OK, just tell me where you are? I will come right now to pick you up,"

What I could hear was her wail. And the sound "click".

She had disconnected. And her phone was dead since then.

I was flipping channels and was stunned to see Urvi surrounded by the media at her office building.

"That's rubbish! We only suggested our client to invite minister Kadamb so that we could get good media coverage," she clarified, controlling her ire. Her eyes were red and swollen. She had not slept whole night, nor had I. But she looked confident than last night.

"But why did you recommend only minister Kadamb to your client? Are you working for him as an agent to lobby for the corporates?" a male journalist asked. I wanted to knock him down, the rogue!

"This is ridiculous! My management and client mutually agreed upon minister Kadamb. And you are a journalist; you should know how a PR agency works. We do know many politicians and corporates, but we do our job professionally. And if you want more information, please ask Mr Abhiraj Chaturvedi, the CEO of our company,"she said and started walking towards the lift.

"You got a promotion really quickly; obviously you broke a big deal with your client and also with the minister. Can you tell me if this tape conversation is correct…" a lady journalist asked.

Urvi stopped, looking stunned. Her eyes were filling up with tears and she ran towards the lift, wiping her eyes. I felt like slapping the journalist.

◎

"Is it true that you gave four bungalows to minister Kadamb for clearance for the Hill City project?" a journalist asked Vimal Talwar, who was standing next to his car outside the office building.

I was watching news on television since last 48 hours.

Deepak and Siddharth, both unshaven and without hair gel emerged from the car and stood beside Vimal Talwar.

"No, it's not true. We got a clean chit from the environment ministry and all the compliance requirements of the ministry have been met," Vimal Talwar growled with a straight and confident face.

I knew that it was a bald-faced lie. He had shown me the green file.

"Then how did you get the clearance from the ministry in just two months, when many other projects have been awaiting approval for more than a year?" a lady journalist interrogated Talwar.

"That I don't know. You can ask the ministry, not me. All I can say is that we have met all the compliance requirements of the departments," Talwar replied coolly.

Suddenly, something else flashed on the screen.

"*KADAMB RESIGNS!*"

"Excuse me sir, Mr Kadamb has just resigned, as the high command has asked him to resign on moral grounds, till he comes out clean and has called for a CBI inquiry. Can we assume that he has accepted that he had received a bribe? Will you also resign from the post of the chairman?"A journalist asked. All the three looked shocked.

"Excuse me, let us go. I don't want to comment on this," Vimal Talwar said and pushed his way into the office.

◎

"Boss is calling you," Rita called and hung up the phone. I sprang from my seat like a missile and loped towards Talwar's lost chamber.

"Sir the media has been creating panic," I said without preamble and immediately took the chair beside Deepak. I offered him my hand. He smiled and gave his hand softly for the first time.

"Manav, you know Banerjee is not reachable. And if we are not in the office, you have to take charge of the Hill City project and the office. I think this issue may take a serious turn," Vimal Talwar said taking a sip of water. He was dripping with sweat.

"But Sir, I don't have much information about the project and the advertisement contracts," I said, looking at Talwar. "And my job..."

"Don't worry, you are Chief Operating Officer from today. I will make you CEO soon," Talwar said quickly and started to dial a number on his cell. Deepak looked jaundiced.

"But sir..."

"Nope, now only your honesty can save us," Talwar said and without waiting for my response, gave orders over the phone. I remained silent. Deepak kept his head down.

I became the Chief Operating Officer of a sick company.

"Dad, I want to go back to America today itself," Siddharth yelled, jumping on the chair. Deepak looked very nervous; this was the first time that I saw him looking so nervous.

"What is the media doing?"Deepak booed, "Why are they acting like bees?"

"I had told you, man, stay away from the media, be realistic," I said.

"This is because of Baweja," Talwar yelled, wiping his forehead. "And your Master of Fucking Business Administration strategy!"

Deepak looked shocked and bowed his head down.

"Sir, we corporates are also responsible for not only environment-friendly developments, but also a corruption-free society,"I discoursed.

"Let's not criticise each other. It's a testing time for all of us," Vimal Talwar said and lit up his cigar.

"Sir, but the big question is; how we will continue the Hill City project? The bank had already released the loan, the interest has already started. Our other projects in Delhi and Bengaluru are already sold out. If we don't start selling quickly, we will not be able to sustain the interest cost and salary cost," I exclaimed, "I think the advertisement campaign is going to start after a few days. But who will buy now?"

Talwar didn't respond, looking into my eyes. He turned pale.

Siddharth and Deepak turned towards me.

"We have already signed and paid the advance to the advertisement agency. All hoardings are ready. They will not refund the money," Deepak said, looking at me.

"We have borrowed from the market as well. If this scandal continues for six months or more, we will go bankrupt," Siddharth said quietly, looking at his father, "Baweja has screwed us dad!"

Talwar's expression changed to white as a sheet. He looked grimly at Deepak and then Siddharth. He took a giant drag from the cigar and before he could release the smoke, he started coughing. He kept his hand on his chest. We all sprang up from our seats.

"Call the ambulance! Daddy is having a heart attack!"

Blame. Blame. Blame.

Vimal Talwar passed away that very day. He got three heart attacks before he reached the hospital.

A leading newspaper's headlines screamed,

THE FIRMAMENT HILL CITY UNSHIELDED

Flamboyant management used kickback to minister.

Kadamb, Siddharth, Deepak and Urvi all quoted that they were innocent. Kadamb said it was a conspiracy by the opposition party. Urvi blamed her boss Abhiraj. Siddharth blamed the CEO Deepak and Deepak blamed the management, and Vimal Talwar had already gone to a better place.

Am I a Scapegoat?

"No, I didn't meet her. Ramanbhai was hospitalised," Bapuji advised me over the phone, "Leave her alone for the time being. Time will heal the pain."

And Ba said, "Don't worry; if God closes one door, he will open another."

Urvi had returned to Ahmedabad. I could not meet her though I tried very hard. I thought bapuji had a point. She was safe at home. Also my life was living hell. And that was the reason I had asked Bapuji to visit Bhuvi, as they had disconnected their telephones. Her father had taken VRS (voluntary retirement) to avoid embarrassment in the office. He had suffered a minor heart attack, I am not sure whether it was because of gastrointestinal distress due to the overeating of chaat, bullying by the media or the hearty hammering by aunty.

After a blame game that went on for a few weeks, the police finally arrested Siddharth, the Machiavellian philosopher. Deepak and Kadamb were arrested as well. Soon the media lost interest and moved on to other sensational stories. I planned to see Urvi and on Sunday morning I reached my home in Ahmedabad.

But bapuji surprised me.

"Their house is locked since few weeks. I think they might be travelling to avoid embarrassment," he said quietly.

"Dont's worry, you will get many good marriage proposals," Ba said caressing my hair. And then she added, "Can we talk to Riya's parents?"

I ignored Ba and rushed to Urvi's house, Bhuvi. It was locked. I asked a lady neighbour, standing at the door, watching me inquisitively.

"Excuse me, can you tell me where they have gone?"

"Himalaya or Hell! We don't care! And we have no more relation with corrupt people," She said and closed the door hard.

I felt disgusted. Nothing was going my way. I know she needed me. I could not figure out where to focus, Urvi or office! It was going to be a life and death decision.

Riya's words hovered in my head. "Leader has to be fit to deal with stress, conflicts, and crises...."

It's very hard to practice what we read in the books. But do I have a choice? Urvi has rightly said, "Life is one way, you can't stop." I thought and resumed the work.

I returned to Mumbai the same day and focused on the office, lawyers, courts, banks, lenders and the environment department. The bank had given a notice to clear the debt or else to auction the land to recover the money. The environment ministry compelled us to follow the guidelines and build a canal for the villagers, which meant an additional investment of Rs 700 crore. The company debt piled up. We were not able to sell the property.

But Ba was never wrong; God opened not one, but two doors. Banerjee Sir and Riya returned.

Riya had been charged for using cosmetic accounting gimmicks to make the company's finances appear less shaky than they really were and she had been held by the FBI. However, she was able to prove her innocence, thanks to Banerjee Sir's advice which she had followed by maintaining all the correspondence and records in writing.

My mobile rang. The Bengaluru office was calling.

"Good morning, Manav," Banerjee Sir said quietly.

"Sir, everything is in a mess here!"I said disconsolately.

"I know the management has paid the price for not listening to your advice. I should accept my mistake too," he said quietly.

"Sir, but our company's name has been affected. I don't know how we will sell properties and get out of this financial mess," I said concerned.

"Don't worry. I have called director Rakesh Padukone. Let me take account of the situation. I will organise a meeting in Mumbai very soon," he said and hung up.

"Good evening," I said, as we entered the conference room.

Meeting attendance: Rakesh, Sachin, Manjunath, Pankaj Banerjee, Gill, Manav Modi and Harish Shukla.

Harish gave me the copy of the agenda.

1. Environment clearance: to check and discuss with architect.
2. Legal proceedings to discuss with lawyer.
3. New acting CEO to be appointed.
4. Possibility of arranging finance or entering into a joint venture to resume work, if viable.

"Rakesh, if things were out of your control, then why did you not inform the board of directors?" Manjunath almost scolded him.

Rakesh cleared his throat.

"You all know how Siddharth is. Most of the meetings with the government officials and ministers had been arranged by Siddharth and Deepak, I was not involved. Hence, I had no information about the gifts to minister," Rakesh said nervously. His hands were trembling.

"Sir, Siddharth had told me that the four properties had been offered to the ministers,"I replied quietly. "In fact, he showed me a green coloured file with the allotment letters that were signed by Deepak and Siddharth."

"Mr Rakesh, can you explain what the problem was with the designs submitted?" Mr Gill interrogated in his loud voice before Rakesh could answer, "And is it true that we offered gifts to clear the project quickly?"

There was absolute silence in the room. Rakesh grew paler.

"Where is that file?" Banerjee Sir asked me.

"It was in Vimal Talwar's chamber, but I could not find it thereafter," I said as Rakesh remained silent, his head down.

Everybody looked melancholy. After a few more distressing seconds of silence, Rakesh spoke up, "I am sorry about that, but everything was going so fast, and I trusted the management and Deepak."

We called the architects in. They confirmed that the ministry had asked them to build a water canal, but when the approval was sent, they were surprised that some minor changes in the design like cutting the hill and forests were made, but building the water canal had been waived. They had no knowledge of how that had occurred. They left.

"Hmm, there are no complete records and transparency was not maintained," Sachin said, thinking.

We discussed this for another thirty minutes. We took a break and asked Rita to send Ajit Vaghle, the lawyer, after the break. You have to be at your best to face lawyers, and he was a legal juggernaut!

"Rita, ask Raghu to bring some coffee to my chamber," I said, as I reached my chamber during the hiatus.

"Sure," she said.

Raghu entered with the coffee, placed it on the table and left.

I heard a knock on the door as I took the last sip of the coffee. Suresh entered the room.

"You here? Hope all is well with the network," I said, starting to leave.

He smirked.

"I just came for the routine inspection. Anyway, if you are done with the meeting let's have coffee together. It tastes better when I drink coffee with you," he said, trying to flatter me.

"Sorry, the meeting is not over and I have just finished my coffee. You are welcome to have a coffee here though," I said and chuckled.

"Wait... I need to help. I mean I... need help" he said hesitantly, looking at the door nervously.

Help! Why not, we are running a fucking NGO over here, I thought, recalling Ba's acerbic comments to Bapuji.

"Can we discuss this some other day?" I said instead, and stood up to leave..

"Sure," he said, clearly disappointed.

I asked Rita to send Ajit Vaghle in. He was middle aged with a French beard. He had orange eyes and his fussy habits in some way reminded me of a fox. He entered as if he was entering the court and "lawyer" was displayed all over his skin like a tatoo. He arched his eyebrows; this caused the entire conference to nearly spit out their coffee.

He raved and ranted. He created further panic to create a milieu with the aim to increase his fees.

"When will Siddharth get bail?" Sachin asked casually.

"Actually you know the judge Mr Alok Sharma is very strict; he will review each case with *parri passu*," he said vaguely.

Everybody looked more puzzled. I hate lawyers!

"Can you explain it in simple human language," Gill ordered.

"I don't see how Siddharth can get out quickly. It's a difficult situation but we have to accept it. They have to stay in jail for some more time, otherwise the media and the opposition party will create more drama," the lawyer said melodramatically.

CAs should learn from lawyers – to strike while the iron is hot; they know how to milk an opportunity to squeeze more fees from their clients.

"If this case continues further, we will go bankrupt," Gill said looking dismayed.

I guarantee that if we CAs become lawyers as well, every client would go bankrupt.

Vaghle stood up to leave after creating striking fear in all the directors. He knew that not a single person in the room – or on the earth – liked him.

"All right," he said, and frowned at all of us. "I will send my bill tomorrow morning."

A lawyer will always be lawyer, even if he is wearing skirt like dhoti. If a lawyer looks at you, he is thinking how to dismantle your balls. We have seen this happening to the British Empire by a thin but determined lawyer just by fasting and with the help of a stick.

I stood up to escort him out.

"I hate it when records are not maintained," Banerjee Sir muttered, taking a sip of the coffee. I nodded in agreement. After the lawyer had left, we ordered some coffee again to regain our senses.

"There are no minutes of the meetings; we are the number one paperless, environment-friendly company!" Gill said and giggled nervously.

"Gill Sahib, we need to start the project as early as possible, otherwise we will incur more losses," Sachin said. It was obvious. Even Raghu and Rita were thinking the same. I could read their faces.

"But then we need to agree to the environment ministry's terms and conditions to build the water canal that'll cost us an additional Rs 700 crore," Manjunath said, looking worried.

"Sir, we should arrange for an investing partner. We may have to sell some equity shares," I said, taking a sip of the coffee.

Each person in the room looked at me as though I had lost my mind.

"A legal case is going on, the chairman has died, the CEO is in jail, the ministry has already blacklisted the project, and recession has begun everywhere," Gill said, counting each issue on his fingers.

"Which crazy person will finance or invest in this sick project? Yes, only if he wants to commit suicide."

"Sir, can we move to the next item of the agenda?" Harish Shukla spoke.

"Yes, can we first appoint someone as the CEO so that he can lead this titanic project?" Manjunath said, looking exhausted.

Banerjee took the last sip of the coffee and taking a deep breath, he spoke loudly, "I think the CEO should have big cojones to accept this position and stay in this business. We need a brave person, a risk-taker. Someone who knows this company and also this project."

He paused, raising his hand to drink some water, but the glass was empty. I offered him my glass. He gestured thanks and continued.

"And also, someone who can maintain transparency and have the ability to pull the company out of this financial and legal mess," Banerjee Sir said and moved his head from left to right and again from right to left.

"As Rakesh Padukone was involved in the project since the beginning, and as the CBI enquiries and police enquiries are still going on, he should support the new acting CEO... Mr. Manav Modi, until the Hill City project is revived and starts operations smoothly."

Silence!

I felt completely numb. But soon I heard clapping. Yes, everyone was clapping. Was it an opportunity? Or was I being made a scapegoat? Was it a dream come true or a nightmare.The race with Deepak was over. Deepak had lost to Manav; MBA had lost to CA.

It was an opportunity, and I seized it. I couldn't believe that I had become a CEO, albeit an acting one. If I gave it my best, I could be the CEO till the cow comes home. I instantly thought of telling Urvi to bring joy to her face. Her parents' faces. All Modis' faces.

"You have to perform miracles to save this company," Manjunath said.

"Let's be positive, we are together in this. Do or die!" Rakesh said beaming at me.

"Don't worry; you CAs know the financials; restructure the company and bring it back to business from the dead," Sachin said and offered his hand to me. I was still sitting on the chair.

"Manav, you are a born entrepreneur and the next Dhirubhai Ambani of Gujarat. You have to prove it now," Gill said, and kept his heavy hand on my shoulder.

Everybody offered commiserations instead of congratulations.

"But Sir, it's a big project and I don't have any accounts of the Hill City project; everything is with Deepak," I said composing quickly. "And with the legal case going on, who will invest in our project? We need money urgently..."

"What is the big deal? You can visit the jail to see Deepak. And don't worry about the money, have trust in God,"Gill announced. "*Wahe guru ji da khalsa, wahe guru ji di fateh*!"

"I promise that we will comply with the guidelines of the environment ministry. And we will ensure that we will not do any injustice to the poor who will be affected because of this project, as we are all a part of this society. Also, we will cooperate with the police and CBI enquiries until justice is done," I said, finishing the tenth interview after formally accepting the positionof the CEO.

But it was just the beginning, the job was not done yet. If the company failed to survive, the CEO would not survive either, I reminded myself a thousand times in my head.

My interview was telecast on all the TV channels.

The first SMS I received was from Riya: "You looked hot on TV. Good luck, you macho man. You can do it."

I received calls from Ushaben, Umesh, and the entire Modi club. Everyone wished me the best of luck.

An SMS from Krishna: "Dude, you have done it! Keep it up. I have to catch a flight. Call you later. I am coming soon to fix my marriage."

"I will go to *Mata na madh* and after that we will celebrate at home," Ba said impatiently over phone.

"Ba not now, I have to work hard," I said. "I am only the acting CEO."

"You are acting?" Ba asked, confused and handed the phone over to Bapuji. I explained to him how hard I would have to work if I had to pull the company out of this financial mess to survive. He instantly understood my situation.

"Don't worry," he said. "Trust in God, in Krishna."

"What about Urvi and her family, are they back?" I said.

I needed her back, I felt strong whenever she was beside me.

"Hello, Papa?" I said as he had not responded, "Are you there?"

"Beta, sorry I didn't mention this to you. Ramanbhai and his family have sold the house and have left," Bapuji said meekly.

I felt blank and paralysed.

"Hello, Manav beta, can you hear me?"

"Left?Where? Who told you?" I quizzed, composing myself.

"I tried hard but I could not reach them. Maybe they have left Ahmedabad...or the country itself," Bapuji whispered like a ghost.

"What!" I yelled in disbelief.

I completed my CA for Urvi. I came to Mumbai for Urvi, and now Bapuji said that he was not aware of her whereabouts? I felt like shouting, but instead disconnected the phone.

My school, college, and now professional life had been screwed up by Deepak and only Deepak. I hate you! I used bad words in my head and jumped into the car, hit the ignition, slammed into gear and stomped the accelerator, yanking the wheel hard right. The car boomed forward on the road.

I have to work hard. It would be my last meeting with him; I wanted to close this chapter in my life. I hummed to myself, as I headed towards Arthur Road Jail to meet Deepak

I jumped out of the car as I reached the jail but was taken aback to see two familiar faces coming out from the jail. Yes, Parthivbhai followed by the nobleman wearing gold plated spectacle. They must be involved in charity work at the prison, I guessed.

I hurried to reach them but suddenly a BMW car stopped in between us; both jumped into the back seat, and the car sped away.

I stood dazed for a few nanoseconds; suddenly horns honked around me and I realised I was in the middle of the road. I jumped to the pavement and ambled slowly to the jail, pondering.

"Tell me the number," a khaki-dressed man asked in irritation, as I entered Arthur Road Jail, wearing black suit, still puzzled.

"Sorry, 714," I said recovering. Deepak hated numbers, now his identity was a number – 714.

I reached the common meeting area, where folks were talking to jailbirds behind the fences. There was no separate bigwig wing for a CEO to meet with criminals, so I had no option but to wait with the families of felons. It was the first time in my life that I was visiting a jail. I was sweating. And jail in Bollywood movies is way better than jail in real life. I was sure that Deepak and Siddharth were having a hard time.

They deserved this for humiliating me and our accounting profession! I was feeling proud to be a CA that day.

And very soon a hawaldar asked me to follow him. He left me in a secluded cell. If it was not official or important, I would have run away as I looked around in the small lavatory-sized cell. There was a cement bench to sit on in one corner, a small pot on the other side with a stone fixed beneath it. A small carpet was spread on the floor on the other side. There were bugs crawling all over the place. I looked at the small window. Instead of fresh air a foul odour was coming through it. And bat-sized mosquitoes started hovering like choppers above my head.

I don't understand how the brain's memory chip functions; I should ask Mr Microsoft. All the crappy memories surfaced as I saw the bugs moving on the carpet.

"*You CAs are like cockroaches,*" Deepak had told me at Manek Chowk for the first time.

"*I will rule this city!*" Deepak had yelled after. But he was in jail now.

I heard footsteps.

And what I saw demoralised me further. If he had not come with the same hawaldar, I would not have recognised Deepak. He had a long beard and he was dressed in the white attire for prisoners – a white kurta and short pyjamas with black lines. For a moment I forgot that he was my foe. But I controlled my emotions. It was my day.

He scanned me from top to bottom and smiled the way a loser would.

"So you have come to show me where you are today, a successful CEO while I am a criminal, a loser," he said, the smirk did not escape me, but I ignored.

"Have I not earned this position?" I asked with pride in voice. I deserve this, I thought.

"And for how many days will you hold this position because you don't think beyond numbers," he said giving me a smug smile.

"So far life has taught me everything and it is not important how long I will be a CEO," I said, my voice stern. "As long as I hold this position, I will give my 100% and will not indulge in any unethical practices like you."

"Ha ha...so you have come to tell me your philosophy?" He said mockingly again. This triggered my temper. I felt angry but controlled.

"I have come here to discuss the mess you have got us into," I said sternly, looking into his eyes. He could not look back into mine, not yet.

"You too think that I am criminal and I have bribed the minister?" he asked, turning around back and walking towards the railing. Obviously, he could not face me.

"Why not... you can go to any extent to become rich and famous," I said. "For you, money is everything."

"The whole world is after money," he said, turning towards

me quickly. "And I am not the monk whose success is measured in welfare of humankind."

"Do you know the business which generates only profit and money without creating values for society is like a monster to humankind," I said coming close to him.

He kept quiet. And suddenly Ba and Bapuji's doleful face hovered in my head when Bapuji was struggling for money because of the loan and the failed deal with Ranjit Mehra. Now I was struggling for money.

"You criticised me, my profession and ruined the image of the company and put thousands of employees and shareholder's money *at risk.*" I yelled as I spoke, "Like father, like son. You can go to any extent to make money like your father. Your father spoiled my father's business and now I am suffering because of you and you alone. People like you and your father are a curse, and dangerous for the society."

I paused to breathe.

"Though it's late but finally justice is done by God," I said with acid in tone. "Consider this as even."

Deepak winced.

"You became part of a corrupt system. Shame on you and your profession," I said loudly, "And do you realise that you spolied Urvi's career and her life."

"What is wrong with Urvi?" he asked sounded anxious, "Where is she?"

The image of Urvi crying and running from the media flashed before my eyes. And Bapuji's words that she has left this country hovered in my head. I got even angrier.

"Please tell me where she is," Deepak exclaimed, keeping both hands on my shoulders. I looked sideways.

"Only God knows where she is," I said inaudibly first, but raising my voice as I spoke. "She has left Mumbai. Her family has left Ahmedabad and they might have left this country and that is *because of you and you only!*"

"Oh my God!" he said as his eyes filled up with tears, "Please forgive me."

Deepak was in deep thought for a few seconds.

"I was... never like this before," he said quietly, turning towards me. He trudged to the bench and sat on it. "I never wanted this. I had promised my mom that I would be a good person."

Suddenly he began sobbing like a child. I softened towards him but was not ready to forgive him. His sins could not be forgotten.

He went further. "I had promised Anu, my sister, that I would be rich and famous but not like dad. I have let down my nana as well. He had said that I came to this earth to do a special task."

Suddenly Yogi Bhardwaj's words aired in my head. He had said, "Remember there are bad people who will discourage you and there are good people, who will encourage you, but be humble. You have to face both, accept the criticism and keep striding towards your goal. You are lucky as you are on this earth to do a special task. Recognise the opportunity and grab those opportunities to be a successful person in life. You have to serve your loved ones and society at large....."

Deepak stood up.

"I am sorry Manav. I wanted Urvi to be happy and successful. I had a grudge against CA as a profession but I never used any trick to outplay you. I have not done anything wrong. I am innocent. Please trust me."

He jerked my shoulder hard, looking into my eyes. I became soft.

"I feel sorry for you, but you have to pay the price for your mistakes. The whole company has to pay the price for your greed. I can't do much for you."

"No man, I didn't offer any bribe to the minister. Siddharth lied in court!" Deepak exclaimed, looking into my eyes.

"But how you will prove it? There are no documents," I said.

"I just did what Siddharth and Abhiraj instructed me to do. They are the real culprits, not me," Deepak said. "Am I guilty of signing the allotment letter for the bungalows to Kadamb when the booking forms were already approved by Siddharth?"

He alarmed me. I thought for a while. He had a point. If I cleared the legal problems, the company's reputation would be restored and it would help raise funds. I could then focus on Urvi.

"Where are these booking forms and where is that green file?" I asked edgily after discussing accounts and project related matters.

Deepak pondered for a while, and squinted his eyes.

"I kept the file in the car and it's at the service centre, where the police caught me!" Deepak said and jumped up as well.

"Do you know that green file can save your life?" I whispered.

"Really?! Yeah, Siddharth had signed the booking forms in his handwriting," Deepak said as his eyes glittered in hope.

"Man, I should leave now. I have got work to do," I said and stood up to leave. Manav on a mission!

"Sorry man, I always cursed you and the CA profession. I owe you," he said again.

I started to leave in repulsion.

"Excuse me, Manav," Deepak said, pulling out an envelope from under the carpet.

"What is this?" I asked.

"My... confession," Deepak said. "I trust you. Promise me that you will not show it to anyone."

I opened the envelope to read the letter. I felt dazed and my body was covered with goosegumps as I went through the letter. I looked at Deepak; his eyes had filled up with tears. He folded his hands to say sorry. Suddenly Ba's image lying under the debris during the earthquake flashed in my head. Even my eyes got moist. I felt sorry for Deepak.

I heard a knock on the door. The hawaldar signalled to say that the meeting time was over.

I kept walking. And thinking. And mourning.

And regretting.

Hats off to IT

"Sir, we can't help it. We need at least one week's time to get the car back from the garage," the receptionist and the head of the service centre said in unison.

I had started reviewing all the documents and files, as if I had to appear for an exam. Rakesh and I were dead to the world for the entire week. I asked Rakesh to renegotiate with the ministry to revive the project and we had various meetings with the environment ministry along with the architect.

I called investors, bankers, financiers, supporters, backers, and angel investors to discuss solutions to help us get out of the financial mess. This included asking for loans, credit, advance, and partnership. Everyone gave us reasons, excuses, and stories. Time was of the essence; just a few days were left before the bank would auction the land to recover the money.

I figured out that my major problem was environment clearance and the arrangement of funds to start the sale of the project, once the legal case was sorted out. There was no news about Urvi. She was not a priority at that time. I cursed myself and my position as a CEO.

I was immersed in the files, when suddenly Suresh, the IT head, entered.

"Congratulations my friend, you've became the CEO! We deserve at least one in-house coffee," Suresh said, and offered his hand to me.

I reciprocated and called the pantry for some coffee. Raghu brought the coffee and left.

"I heard that we are in a big financial mess and if the Hill City project does not start soon, we may have problems receiving our salaries as well?" Suresh asked, taking a sip of the hot coffee.

I was irked by his remarks, but it was a fact. The staff was understandably restless and had to be dealt with skillfully, hence I ignored his remarks.

"You call me a friend, so have trust in me," I said and took a sip of the coffee. "If you won't get your salary, I will step down from the CEO's post."

"I am impressed with you, man! You are the only smart CA I have ever met," he said smiling.

Oh no! Why do people think that all CAs are nerds? Why can't CAs be cool?

"Man, are you trying to flatter me?" I said and smiled.

"No man, seriously. The whole office is impressed with your interview," Suresh said, smiling.

We discussed for some more time and finally I told him that I would have to leave.

"Are you in a hurry?" he asked.

"Even bachelors have to go home," I said smiling.

Suddenly the intercom rang.

"*Sir, thereismailforyou,*" It was Raghu.

"Now?"

"It has been at the reception since the last two days," he said slowly. "I think it's very confidential and important."

Rita had been absent since the last few days. Without women even an office cannot function well, forget life.

"Bring it quickly," I said. I wondered if any legal notice had been sent by the bank.

"Siddharth is the real culprit, not Deepak," Suresh said and kept an envelope on my table.

"What!" I almost yelled, "What is this?"

"This is the CCTV recording and telephone conversation between Siddharth, Abhiraj, and the minister," he said softly. I couldn't believe what I had heard.

"But why have you given this to me? You could have given it to the board of directors," I said, opening the envelope. It contained some CDs.

"I trust you. I don't trust them," he said quietly. "And I know you love Urvashi. She is innocent."

I wondered how he knew about Urvi. Yes, she had called me on the office landline once.

But how did he know that she was innocent? The IT department had an automatic phone recording system and a 24x7 CCTV camera recording system.

Another envelope was brought in by Raghu.

I gazed at the envelope; it said 'Private and confidential'. The hand writing was familiar. It was none other than Urvi's. My eyes widened.

"Everything all right?" Suresh asked. I didn't react.

"This is a recording between Abhiraj and Urvashi." Suresh said and kept another envelope on the desk.

"What!"

I was nervous and wondered which envelope to open first? I kept Urvi's letter in the drawer and opened Suresh's envelope quickly. It contained more CDs.

I inserted the CD in the CD drive.

Siddharth: "Sir, if we build the water canal for the poor, we will become poor. Let's settle with four bungalows for you and your children."

Minister Kadamb: "Please understand. It's very risky. I have to answer to my party and the opposition. And many projects are in the pipeline. Let's meet and discuss this... not over the phone. Ask Abhiraj to speak to me."

Siddharth: "Wait... he is here."

Abhiraj: "Jai Maharashtra Sahib!"

"Woh sab theek hai..." the minister said and paused, "You fix your cut directly with them. I am okay with four bungalows."

We started watching the CCVTV footage.

The minister and his wife entered the office reception. Raghu showed them to the small conference room.

Very soon, Abhiraj and Siddharth joined them with the design layout, and both spread the plan on the small conference table in front of the minister and his wife. Both debated and after arguing with the minister, the wife told Siddharth to book four bungalows. Deepak was not present at the meeting. Abhiraj and Siddharth filled up the booking forms. And then Siddharth signed all the four forms. He dialled the intercom. Deepak entered and after shaking hands with the minister signed the forms.

I played the second CD.

Abhiraj: "Urvashi, how are you?"

Urvi: "Don't ask me this; you know I am working like crazy for the Hill City story."

Abhiraj laughed hard.

Urvi: "When you laugh like a monster, I feel like resigning. You know, my personal life is in a mess! And there is no response from Minister Kadamb's office. I cannot complete the story if the minister doesn't agree to grace the inauguration. The media will throw the story in a dust bin. I don't understand your logic! Why don't you invite some other minister?"

Abhiraj laughed and after a pause said: "Cool down. Listen, there is good news. Minister Kadamb has agreed; his office called me just now. Call his PA now and get all the details you want."

Urvi: "Are you serious? His secretary was haughty; she didn't even answer the hundreds of calls I made to her phone. How will they serve the public then?"

Abhiraj said in a firm voice: "We are not the public, Urvashi; I am Abhiraj, meaning fearless king. And you know our goal; we have to rule all over India ..."

Urvi: "Okay, okay! Listen, I need a break next week. I have to go home. Mom and Dad cannot come here. It's something personal."

Abhiraj: "Why don't you call your mom here? I want to see who is more beautiful."

Urvi "Shut up, you crazy..."

Abhiraj laughed and the phone was disconnected.

"Man, is this genuine?" I asked. I still could not believe it!

"100% man!" he said and showed me a thumbs up sign and left.

I hurried to the drawer and pulled out Urvi's letter.

My love Manav,

Honey, I am so sorry for not being able to keep in touch with you. But we have to get used to living apart. I have learned a lot after my fall. But now, I can't swallow my pride and correct my blunder. I have let everybody down. But whom should I blame? The media, who blamed me even though I was innocent? My boss, who used me? Or my own ambitions? I don't know. I don't want to know either.

But it is so strange that men at home enjoy success of the women. But outside in the corporate world, men are different, they are biased and don't accept women's success. Just take Papa's example: he is dutiful towards mom. Though he is a banker, mom controls his personal bank accounts, she monitors his food habits and we both decide his clothing and he loves both of us. Papa supported me when I decided to work in Mumbai. Even Bapuji surrenders to Ba, just like the men in your Modi clan remain docile to their wives. Don't we live in a hypocritical society? Sorry, I am asking you questions like a journalist. Leave them; I don't want to talk about them.

I had ambitions to be successful, but I had no intentions of being unethical. I ignored your advice and also knowingly turned a blind eye to Abhiraj's unethical business tactics and just focused on my job. And I had to pay the price for it. Yes, a big price. I am hurt. I have let my parents down too. They are hurt and embarrassed because of me and want to leave this city, in fact this country.

I have let you down too. I am going away from you. I know life without you will be hard, but I deserve that, I have earned that, my punishment... to live away from you forever and ever. I am crying, darling.I miss you a lot. I miss every single moment since I can remember.

I am looking at the sorry card you had given me. But now, it's my turn to say sorry, to cancel out the effect on our life's account, yes contra entry is completed. See wonk, I also know a little bit of accounting. I just laughed after ages. But my heart is crying. I think I am mad. I am mad in your love.

Baby, I am missing your golden touch. I can't tell you how fond I have become of you, and of course your massages.

But all good things must end just as my dreams have ended... because dreams are dreams, they never come true. But my love is true and it will always remain with you forever until death does us apart and even after that. Sorry baby for being negative today.

Honey, I have to go now, mom and dad are waiting outside.

With lots of love, hugs and kisses,

Goodbye,

Urvi

"No darling, don't say goodbye. I am sorry for not being able to give you top priority. I have always trusted you more than I have trusted myself and more than my life. And how could you think that I could be upset with you?" I murmured to myself. Like a dim-witted fool, I read the letter over and over again to inspect it closely and to see if I could get the address from where the letter was sent.

My eyes grew moist. The last word 'goodbye' blew up like a bomb in my head. I felt numb and collapsed into the office chair.

Suddenly the intercom rang. I picked up the receiver in a daze.

"Sir,canIorderdinnerfromSubway?"

CEO till Doomsday

"Even if the legal case is solved, where are the investors to invest in the company?" Banerjee Sir asked.

We were sitting in the conference room with the other board of directors. I had summoned everyone.

Forget gratitude for the excellent job I had done, instead everyone looked at me skeptically. An eerie silence prevailed as I played the CDs and revealed the green file with the booking forms signed by Siddharth.

"I think we should sell the Hill City land and pay off the debt," Sachin said looking at his watch.

"Sir, I think we should hand over all the evidence to the police and our lawyer. Otherwise we will be part of their sins. We have to save public's money and company's reputation," I said looking at Gill, who was still in deep thought after watching the CDs and reviewing the file.

"He is right sir," Rakesh said.

"Only God can help us," Gill said finally, opening his eyes as wide as possible. And murmured, "*Jo bole so nihaal, sat sri akaal.*"

"But how can we declare that our CEO is the culprit? We will submit this to our own lawyer to put his own client behind bars? It's highly embarrassing!" Manjunath said. He had a point, but I had planned for this eventuality.

"As there is strong evidence against Siddharth, he cannot deny it. We will convince him to plead guilty," I said. "I will discuss it with the lawyer so that he can get a mercy plea for him."

Each person looked at me in confusion. Yes, if you cannot convince them, confuse them. All bosses do this to their employees. After all, I was the acting CEO.

"But you had planned to start the project first and now you want to get into legal matters?" Sachin asked, lost.

"Sir, the situation has changed. No one is willing to lend us money or invest because of the legal case," I said firmly and stood up. Everyone looked at me, as if I had dropped a bombshell. I wanted to show them what I was made of. A leader has to be bold, fearless, and inspiring. And with that I went forward.

"What if Suresh himself would have submitted these evidences to the police? And why should we not cooperate with the police and CBI? After all, that's what is expected of every citizen of India. Maybe today the property market has been hit, but it may look up in the future and we may get investors. We should believe in morals and ourselves," I said and started to walk. Their necks turned in my direction.

I continued.

"And I should remind all you gentlemen that our Hill City land is already mortgaged to the bank. We cannot sell it, and if we default, they will auction it for peanuts," I notified them.

Everyone was stunned and silent. They surrendered to my arguments.

"You are right, God will decide the destiny of all human beings according to the good and evil of their earthly lives," Banerjee sir said, taking a sip from the glass of water. "It's judgment day."

Everyone applauded. I even pictured them giving me a standing ovation.

And after a while I received a message on BBM.

"I am proud of you Manav; you are the CEO till doomsday."

◎

"Thanks, Manav. I still can't believe that I am free!" Deepak said to me when the trial in court had concluded on judgment day. He went to London to take a break and come out from his gloomy mood.

Abhiraj was issued arrest warrants. Minister Kadamb was arrested on graft charges. The court sentenced Siddharth to jail. He had pleaded guilty before the judge. When I had tried to convince him to plead guilty, he had claimed that the CCTV proof and the phone conversation had been tampered with, but the booking forms confirmed that he was lying. I told him to follow the footsteps of Ramalinga Raju, the ex-chairman of Satyam Computers who had confessed his financial wrongdoings. And he voluntarily accepted.

Half the problems in the world will be solved if you possess the power of convincing and communicating. But how to communicate with invisible people, I mean Urvi and the investors? My heart ached whenever I thought of her. I wasn't sure how to communicate with the bankers, backers, financier, or fair weather friends – none of whom were coming forward. Even though the legal case was cleared, no one was coming forward to make investments. They gave promises and blessings, but not money and we needed money to survive.

I was still running from door to door to beg for money, and had little time before the bankers auctioned our Hill City land and the directors threw me out of the CEO post and closed down the company. The bank had issued a notice to auction the land; we had just two weeks left.

I was watching television in the conference room. I had become a couch potato, spending time only watching TV and the video CD of the Hill City project.

A documentary, "Can India pull the world out of this crisis?" was airing on one of the channels.

I imagined another documentary, "Can Manav pull Continental Realty Ltd out of this crisis?"

A woman reporter was shouting, "Though the world is facing a global crisis due to recession in Europe and USA, India has established itself as a leading growing economy. After a few months of panic, India's economy, including the real estate market, is stabilising."

My eyes were transfixed on the documentary. After ages, I liked the news.

The headlines read: 'India attracts FDI in real estate'.

"Many foreign companies are investing in the Indian real estate market, as the worldwide property market has crashed. Only India's property market is offering good returns and stability to foreign investors. India's liberal economic policies are being welcomed by foreign companies and foreign direct investment will grow further in 2009-10."

The documentary ended and was followed by advertisements, advertisements, and more advertisements. Many real estate companies had once again started spending on advertisements. I disliked advertisements but I had to change my perception and broaden my outlook. Now that I was the CEO, I needed to think of strategies and think of the growth of the company.

"India is booming, except our company," I said to myself gloomily as I got ready to go home.

A Call Makes a Big Difference

"Hello," I said, still half-asleep.

It was about 5:00 am. I had ignored the cell phone when it had first rung because I was in the bathroom.

But I wondered who could it be calling at this hour. Ba? Some old Modi had passed away? Or Urvi?

Or was it a call from a call centre? I didn't curse the call centres for bothering me early in the morning. My perception had changed, in fact, I was thankful to foreign companies for creating jobs.

I ran out of the bathroom to pick up the phone when it persistently rang for the third time.

"Hi pal, what's up?"

"Hello…who?" I said, "Krishna?"

"Man, this is my third call! Were you sleeping with a babe or something?" he chuckled.

"I am sorry… No man… But where are you calling from?

"I thought to give you a surprise. I am at the Mumbai airport. I need your car and some shelter," Krishna chuckled again.

"Good! I am happy that finally Deepak's chapter has closed in your life. No more CA vs MBA," Krishna said, keeping his small bag in the back seat of the car.

When you meet an old crony, you tend to tell them every damn thing about the past – college and home – even if they earn millions or become a CEO. I had told him everything even before we had reached the car park.

"But, I am surprised about why Urvi took it so personally. Where is she man?" Krishna asked, looking into my eyes. I almost cried, but turned my gaze to the road and hit the ignition, for the car to move forward.

"I don't know but she and her parents were hurt. They have left the country. I will look for her after I save the company from this financial mess," I said, exiting the parking lot and reaching the main road. "How is your business?"

"Don't ask, it's a horrible situation; real estate has become dead in Dubai. Thank goodness I was not a partner in the Dubai's property market. I am still looking for investments in London," Krishna said and paused. "But my partner wants to invest in India, especially in luxury projects."

I felt like taking a U-turn and driving to Hill City right then and there.

"If foreigners are investing in India, why don't you consider investing in India as well? It's your home country, after all," I said.

"India is our motherland and we NRIs don't do business with our mother," Krishna said and laughed loudly. "Sorry I was kidding."

I looked straight ahead.

"At least now you are positive about India again," he said, looking at me. "We had plans in India, but you see, the corruption... it's impossible for NRIs to do business and make money here unless you break a hundred laws."

I felt like someone had slapped me and my country. But I had to accept the truth. We reached home.

"Interesting; I thought you NRIs have problems with the dust, water, electricity and poor infrastructure in India," I said and dumped his bag near the sofa.

"No man, these are petty issues for NRI business people.The major concern in India is to deal with the system," he said seriously and sat on the sofa,"I mean there is a lot of red-tape. Kickbacks become a necessity if a business has to survive."

I nodded. Talwar had said the same thing, but then who was the culprit? Politicians? The public? The system.

And who makes this damn system? Politicians? Or corporates? Or we the people? I think that all of us together make up the system, but then why do we always blame the system? Because a few crooked people twist the system for their own benefit.

I think that the government is the spitting image of the people. If we the people are corrupt, the government will always remain corrupt.

"How much are you looking to invest?" I asked, coming back from my thoughts, and sitting beside him.

"We have planned to invest roughly up to USD 200 million in real estate,"he said, stretching his arms; he looked tired. I was dazed.

Krishna lay down for a nap and I went for my workout.

"Hey man, you have a good body," Krishna said, as I came out from the shower with a towel wrapped around my waist. Krishna sat idle on the sofa-reading Bollywood masala supplementary newspaper-and scratching his balls, he was on holiday.

"It's intensive workout and a healthy diet," I said, "When do you plan to get married?"

"Beena's parents are insisting on having at least one ceremony in Ahmedabad. That's the reason I am here. We will decide in a couple of days," he said.

"Let's have breakfast," I said. We had bread-butter sandwiches, cereal, fruits and some juice. Krishna munched on some cereal, while I gulped down a protein shake.

"Do you think all corporates in India are corrupt? Even me?" I asked breaking the silence.

I turned on the television.

"No, there are good people in India. I don't want to generalise, but that's the perception among NRIs and foreign investors about India. And you are my bro, I trust you,"he said.

"But bro, that is not enough. I need funds," I thought.

I took four slices of brown bread, spread butter and jam and tossed them on a plate. He ate half a sandwich, and spread more butter on his bread.

"What is your financial problem?" he said chewing.

I told him everything about the Hill City project, the environment ministry's conditions, the funds required, the time frame(only thirteen days were left),and every other damn thing. I showed him the CD presentation on my laptop.I had shown it to a thousand people; everyone could see Hill City in my eyes.

"Listen man, I can put an offer to my partner if I see a good opportunity." He said.

"What next?" I asked.

"*Khallas*! Let's go to Pune."

"Man, the idea is brilliant! I must say Deepak deserves credit for it," he said as we were sitting in the car after we had surveyed the land and the surrounding area, where the water canal was to be built. All the workers cheered and performed a jig like West Indian cricketers, when they discovered that the visitor was from Dubai. Half of them had come back from Dubai during the crisis there and had not been paid their salaries.

"Yeah, but do you think your partner will like it?" I asked, as the car hit the highway.

"Arabs are crazy about such projects. Mr Shirawi will love it!" Krishna said. He was still in deep thought. "Email me the project details and presentation. I will forward them to Mr Shirawi right away. He may fly in tomorrow itself."

"Are you sure he will come tomorrow itself?" I asked when we reached office.

"Yes, but only if he is not travelling."

My heart sank. My prayers were rejected. "I have only limited time, less than two weeks!"

"Arabs make decisions in seconds," Krishna said, hitting a number on his speed dial.

"Assalamu' alikum Mr Shirawi," he said.

I prayed hard to Allah, Jesus, Guru Nanak and Krishna.

"Oh, you are travelling tonight?"

"Makkah, Saudi Arabia?"

"After one week, fine. Pray for us as well."

"OK, I will email the details of the project to you. Check your email if you have time. Yes, I will email them to Simon as well."

"*Shukran,*" Krishna said, disconnecting the phone and my last hope as he announced, "Greg Simon is a shrewd Brit."

Do or Die-Can I do it?

"Usmanbhai, Sahara Star Hotel," I said to Siddharth's ex-chauffeur, who was now my chauffeur. Krishna was sitting beside me. Yesterday night:

"Yes, I have received the travel details," I had said to Krishna, looking at my Blackberry. We were having dinner at Kamat Restaurant. His partner, Mohammad bin Abdullah bin Ahmed Al Shirawi, was travelling. But then he asked the CEO, Greg Simon, BDM, and Amit Khanna, to visit the Hill City project. His son Abdullah had cancelled visit at the last moment because he was busy watching horse race-Dubai World Cup! They were impressed with the presentation that he had emailed to them.

The car moved towards Sahara Hotel. I had hardly slept at night. Twisting on the bed almost whole night, squirming restlessly, unable to stop my brain from thinking about the problems. But I could not come up with any answer, instead, I started talking to myself. And then my brain and heart got into a long debate, both blaming each other. I was stuck between the two as I went to bed. Thoughts of Urvi jumped into my head.

My heart charged me representing womenfolk. And my brain represented menfolk.

Heart: *You left her all alone when she needed you the most! You have to accept that. For you business comes first, not love.*

Brain: *It's not true! You know that I love her.I was left with no choice. And you know that I have a commitment with the company I have to honour.*

Heart: *I know what you truly feel inside. You wanted to prove to the world that CAs can conquer MBAs. And you wanted to beat Deepak because he criticised your profession and his father cheated your father. You took revenge. You are selfish.*

Brain: *Nonsense! I am not selfish. Whatever I did, it was for both of us. Otherwise her parents and society will never accept me and my family. And you stupid heart, if you know what is right and what is wrong for me, why don't you act accordingly and why the hell do you listen to the stupid brain?*

Heart: *Because you believe in calculation like others – it is profit or loss. You just rely on the numbers. You never listened to me. You are a moron, number cruncher!*

Brain: *Accepted, I am a moron but why did she have to leave me? After all I will be with her when all this is over. Hasn't she been reading the newspapers and watching the news on television? Everything is fine now. Why doesn't she come back? Please tell her to come back. Please. Please.*

I kept saying to my heart. My heart beseeched, *Sorry baby, I love you. I need you. But my company, my office needs me as well.*

Suddenly the faces of Ba and Bapuji flashed in my head. Ba was celebrating every small damn thing with the Modi clan.

My brain humiliated me representing the upper-middle class. And my heart represented the lower-middle class.

Brain: *You Modis are born to be small. You don't deserve to be a CEO.*

Heart: *Why can't I dream of becoming a CEO? Is it just because in our big family no one has ever reached the top position?*

Brain: *Nah, not because of that. It's because you middle class people are always surrounded by shallow people, and to reach to the top position, you have to think big and be smart and ruthless. Emotional people just feed their stomachs. They don't even do well in their career, forget becoming a big leader.*

Heart: *Excuse me! Dhirubhai Ambani and so many great leaders have come from similar backgrounds, why can't I become a leader as well?*

Brain: *Well you can dream, it doesn't cost you much.*

Heart: *Yes, we are the young India. We have dreams, everybody lives on hope; so do I. We are educated and work smartly. We don't believe in the boundaries set by the old school of thoughts. We believe in our sincere efforts, in God and in our destiny. I can do it.*

My head and my brain were having a boxing match in my head. I started praying, praying, and praying.

◎

"Pleasure to meet you, Manav," Simon Greg said, as he came out with Amit Khanna from the Sahara Hotel and after maori greetings (we held each other's hands, we rubbed our noses and kissed cheeks, then they asked about their kith and kins and financial crisis in general and in Dubai in particular which took fifteen long minutes) with Krishna and me, like Prime Minister of United Kingdom meeting with Prime Minister of Japan. Now I understood why government works slow; half of the time goes in official formalities.

Anyway Greg was sporting what the British would have worn, if British East India Company would have intrude in present times in India – khaki Bermuda shorts with a black belt and white T-shirt, black sunglasses on his head and white Sneakers. He was carrying a small bag. He was in his mid-forties and was slim and fit.

Amit had a beer belly and was wearing blue jeans and a black Crocodile T-shirt. He was armed with a camera to shoot a video of the barren project, as if he was travelling to a desert safari and expecting a belly dancer at the site. Krishna was dressed casually as usual. He was going to catch a late evening flight to Ahmedabad to meet Beena, and from there he was going back to Dubai. So, if nothing worked out, my dreams would end along with the so-called dream project – the Hill City Project.

I was wearing what the Mughal Emperor Jahangir would have worn in present times to welcome British East India Company – I mean a grey suit and tie, but later dumped the suit jacket to match their casual clothing. They were on leave and were relaxed, but I was jumpy.

Anyway, we all sat in the car and headed towards the site. I showed them the Hill City project. All the labourers sprinted after them.

Later I proposed that they meet with the environment ministry; they liked the idea. We had organised lunch at the site cabin from a five star hotel. They wolfed down all the food. After lunch, I introduced them to the bankers. Greg was delighted and Amit was busy with his camera and mobile phone. We returned to the office in Powai soon after.

Usman came out of the car and bowed low. Suresh, Vasant, James Peter Chikala, Raghu and Rita gave us a red carpet welcome when we reached office for the final meeting. My destiny was going to be decided in the next few hours. My heart was pounding rapidly.

"I am impressed with your friend," Greg said to Krishna when we got back to the office. After an hour's break, we started the meeting in the conference room with tea, sandwiches, samosas, chicken lollypops, some cold canapés, juice and coffee served by Raghu and Rita.

"He is a mastermind. A man with a golden tongue," Krishna said and patted my shoulder. *That's not enough dude. I need money. I will give you my tongue for free.*

"As I can see, the project seems fantastic!" Greg said and picked up a samosa, pressing a tissue over it to squeeze out the excess oil. "But there have been some serious legal problems and huge investments as well. I think we will need to take the advice of the Big Four audit firms."

I felt numb. My heart fell inside my body and broke into a thousand pieces. I started sweating. Even Krishna looked jumpy.

Amit looked dizzy; he was taking notes of the meeting and eating all the snacks heaped on his plate. Why had he brought this dimwit? A business class ticket and five star hotel stay? Waste of money I say!

"But there is a way out," Greg said as I poured some juice into his glass. "Can we meet your lawyer as well?"

"Sure, but aren't you leaving tonight?" I asked quietly.

"Call him now," Greg said and stood up taking whatever food was left in the trays.

I dialled the lawyer's office. He said that he could not make it which I had expected him to say. He wanted his money.

"What do you think about me? I am not working pro bono. I am a reputed lawyer and unlike CAs...." he said.

I ignored his remarks and told him that the party was from Dubai.

"Is it a regular issue or does it require special expertise?"

"Um, regular,"

"How much can you pay?"

I think lawyers are heirs of canidae family from whom they have inherited scheming brains! I mean we CAs – even if we are big four accounting firm – will charge our client maximum his arm or a leg but lawyers will charge full body.

"Nothing," I said, my voice stern. "If you don't support. You won't get your arrears of fees."

"Um, yes...No, I mean it's fine. You can pay me later on," he chuckled, sounded nervous.

He came in a local train to make it on time.

Greg scanned him, then the file and the court judgment. He asked for a copy of the judgment and the lawyer left. Greg left for the washroom and Krishna left to make some phone calls.

Finally both returned after ten minutes. After all, the legal-schmegal and dotting the i's and crossing the t's, Greg said, "Manav, I am impressed with you and your approach. You have the Midas touch,"he winked at Amit. "I had been tracking this project for the past six months, when the first story was published."

Greg paused. Amit winked back.

Greg continued, "But then the scandal hit your company the very next day. You have pulled out your company from the legal mess. I saw the news on the net and on the television channels a few weeks ago. I knew every damn thing about this project, thanks to Amit who had researched and liaised with our advisors after we received your email about the project."

I was stupid. The power of the media was amazing! I kept quiet.

"Krishna, you have a very good friend. Thanks for getting the right people on board,"he said, shaking hands with Krishna and me.

But Sir, what about the money? I wanted to ask. *Let's come to the point.*

"I spoke to Mr Mohammad Shirawi and our auditors, and both have given a thumbs up to this project," he said and looking at Krishna, smiling. "Thanks to Krishna for agreeing just now to invest his share of investment in this project."

I looked at Krishna in disbelief. He smiled and kept his hand on my shoulder. He reminded me of the day he had stepped into my life, when Bapuji was hospitalised and Mr. Yogiraj had appeared like a God thereafter. I heard his eyes saying, "How can Arjun lose the battle when Krishna is beside him!"

What was happening? Did he said they would invest in it?

They would invest in it?

I felt like I was paralysed. I couldn't believe it.

My brain and heart were in sync for the first time. Both were nervous and confused!

Suddenly Krishna's phone rang.

"Hello Dad. Yes, everything is all right. Greg has also confirmed," Krishna said and he gave the phone to me. I didn't know what was happening and what to say.

"He…llo," my voice broke and my eyes filled up with tears.

"Manav beta," Laxmanbhai said. I tried to speak. But what came was only sobs.

"Don't cry, my son. I know that you are a number cruncher. But do you know, God is a big number cruncher as well; he maintains our accounts. Your Bapuji and Ba have enough credit with God. I can't forget those days when I was not earning, and for months I lived in your home and your Ba looked after me and my wife like we were her own children. They have always done good karma and now it's my turn. I want to settle my account with him before… I… die," Laxmanbhai said and paused. He was crying.

He continued, "What Arvind did for me, no one can do without self interest. I owe him. Whatever I am today is because of your father. He changed my destiny. I hope my Krishna will bring good luck to you as well. God bless you all and all the best to you, my son. I am sure you will be a successful chartered accountant and CEO and your parents will be proud of you…" he paused and hung up sobbing. I was sobbing as well.

"Let's meet with the board of directors tomorrow. We will extend our stay for one more day,"Amit spoke for the first time, leaving me numb and speechless.

Krishna and Amit hugged me. Somebody even kissed me. I didn't know who it was and I didn't even care. I can't tell you how nervous I had been since the day I had taken over as the CEO. But that kiss and that hug made me strong. *Yes, I can do it! I will not look back any more.*

I was emotional. The images of Ba, Bapuji and all the Modis flashed in my head. They were crying in disbelief. They were saying to Ba, "Manav has done it! Your Manav has done it, Roopaaa!"

I imagined Raghu, Rita, Usman, Suresh, Vasant, James Peter Chikala and the workers at the Hill City site giving me a thumbs up with moist eyes. And Banerjee Sir and directors showing me the victory sign while Riya jumped blowing flying kisses. Showing thumps up gesture, Urvi was crying and waiving her hand to say good-bye.

I realised a white soul was favouring me and that was my angel, Krishna. I could see rainbow colours in my eyes, as if Lord Krishna was smiling at me.

I snuffled, cried and wailed like a child on Krishna's shoulder.

Was this the second U-turn of my life? Yes, it was.

Epilogue I

"It's amazing! I was never committed to my goal like you," Jiten said, wiping his eyes. I wiped my eyes too, taking a sip of water.

"But I have still not accomplished my goal," I murmured to myself. "Without Urvi, I am incomplete."

An announcement was made. "Flight IC-787 flying from Mumbai to Dubai is ready for departure. All passengers are requested to board at gate number 122." We started to walk towards the gate.

"But how did you become the permanent CEO?" Jiten asked, as we settled in the plane. He had requested the passenger sitting next to me to exchange seats with him.

"The next day, we had a meeting with the board of directors. We worked out the offer and they put in a condition that they would invest only if I would remain the CEO. They changed the name of the company to Falcon Realty Ltd. It took a couple of months to finalise everything."

"But what happened to Urvi? Did you try to look for her?" Jiten asked, looking into my eyes.

I said quietly, "I tried to find her, but failed."

"Dont worry, the world is a small place. Look at how you and I met at the airport and I am sure you will meet her..." Jiten said, smiling, "... one day."

I smiled.

"It's strange how sometimes the world looks very small like a pool and sometime very huge, like an ocean," I thought.

"But what about Deepak's confession... I mean what did he write to you?" Jiten asked, "Why did Mr Parthivbhai and Mr Yogi Bhardwaj visit the jail? Why did Deepak hate CAs?"

"Sometimes what our eyes see is not correct. We should not judge people without knowing their pasts and the reasons for their behaviour," I said quietly. "And I gave him my word that I would keep this confidential. I want to keep it to myself."

Jiten remained silent for the rest of the flight and did not question me further.

The flight landed at Dubai airport at last. It was cold and windy.

And now time had come to bid Jiten adieu. I would remember this journey. It had taken me to my past. I was missing Urvi like never before; it had been more than a year now.

"But how is Deepak doing now?" Jiten asked.

"We transferred him to the Bengaluru office. He is the COO of the south region," I said, looking at him. "Riya and Deepak have become good friends. Some people are successful at their second attempt."

"Wow! That's very good!" Jiten said in excitement, "Even I want a second chance. I want to meet Krishna as well. Maybe my destiny would change as well. I will appear for the CA exams in Dubai for sure."

I patted his shoulder.

"Welcome to the city of gold!" Krishna said and hugged me tight. "Dude, why didn't you take an Emirates flight? It's always on time."

"You know, I am a true Indian, so I should travel by Indian Airlines," I said smiling and looked at Jiten. "But I am happy to be late, for I would not have met this young boy who reminded me that my task is still not finished."

Krishna looked at Jiten and offered his hand, which Jiten held graciously.

"Sir, I want to hug you!" Jiten said, his eyes glistening as Krishna looked at him.

"He is Jiten. A bright CA student. He will be working in Dubai and will also appear for the CA exams in Dubai," I said and looked at Jiten.

"Good luck man! Do attend my wedding reception. It's on a Friday so you will be free." Krishna said, offering his business card, "Email me; I will send you an invitation."

"Thank you, sir and before Manav sir leaves Dubai, I want his signature on my examination form," Jiten said, smiling. "Maybe you both can bring about the first U-turn in my life."

"Don't believe him. I have benefitted from my investment in India. I am a businessman. I should say thanks to him," Krishna said, laughing. We all joined in the good mood.

Krishna's white Bentley arrived.

"Sir, I will go to the institute's branch tomorrow and may call you for the signature," Jiten said, waving his hand as he ran towards the taxi stand.

I waved goodbye to him and the car slowly left the airport.

"Why are there so many lights on the street?" I asked, looking at the Al Garhoud Bridge. We were sitting in the back seat of the luxurious car.

"This is the beauty of Dubai.This country works 24x7 like Mumbai," Krishna said and patted my lap.

"Any news about Urvi? It's been almost a year now," Krishna asked, as the car made its way to Palm Island.

"No, I don't know where she is. And I don't know where to look for her," I said, looking outside the window as we came out of the tunnel in front of the Atlantis Hotel at Palm Jumeirah.

The hotel entrance and reception were gigantic. A steward was serving apples and water bottles to all the visitors in the lobby.

"Nice hospitality," I said as we walked to the East Tower.

"What a great view," I added, looking at the sea from the window, as we reached the huge Ocean Deluxe room.

"This is the marriage schedule," Krishna said and gave me a small ocean themed card.

I stared at the card: 'Krishna weds Beena'. I missed Urvi instantly. I felt so incomplete.

"Don't worry, you will find Urvi," Krishna said, reading my mind. "I had thought that you both would attend my wedding together. See, you think I am lucky for you, but it's not always like that."

"No, don't think that way. I already have everything because of you," I said, keeping my hand on his shoulder. "You are my lucky mascot."

"Fine, if you think so," Krishna said. "I don't want to get in between you and your belief."

He smiled and left.

"On which floor is the gym?" I asked the operator ten minutes after Krishna had left.

"Can I use it at six in the morning? ...Oh 24x7, thanks."

After ten more minutes, I lay down on the bed. I wanted to keep myself busy and not think about Urvi. Working out was the answer to that. I was suddenly startled by a beep on my phone. It was an SMS.

"Reminder, tomorrow seminar at 2 pm felicitating Manav Modi as the youngest CEO. Please be ready at 1 pm at hotel lobby." It was from the chairman of Dubai chapter of Chartered Accountants, Mr NK Gupta.

I cursed him and switched off the light. My mind shifted from Urvi to CA; both were my pride...my only purpose of living.

I reached Dubai Men's College at noon. Nobody paid any attention to me, as lunch had been announced. Chairman Mr Gupta looked at me, and ticked my presence in his diary like a school teacher at the entrance, and completely ignored me thereafter. He was robustly chasing other speakers so that everything could begin on time.

I sat in the front row along with the committee members and other guests.

Secretary Mr Ramesh Nair jumped up on the podium with his notepad and after the welcome speech, said,

"Dear fellow colleagues, we all know that top positions, such as the one of a CEO in any organisation, whether in India or in Dubai or globally, are mainly held by top ranked MBAs. These MBAs dominate the corporate world. And we CAs restrict ourselves to second level positions such as auditing, finance and accounts executives and CFOs. Most of the time we are underpaid, and our hard work and meticulous approach remain ignored or unaknowledged."

The crowd didn't seem to be listening to him, some people even booed. He noticed the reaction, paused, and took a sip of water.

"But CA Manav Modi, a man with a golden tongue, has proved that we CAs are not only good at numbers, but also at communication and equally good, if not better, than MBAs in managing people and any organisation. He is smart and handsome and he is one of the youngest CEOs of a public listed company with a 10,000 crore net-worth. Our institute and the CA fraternity are proud to have contributed such an entrepreneur to the business community. Please give him a big round of applause. Welcome him to say a few words and also to share with us the formula of success, and more than that, how to think beyond numbers."

The crowd applauded feebly, as if fighting to stay awake after guzzling a lavish lunch.

Chairman Gupta and the other committee members led me to the stage. The photographers like paparazzi flashed their cameras in front of my face. I looked at the audience; very few people were in the hall, scattered randomly here and there. I didn't know whether they had come to hear me or to treat themselves to free food.

I started, "Dear fellow colleagues, good afternoon."

There was a mild response.

"Friends, before I share my success story with you, I would like to know how many of you believe in destiny or God. Do you think God actually exists?"

Almost everybody raised their hands and roared, "Yes, God does exist!"

I smiled. I was expecting this reply. More people started trickling in steadily.

"Very good. Tell me, how many of you have seen God or met God?"

There was pin-drop silence. Nobody raised their hands. Everybody looked at each other. Everyone seemed confused and hypnotised. *Yes, now I can rule them,* I thought.

"How many of you believe that we humans can do anything we want to, and that we do not need God's help?"

Silence still reigned. All eyes were fixed on me.

"If we don't do anything but just wait and watch, can God help us?"

"Nooo!" the crowd thundered.

All were roused again. That's what I was looking for. The hall was jam-packed and many people had to stand at the back.

"Friends, I have one last question: If we put in effort and work hard, is there any assurance that we will be successful and we will get the desired results?"

"Nooo!" the crowd roared even harder. I like it when the crowd is energetic and engaged. It was time to start.

I took a sip of the water and walked to the podium.

"Dear friends, don't you think it's strange and interesting at the same time that we have not seen God, yet we believe in him? And also, if we don't put in effort, we will not be successful and even if we put in effort, if God isn't kind to us, we will still not be successful?"

"Yesss!" the crowd roared.

"That means hard work or sincere efforts are not enough to be successful in life; we all need God's help and are dependent on destiny. That means we all are puppets of God."

The crowd nodded understandingly.

"Friends, ever since I recognised that I was a number cruncher, I realised that to be a successful CA, not only did I have to qualify the exams conducted by our institute, I also had to pass the litmus test of 'CA vs MBA'– a battle or myth or whatever created by our CA fraternity or by our internal weakness."

I paused; the audience's eyes were transfixed on me.

"Before I start talking about my success story, let's evaluate ourselves, our weaknesses, and our training system with the training system of MBA in general."

"We CAs think that MBAs are paid higher salaries in the corporate world, or that CAs are underpaid compared to MBAs, or that we CAs deserve an equal package like MBAs. But we also know that MBAs have better marketing and presentation skills than us. Correct?"

The mass nodded their heads in unison.

"We know that MBAs don't have a uniform education system or a single institute like the ICAI, and they are dispersed all over, handing out degrees without maintaining standards and a uniform syllabus. We don't know which one is a recognised institute or a blue institute, do we?"

The crowd was listening intently.

"Though we have one institute-ICAI-but we all know that we don't have uniform training standards or any training manual or guidelines for CA articles either. There is no mechanism through which our institute ensures that each article has been properly, fairly and uniformly trained by his or her employers scattered all over India, in cities, towns and metro cities.

"Apart from that, many CA firms specialise in different fields such as income tax, sales tax, direct tax, and some deal with auditing and other services. The articles are at their mercy; they may or may not give the articles exposure.

"Students aspiring to be CAs may join big firms with big clienteles in metros and they may get better exposure compared to CAs working under sole proprietors in villages or towns. This means that the conditions, environments, and circumstances are different for different students and there are no uniform standards to train students by these practicing CAs? Correct? "

There was an eerie silence.

"Let's analyze further. Many of our CA students in small towns can't even speak in English. One CA student might join articleship under a sole proprietor in a village with a few small clients. There would be no corporate culture in the CA's office. And he may not get any access to facilities like this beautiful auditorium..." I said, waving my hands. Everybody looked around.

"However, MBA campuses have world class facilities, libraries, fitness centres, lecture theatres, and seminar rooms. They undergo a rigorous academic course which comprises general management themes that include tools and techniques of managing an organisation and engaging with the world.

"This means that we are responsible and should blame ourselves and not MBAs. We should evaluate ourselves and our weaknesses. We should work on our weaknesses if we want to compete with MBAs or aim for the top posisions in organisations."

The crowd applauded. I gestured to them to calm down.

I took a sip of water.

"Now I will speak about my success story and formula for success in life.

"We all have to pass the acid test of life. Nobody is immune to it, including me. We all have goals in life; we want to become a CA, MBA, doctor, or an engineer to give a better life to our loved ones or to fulfil our own passions.

"We have to face challenges to achieve that goal. Those challenges might be manmade or natural. Life can slap you in the face sometimes. To overcome those challenges, we need to push ourselves as hard as possible. We may give up or we may succeed. I successfully overcame those challenges, partly due to my hard work, partly due to positive people around me and partly due to luck and my destiny."

The crowd was silent and moved their necks in the direction I moved. I stopped at the edge of the podium. "My teacher advised me to pursue CA; she gave me my vision. And my love inspired me to get going. And my race with an MBA inspired me to be the best and greatest chartered accountant." I thought of Deepak and continued, "If he hadn't been in my life, I would have never aspired to be where I am today."

Yes, I had tailed Deepak like his shadow. But sorry Deepak, I misjudged you completely. I owe you, brother. I stopped looking at the crowd and recalled Deepak's letter.

Hey Manav,

You have no idea how much it hurts to write this. I feel ghastly about what I have done to you. But you have the right to label me a bad guy or bad MBA, because I had hated you and your profession. But why did I do that? Why did I not come to Urvi's birthday party twice? And what do you know about my past in Delhi before we shifted to Ahmedabad? Nothing, man, nothing; but I don't blame you either. How would you have known?

But man, now I have to tell you about my past. After a great deal of anguish and soul searching, I feel suffocated and guilty about being so negative. I have accepted that the only way to overcome this stifling feeling is to confess my feelings to you.

I was a very different person earlier. I had a loving mom Ayanna and a beautiful older sister, Anamika, who everyone lovingly called Anu. She was beautiful and talkative like Urvi and equally ambitious like her. We didn't have much money but had a happy life. One day life changed in the blink of an eye. It was utter hell! My father betrayed his wealthy client who trusted dad like his brother. But dad, along with his client's personal secretary, robbed him by fabricating and preparing a false will.

And that was just the beginning; dad ditched mom for that personal secretary, a wanton woman. Sorry, excuse my language. It was embarrassing for us. We were hurt and mom sank into atypical depression. But that was not enough and my father along with that secretary poisioned my mom and my sister with Death Cap Amatoxin. We tried hard to save them but it was too late. And dad with his political connections and money in his pocket fabricated autopsy reports and proved it to be suicide. I saw two dead bodies lying in front of me. And that date coincides with Urvi's birth date. And that was the reason I avoided her birthday parties.

But tears didn't roll out from my eyes; they remained somewhere inside and turned into anger and then into negative thoughts and ultimately into hate towards my father, towards that wanton woman and towards my father's profession – chartered accountancy. Yes, he was a practicing CA and a real crook. I hate him even today.

Dad shifted to Ahmedabad after that promiscuous woman ditched him. He started his business. When I came to know that your dad wanted to work with mine, I thought he may cheat your father as well. I had come to Shambu Cafe to warn you before going to London, but you didn't allow me to utter a single word. But when I came to know after the earthquake that dad had cheated your father and you had become an insurance agent, I felt bad and terribly guilty.

I decided to repent for my father's sins. My grandfather, my nana, Yogi Bhardwaj was based in London. We met your C.A. Parthivbhai and we settled your debt. We kept it a secret from you so that dad should not come to know, as he was claiming his right to my mom's share. She was the only daughter of a rich father. Her assets have now been transferred to the Ayanna & Anamika Foundation Ltd.

I wanted to become big, in fact, bigger than my father. I didn't want to stay with dad in Ahmedabad so I decided to shift to Mumbai to chase my dreams. But my plans crumbled and I blew up my career. I forgot that anger and hate eradicate intelligence. I was in the company of people who were dishonest. But I am innocent and did nothing illegal.

I am sorry I pushed you hard on many occasions, but you really proved me wrong; you have changed my perceptions about your profession, I must admit. But, man, you owe me for what you are today. I egged you and to beat me, you worked even harder. If I hadn't challenged and criticised you and your profession, you might have remained complacent. I think my negative boosting worked for you.

Sorry bro, I have never opened up to anyone. Now I leave it up to you to decide whether I am a bad guy or a good guy!

But pal, nothing personal.

Yours,

Deepak

I emerged from my reverie and continued, "I had raced with an MBA, someone I had thought of as a rival, until recently. But I want to confess today that without him, I would have remained complacent. He challenged me. I hated him and worked hard to face his challenges. I became passionate about working out so that I would be as smart as him. I was shy and introvert, but my character, my persona was influenced by that man. I must accept today that I would have never achieved my goal, or forget that, I would have never dreamt of becoming a CEO if he hadn't been there and if he had not challenged me. He gave me a vision and he showed me the path.

"But I never cheated to beat him. And today I can say that I loved to race with him. A healthy competition brings out the best in us. I was positive, honest, and probably that was the reason destiny favoured me; first, when I was almost on the verge of dropping out of school, and second, when my company was hit by scandals and was on the verge of bankruptcy.

"Friends, if you ask me, success is not the same to everyone. But the road to success is the same for everyone. And that goes via hell. The the formula for success are the 5 Ds – Dedication, Devotion, Discipline, Determination and Destiny. I think without destiny, no matter how hard we work and how smart we are, the formula for success will remain incomplete. Therefore, I think that we all are puppets of God, the Big Puppeteer, who controls us and our destiny."

I completed my speech with moist eyes. The faces of Deepak and Urvi hovered in my head as I reached my seat. But neither was present at that moment.

The ringing phone startled me awake. Hell! I had woken up late and it was already 9:00 am. I jumped off the bed, thinking about my nightmare. Thank God! I didn't want to change our CA fraternity, and nobody could change it even if they had wanted to.

"Good morning, sir. Sorry to bother you. I have to submit my examination form," the voice of Jiten said with excitement. "And I want your signature; you might be lucky for me."

"But can't we meet at the reception on Friday and finish the formalities?" I said, standing beside the bed.

"No sir, I want to submit it this evening itself. It's the last working day here. I want to submit the form before 5:00 pm today."

"Fine, we will meet after the speech at the Dubai Men's College."

Epilogue II

I finished my speech and came out to the lobby, avoiding the crowd and looking for Jiten. The members rushed to share their cards and the photographer swung into action.

My phone rang.

"Sir, I am outside in the parking lot," Jiten said. "I was not allowed inside."

"No, problem, I will come to the parking lot," I said and ran towards the gate. It was cloudy outside.

Suddenly it started pouring cats and dogs. Loud claps of thunder along with the howling cold wind made it difficult to walk or talk. My body shuddered in the cold which was so unusual in a desert.

"How did you come?" I asked Jiten, who had been waiting in the parking area.

"Along with that lady, she works at the Institute's branch," Jiten said signalling towards a woman waiting near the car far away. "She has the forms."

I hurried towards her. Jitend followed me.

"Sir, isn't it amazing that it is raining in the month of January?" Jiten said, shivering and smiled, "Maybe it's a message from God."

Without Urvi, the rain held no charm for me. I was missing every single moment I had spent with her in Ahmedabad and in Mumbai. I felt hollow deep within.

People from around the world come to this wasteland turned wonderland to see the marvellous infrastructure and to buy gold.

All I did was think of Urvi. I neared the woman who Jiten had pointed out. I went very close but still could not see her face. She turned around. And suddenly the heavy wind blew her hair and covered her face. After a few chilling moments, she removed the strands of hair from her face and looked at me. Time stood still. The cold was gone and the wind stopped blowing.

I stood thunderstruck because it was a known face – one that I had known since childhood. I became numb and my breath stopped… because the girl standing in front me was none other than *Urvi*!

She began to cry as soon as she saw me. I could not control myself and my eyes overflowed with tears as well. I raised my hand to touch her in disbelief. She raised her arms and buried her head into my chest. I forgot the heavy rain. Her touch was so warm and comforting. She hugged me tight and cried, cried and cried. I joined her and we both cried like babies.

You forget the world around you when you are in the arms of your sweetheart. It feels like the safest place on earth.

"Where…were you... all this time?" I stuttered.

She didn't reply. I rubbed her shoulder and held her close. She didn't resist.

"I am sorry; I was so caught up in the affairs of the company that I ignored you completely," I said. "I missed you a lot ever since you left me. I can't think of a life without you. There is not a single moment that I didn't think of you."

"I am… sorry b-a-b-y," she said, crying louder. "I love…you more than my life," she said looking into my eyes.

"I love you too," I said and squeezed her tight. She rested her head on my shoulder and I rested my head against hers. I felt warm and happy. I had found peace.

"You didn't read the news about me and our company?" I asked, getting sober.

Still we stayed in the same position.

"Yes, I did."

"Then why you didn't call me or came back?"

"I was waiting for you to come. You took so long."

"You are stupid," I said and held her tight.

"I know. But you are a tubelight."

"How are your mom and dad?"

"You will meet them tomorrow in Krishna's wedding reception."

"What?" I said surprised, releasing my grip.

Suddenly a voice brought us back to reality.

"Sir, I had gone to the ICAI office at the Dubai Knowledge Village to fill up the examination form, and I was surprised to see someone called Urvashi Doshi there," Jiten said with excitement. "She works as an administrative manager there."

"He then called me to bring the third U-turn in your life," Krishna said coming out from the car. "I met Urvi and her parents thereafter and we decided to give you the most pleasent surprise of your life."

I was so surprised to see him. He hugged us.

"See, I told you that you that you would attend my wedding together."

I nodded as I looked into Urvi's eyes. I could see the rest of my life in it.

I could not believe my destiny! My lucky mascot had once again brought a U-turn in my life.

Was this the third U-turn in my life? You bet it was.

Epilogue III

"Hey sugar! We have a surprise for you," Riya said, clasping Deepak's hand. Urvi and I had reached the reception party at Spice Ballroom in Atlantis. Urvi was looking lovely in a pink sari.

Urvi's mother was chasing uncle to stop him from eating more chaat in excitement. Krishna had called Ba and Bapuji secretly too. Both were busy chatting with Laxmanbhai and Kalpana Aunty. Banerjee Sir and Sony aunty were busy inquiring from the chef about calories in the food. All the directors – Gill, Manjunath, Rakesh and Sachin – were performing maori greetings with Mr. Mohammad bin Abdullah bin Ahmed (breath)Al Shirawi since they had arrived in the morning. Amit and Greg Simon were watching a belly dancer. She had kept a sword on her head and was shaking her hips like Shakira.

"What is the surprise?" I asked.

"Deepak has proposed to me!" Riya said and winked, "And we will be getting married soon!" she announced looking sizzling in a red sari.

"Wow! Congrats! This is good news!" Urvi said, offering her hand as she smiled at Deepak and Riya.

"Let's celebrate!" Deepak said, signalling towards a steward. He picked up two glasses of red wine. I picked up a glass of orange juice for myself, and Urvi did the same.

"Cheers!" we chorused.

Epilogue IV

Deepak and Riya got married the same night itself, in Laxmanbhai's Rolls-Royce. Both went for a long drive and came in the morning in a Dubai Police car. Deepak became CEO as I had resigned after marrying Urvi and to start my practice back in Ahmedabad to live with Ba and Bapuji.

Jiten passed his CA exams and left for Lagos, Nigeria, to earn some quick money. He got another lucrative offer from the Kingdom of Suadi Arabia and joined Saudi Bin Laden Group!

Raman Doshi, sorry dad, has started workout daily to have chaat once in a week. He works as freelancer (in Latin, "free" meaning "Lone" and "lancer" meaning "Ranger") financer. Banerjee Sir has become director at CRL. Mom, I mean Ramola Doshi, and Sony aunty have become friends and both post (on Facebook) images of new interior designs on every month on a salary day.

Usmanbhai became a father again and he is blissfully driving Deepak in his Mercedes-500. Deepak is doing very good and his confidence level is very high once again. Deepak is also planning another project to build world's tallest tower, higher than the Burj Khalifa, in Mumbai worth USD 10 billion. He announced USD 1 million royalties to author Amrish Tripathi for writing his autobiography (titled *Wolf in the desert*). Taran Johar announced to make a movie (*Bluff Master*) on Deepak's life after the release of the book. I announced this news to Urvi; she whispered "Abracadabra".

Bhavesh has started his own practice in Mehasna. He had proposed me to join as a partner, but I rejected because he stopped wearing the hairwig. He said, caressing his hand on his bald head, "If CA looks more mature, client will trust you more and give you more business." However, after waiting for nearly two years, finally he bought his dream car-Tata Nano for two lakhs.

Manoj and Rajesh couldn't complete CA. Instead, both qualified LLB and started practice in sales tax. Now both visit my office to seek the clients for book writing and to have chai.

Sanjay and Kavita were not sure to pass CA; hence they dropped out and appeared for bank exam and topped. Now both have been posted in Daman and Diu, respectively. Kavita has taken medical leave from the bank since last two years and lives with her husband in Daman.

Sonal passed CA and is married to an NRI in USA. She works for Citi Bank (Motto: Citi never lets their clients sleep) at Wall Street (Motto: We are leaders in financial scams).

Kalpana passed CA and married Umesh Sunder Acharya. He is running CA coaching classes – "Abimanyu Institute of Chakravyuh of Ahmedabad". His grandmother (or great grandmother) still watches *Mahabharata*.

Krishna and Beena became parents of a cute girl. Both are happy. Ba had sent some special sweets and Adadiya when Beena was pregnant. Now she is weighing more than Bharati Singh, comedian.

Neelam, my cousin's son went to Africa and he remitted some dollars via Dubai. Now she is running a tailoring and garment shop.

Ishwariben is happy with Bapuji's personal services and everytime Bapuji visits her home, she gives him a KitKat.

Manu Mama has become number one Development Officer at LIC (Motto: Even we don't understand policy terms and conditions) because of millionaire Agent Vinod. Bapuji gets more commission than what chairman of LIC earns. But he has to ask Ba for his pocket money.

Rita and Raghu still work at CRL. I meet them whenever I visit Mumbai to audit their accounts. They are my biggest client.

Suresh has started Security Solutions Company and sells CCTV cameras and alarms to shopping malls and parliament. Vasant has started a travel agency (Motto: you can chew tobacco in India, but you cannot spit) and he books my air ticket whenever I visit our common client-CRL.

James Peter Chikala has changed his family name; now he is James Peter Chaco. But he still drinks tons of water and beer to pass kidney stones from his bladder.

PIA is split. Parthivbhai is practicing as a sole propertier. He is still kind to me as he refers me to all his clients-Charitable Trusts-whome he is serving pro bono.

Indrajit Sodi and Tripathi have started a partnership firm together and practice in Income Tax. Our city is progressing and now anyone who arrives in Ahmedabad by air or by rail or bus or car or space shuttle gets an income tax notice.

A.K. Fuliya is working in a private bank in Private Wealth Management department and sells mutual funds (for more information contact Toll Free number 1800-LASVEGAS-8181).

Ushaben visits my office with her husband in a Hyundai car to file their income tax return. I don't charge them fees. I mean I serve them pro bono in legal language. Except when they were served income tax notice – under section 139 – just before Diwali, I asked them Rs one lack only for the income tax officer.

Mehra Sahib Volutanrily gave away all his wealth and Mehra house at Satyagrah Chavni in Vastrapur to his Nepalese domestic servants and left for the Himalayas, Nepal to repent for his sins.

Directors – Gill, Manjunath, Sachin and Rakesh – still sweat in the conference room when I grill them during the audit (because they haven't yet cleared my cheque).

Ajit Vaghle's practice is thriving as corruption erupts almost every month into India and he has contested in Lok Sabha elections and became Law Minister too.

Siddharth and Abhiraj both are out from jail on bail. They have appealed to the higher court and appointed Mr. Ram Jethmalani as their lawyer. Both have started Yin-yang Real Estate Co. Ltd, and they announced their first project PMIGC (Profesional Middle Income Group City). They borrowed money from Naresh Joshi at interest rate of 5% weekly. Siddharth called me to appoint me the auditor for their company. I was not keen to take his assignment but Ba said clients are like God. So I accepted ecstatically and signed the offer letter and called him but his cell was off. Both were in jail. Both became bankrupt. They sold all of the properties to pay the financer and lawyer's fees.

Victor is now the personal trainer of Jai Hemant Shroff a.k.a Tiger Shroff.

Urvi and I visited Manek Chowk on her scooty to have chaat at *Rajasthan Chaat Bandar* and then have kulfi. Because Urvi was pregnant and the little one inside her was craving for chaat and kulfi, I couldn't say no to them.

Hey guys! I became a father of a baby boy. Ba and Bapuji said, "He is an angel, and the lucky mascot for his father. So his name should be...Krishna."

Upcoming title by the same author:

The Three Wise Monkeys

Amar, Akbar and Anthony – aspiring chartered accountants with IQ the size of a button – took almost equivalent to the two world wars put together to defeat the Institute's motives of keeping them away from the degree. But that was the beginning as the honest and dim witted trio struggle endlessly to earn and could only afford a more extravagance feast than Mumbai's Irani cafe.

That's when they fall in love and realise that honesty alone cannot keep girlfriends happy. So they turn a blind eye to the philosophy of: "see no evil, hear no evil and speak no evil".

They grapple with a Swiss bank, their respective girlfriends who seem and behave like estranged sisters, wealthy clients trying to save their asses in tax evasion, income tax raids, being pursued by the police, goons and guns. The turmoil will send them running for life, and push them into Halloween costumes of Batman, Joker and Scarecrow.

Because ultimately, who dares...wins.